Acclaim for
A Regency

LYN STONE
"Lyn Stone masterfully blends excitement,
humor and emotion."
—*RT Book Reviews*

"Stone has done herself proud with this story...a cast of
endearing characters and a fresh, innovative plot."
—*Publishers Weekly* on *The Knight's Bride*

CARLA KELLY
"A powerful and wonderfully perceptive author."
—*New York Times* bestselling author Mary Jo Putney

"A wonderfully fresh and original voice."
—*RT Book Reviews*

"Kelly has the rare ability to create realistic yet sympathetic
characters that linger in the mind. One of the most
respected...Regency writers."
—*Library Journal*

GAIL RANSTROM
"[This] dark tale...neatly juxtaposes
the seamier side of the Regency period with
the glittering superficiality of 'polite society.'"
—*Library Journal* on *Lord Libertine*

"Ranstrom crafts an intriguing mystery, brimming with a fine
cast of strong and likable characters and a few surprises."
—*RT Book Reviews* on *The Rake's Revenge*

LYN STONE,

a painter and writer, finds many similarities in the two creative efforts. She admits, "There's nothing like losing yourself in a story, whether you're putting it on canvas or computer. And completing either work is a wonderful natural high nothing can replicate. It is a real joy to do what you love."

After living for four years in Europe, Lyn settled in north Alabama. She enjoys an enduring romance of her own and is currently dreaming up more happy endings.

CARLA KELLY

has been writing award-winning novels for years, stories set in the British Isles, Spain and army garrisons during the Indian Wars. Her specialty in the Regency genre is writing about ordinary people, not just lords and ladies. Carla has worked as a university professor, a ranger in the National Park Service and recently as a staff writer and columnist for a small daily newspaper in Valley City, North Dakota. Her husband is director of theater at Valley City State University. She has five interesting children, a fondness for cowboy songs and too many box elder beetles in the fall.

GAIL RANSTROM

was born and raised in the wild west of Montana, and has always enjoyed a good tale of danger, adventure, action and romance of long ago times and distant lands. When the youngest of her three children began school, she finally had a moment to herself and she has been writing ever since. She is an award-winning author of eight novels and two novellas.

After surviving earthquakes, mudslides and wild fires in southern California and dodging hurricanes and alligators in Florida, Gail has returned to Montana where the long winters give her more than enough time to tell many more stories. She loves to hear from readers, and you can reach her at gail@gailranstrom.com.

A Regency Christmas

LYN STONE
CARLA KELLY
GAIL RANSTROM

HARLEQUIN®

TORONTO • NEW YORK • LONDON
AMSTERDAM • PARIS • SYDNEY • HAMBURG
STOCKHOLM • ATHENS • TOKYO • MILAN • MADRID
PRAGUE • WARSAW • BUDAPEST • AUCKLAND

Recycling programs
for this product may
not exist in your area.

ISBN-13: 978-0-373-29567-8

A REGENCY CHRISTMAS

Copyright © 2009 by Harlequin Books S.A.

The publisher acknowledges the copyright holders
of the individual works as follows:

SCARLET RIBBONS
Copyright © 2009 by Lynda Stone

CHRISTMAS PROMISE
Copyright © 2009 by Carla Kelly

A LITTLE CHRISTMAS
Copyright © 2009 by Gail Ranstrom

CONTENTS

SCARLET RIBBONS   9
Lyn Stone

CHRISTMAS PROMISE   93
Carla Kelly

A LITTLE CHRISTMAS   179
Gail Ranstrom

SCARLET RIBBONS

Lyn Stone

Dear Reader,

Sometimes we don't believe what we can do until circumstances force us to do it. And there are other times when we overestimate our ability because we want to do something so desperately. This story is about realizing potential and also accepting limitations with grace. Someone who loves you can help in either case.

Love can unfold gradually or it can spring forth at first meeting. If the chemistry between two people is there, it will happen, whether by chance or design. In this instance, it's the result of a misunderstanding gone right!

I do hope you enjoy meeting Amalie, Alex and their families, celebrating with them and sharing their story.

Here's wishing you a wonderful holiday season filled with love!

Lyn

This story is for Charlotte Ballard who believed I could write a book even before I began. Thanks for being such a good friend!

Chapter One

*British Hospital at Salamanca, Spain—
September 1, 1812*

"**I**'ll not be going, Harlowe, and that's the end of it," Alexander Napier declared. He ignored the English lieutenant and concentrated on the exercises he performed almost hourly. "Ouch! Damn!" Again, he stretched, teeth gritted, eyes clenched.

"Will you cease that self-torture for a moment and listen to me?" Michael Harlowe demanded.

Alex stopped what he was doing, glanced up at the lad and frowned a warning. "You're a trifle loud at the mouth for such a banty-rooster. I'd advise you to grow another foot before you take on someone my size."

Michael shifted on his narrow cot as if giving up. Alex knew better. Nothing intimidated the lieutenant, even a captain almost twice his size and weight and with six years more experience. Now would come reason since barking demands hadn't worked. The wee fellow was nothing if not predictable. They had been round and round on this topic for days now as time drew near for them to ship home from the primitive hospital at Salamanca. He never let up. He'd find a new argument.

"If you refuse to go to Balmsley with me to recuperate, then what *will* you do? No point in returning to Kilamahew, is there?"

Alex stretched out and pressed back against the pillowless bed, willing the pain in his leg to subside. "I hadn't planned to go there." He had thought to secure a place in London and see if he could manage on his own.

His friend smirked. "Edinburgh then? And live with your uncle? You're coming up on thirty, y'know. At least I can offer you employment." Suddenly he turned earnest. "Please let me do this for you, Alex. You saved my life!"

Alex snorted. "If I had lain here and let you bleed out lying right next to me, how would I face myself in a mirror to shave?"

Michael waved that off with a flick of one hand. "You are coming with me, see if you don't. If I have to pour laudanum down that tree-trunk neck of yours and have you hauled there unconscious!"

Alex wondered if the lad actually would go that far to have his way in this. What could it hurt to relent? It obviously troubled Michael to owe such a debt, though Alex had never considered it such. Michael had prevented the amputation of Alex's leg. As far as he was concerned, they were square. Saving a life or a leg or anything else here in this misbegotten place where there were dead and dying all around them seemed a damned miracle.

There was another consideration in Alex's decision to acquiesce. Maidstone would not be that distant, closer actually than London, and he did have fences to mend there if he could. "If you'll leave off badgering me, I'll come for a short visit. Until I'm back on my feet again."

He hated the way Michael's gaze slid away from his, the way his lips tightened.

"I know what they say, but I *will* be walking, make no mistake," Alex insisted. He said it often and worked like the devil to make it so. It had been almost six weeks and he could feel his progress.

"You'll see the best doctor in England when we get there," Michael promised. "What do these leeches here know? You'll be dancing by year's end, I warrant."

Alex grunted in assent. The new year was almost four months away. Surely by then…

Michael sat up, the flimsy cot creaking beneath him. "Until then, I could really use your talent with a pen. I'll be doing my memoirs, y'see."

Alex laughed out loud. "All twenty-two years of 'em or just the important parts?"

Michael chuckled sheepishly at himself. It was one of the main things Alex liked about Harlowe. A man who could laugh at his own folly had learned the secret of survival. Sometimes laughter was the only defense a man had left.

It was late October when they finally arrived in London. Michael promptly and without a qualm sold his commission. Alex grudgingly followed suit. Though convinced he eventually would walk again, he also realized his army days were a thing of the past. He'd had enough of it and then some.

He admitted to himself that this visit was a delaying tactic. It was high time he faced what he must and set the past to rights, but he needed a few more weeks to prepare, to ease back into civilization and become human again.

Alex had not asked, but he wondered what Michael's

family, especially his father, the second Baron Harlowe, would think of the eldest son bringing home a Scot for a house pet. Not much, he reckoned, but it was to be a short visit anyway.

The day was wicked cold and sent a chill right through his bones as their carriage rocked over the twenty miles to Balmsley, the Harlowe family seat.

Alex thought of the fancy wheeled Bath chair Michael had insisted he purchase from a London maker. They had stayed nearly a week while it was modified so that Alex could wheel it himself. Odd they were not made that way to begin with, but Michael's idea to set the seat back a bit and give access to the big wheels was brilliant. It tended to tip over backward if he wasn't careful, but it did give him a small measure of independence. Of course it was merely a short-term necessity. It could be sold when he no longer needed it.

No crutches could be found to accommodate his height of well over six feet, but that could be remedied as soon as they got where they were going. He'd whittle them himself if need be.

Michael had grown unusually quiet as they rode. Alex knew he must be planning his strategy for explaining the unusual guest he had in tow.

If the family resented Scots enough to order him gone, at least he could afford to travel. His back pay amounted to more than he had figured and the fee he received from his captaincy was substantial. He could live on that for a while.

If all else failed, he could apply to his uncle for some sort of clerical work with the city commission in Edinburgh, he supposed. Whether it would be forthcoming was another matter altogether. They'd never got on well in the best of circumstances. Uncle William had resented Alex donning the Blackwatch and serving under the English flag. Called it running away and Alex guessed it was, but he knew naught else to do. The only thing he had trained for, he could no longer do.

"There!" Michael cried, pointing out the window. "See Balmsley's towers above those trees?"

Alex sighed. "A castle, is it?"

"No! No, only a manor house. But it is big, isn't it! I love the place. Who would have thought I'd miss it so much?" He shook his fair head in disbelief. "I was so bloody eager to get away. But Father will be damned glad to see me now, see if he ain't! Glad to have *you* there, too, I'll wager, since you saved my sorry hide. I'm all he's got to carry on, y'see. Amalie's just a girl."

"How old is your sister?"

"Twenty-four," Michael answered absently, his gaze still glued to the manor house looming closer every minute as the coach rolled down the long tree-lined drive.

"Two years *older* than you? Is that a fact? All this time I thought she was a child the way you spoke of her."

"She is. Women never grow up."

Alex shook his head and rolled his eyes. "Ah, Harlowe, but you do have a great lot to learn."

His words went unheeded as the coach drew up in front of the enormous red sandstone edifice that boasted double-arched doors of stout dark oak. Even as he watched, one portal flew open and a short, white-haired gent dashed out to meet them. Hatless, his brocade waistcoat unbuttoned and his neckcloth loose and flapping in the stiff breeze, he shouted, "Michael!"

With a crow of delight, Michael threw open the coach door, hopped down and embraced the older fellow. They danced around like fools, slapping each other on the back.

A rider had been sent ahead from Hartlepool to announce their arrival, but surely this could not be the baron himself.

Alex sat waiting like a piece of the baggage, watching through the open coach door until the excited Michael finally recalled he was there.

"Oh, Father, I've brought Captain Napier. Alex saved my life. Sorely wounded himself, he rolled right off his cot and stanched my bleeding until they could sew me back up." Michael carefully patted his shoulder where the bullet had struck him and passed through. "He's welcome, is he not, sir?"

The older man nodded, tears in the light blue eyes so like his son's. He hurried forward and stretched out a trembling hand. Though his Adam's apple worked up and down, he seemed speechless.

Alex gripped the much smaller hand and shook it firmly. "At your service, milord."

Michael shouted for two footmen who came to take down the bags and Bath chair lashed to the coach's roof. They brought the wheeled contraption around to the door of the coach. Alex had already levered himself off the seat and gripped either side of the coach's door frame while he balanced on his good leg. The other hung there, useless and aching like mad.

The two brutes assisted him down and set him in the chair. "Devilish awkward," he said in an aside to the baron, who stood wide-eyed and openmouthed, obviously not expecting a cripple. "Temporary condition," Alex assured him, forcing a smile.

"Yes, yes, of course," Baron Harlowe answered rather absently, then perked up. "Well, let's get you two inside and thaw you out, eh?" He shivered to make his point.

"Matil…da!" the man shouted the instant they entered

the double doors. "Our Michael's home! Hurry down!" He turned to his son. "She's primping. You know your mother!" He winked at Alex and confided in a stage whisper. "Ladies have to look their best, eh?"

One of the footmen wheeled him from the chilly entrance hall into a good-size library. Books covered the walls on three sides, all the way from the waist-high wainscoting to the carved molding that graced the ceiling. Large, high-backed, overstuffed chairs sat in a grouping facing a huge fireplace with an elegant oak mantelpiece. A roaring fire burned in the grate, shedding its warmth like a blessing on all who entered.

He closed his eyes and inhaled the scent of burning wood, lemon oil and leather. When he opened them again, his chair had been rolled near the hearth. The footman had parked it there before departing.

In the chair closest to the blaze and right next to his own sat the most beautiful woman Alex had ever seen in his life. He felt as though something—the unexpected heat from the fire or perhaps the very sight of her—had sucked the breath right out of his lungs.

Michael was speaking, but his words might as well have been Greek. The winter sun shone through the window behind the lass, gilding the fine golden curls wound up with bright red ribbons. He could swear angels played harps to augment the vision.

Her sky-blue eyes met his gaze directly. However, belatedly, Alex noted something less than angelic in their depths. Scorn, was it?

Oh, well, that was to be expected. He wouldn't be garnering any expressions of interest as long as he sat in the blasted Bath chair. It bothered him more than he wished to admit. Women usually displayed some wee spark of curiosity, at the very least, if only due to his great size. A prurient interest, to be certain, but he was not averse to it all the same. He had grown spoiled to being noticed in such a way, he reckoned. Of course, this one was a lady and such thoughts were usually bred right out of her kind.

He watched Michael lean down to kiss the beauty on her rose-tinted cheek and take her hand. She looked up from beneath her long lashes, offered a smile and a soft, "Welcome home at last."

"Thank you, Amalie." He turned to Alex. "This is Captain Napier who saved my life. He's consented to a visit with us. Could I impose on you to entertain him for a few moments? I would like to speak with Father alone and regain his good graces."

"As you should," she said, sounding less than enthusiastic about it.

Together he and the lady watched the door close, sealing them inside the library alone. Alex braced his elbows on the chair arms and clasped his fingers together. "Your brother is a fine young man," he offered in an attempt at conversation.

"He's a fine young idiot and nearly broke my father's heart," she replied succinctly, thumbing rapidly through the book in her lap. "If he had died, I would never have forgiven him. I suppose I must thank you for preventing that."

Alex cleared his throat, uncertain what to say next. She had a sharp tongue, this one. "Then I suppose I must say that you're welcome."

She flicked one hand toward the wheels of his chair. "How long are you condemned to that?"

He concealed his surprise. The minx was straightforward if nothing else. "Until I find crutches to fit me."

"And how long on the crutches?" she asked brusquely.

Damn the woman. People rarely asked such a thing of a person in his fix. But he answered her rudeness honestly. "Until I can walk without them."

She blew out an impatient breath. "You know very well what I mean. What do the doctors say?"

"That I'll never walk," he admitted. "But they're wrong."

Her sudden smile was wry and humorless. "They say I *will*. And they're also wrong."

His gaze flew to her legs which were well concealed, of course, by the soft red wool of her skirts. The toes of her small matching leather slippers peeked out from beneath the hem. Side by side, her feet perched motionless on a green velvet pillow with gold tassels.

"Riding accident," she explained with a sigh.

His heart sank inside his chest. "I'm so sorry," he said sincerely.

She nodded and gave a small shrug. "Well, what happened to you?"

"Bullet caught me just above the knee at Salamanca back in July. They set the bone, but the muscles were damaged. Infection set in. Almost lost the whole thing ten days after they set it, but your brother persuaded the surgeon to take time to treat it instead of lopping it off. Bribed him, too, I believe, though he won't admit to that."

She inclined her pretty head and pursed her lips as if studying him for a while. "Do you know why he brought you here?"

Alex shrugged. "He has some strange notion he owes me. I think it bothers him, so I thought I would humor him for a few weeks."

She closed her eyes, sighed and shook her head. "No, no, no, that's not it."

"What other reason could he have?"

"He brought you for *me*," she said wearily, then quickly added, "but he won't admit to that, either, so you needn't bother to protest to him."

Alex smiled at her outrageous assumption. "And why would any man in his right mind even think to protest?"

She didn't seem at all offended by his sarcasm. "I can see that you don't believe me," she said, a hint of dry humor in her voice. "But I know my meddling little brother better than he knows himself. I recognized that look in his eyes when he left us in here alone."

"You have a delightfully warped imagination," he told her politely.

She wriggled uncomfortably, then settled herself. "Well, I suppose you would doubt he's capable of such a thing. However, I must confide to you that Michael spent the better part of his school years dragging home friends and attempting to match me up."

Alex frowned down at her legs. "How long ago did this happen to you? He never mentioned it to me."

She brushed her hands over her skirts, then clamped her fingers around her book as if to still them. "A scant two months before Michael left us. That would make it eight months, two weeks and four days ago, but who's counting?"

"You are, obviously. So this matchmaking of his is not a result of…" Meaningfully, he glanced at her legs again.

She scoffed. "No. You have the dubious distinction of being the first nonambulatory candidate he has presented. I will concede he has always attempted to choose carefully."

"So, should we tie the knot and roll through life together in our Bath chairs?"

Her eyes flew wide.

"A jest," he assured her with a grin. "Don't you ever laugh? How else have you borne that brother of yours?"

She did laugh then, and Alex joined her. That was how her father and brother found them.

Alex was ready to kill Michael the next time he got within reach. But for now he hid his frown and winked at Amalie. The sight of her dimples provided his reward for enduring this farce.

"Well!" Michael crowed. "You two certainly are getting on famously! Somehow I knew you would." He looked to his father, probably for his approval.

The baron frowned from Alex to his daughter and back again, distinctly uncomfortable and at an obvious loss for words. Worried, was he?

Alex wondered how the man would tactfully explain to Michael in their presence that this would be a match from hell? His only daughter and a crippled ex-soldier who was a Scot to boot? It should prove interesting.

Alex wondered if the hired coach was still outside resting the team and whether he could get to the damned thing without a push. There was no place on earth he'd rather not be right now, save a battlefield or the presence of his mother-in-law.

Chapter Two

Amalie had recovered from her mirth enough to notice the muscle ticking in the Scottish captain's jaw. He played well at hiding his anger and kept his wits about him. Knowing firsthand how difficult that was, she admired it enormously.

He was a handsome fellow. More than that, really. He seemed imbued with strength of character, if she was not mistaken, and was certainly blessed with a ready sense of humor. He had remained congenial even though she had purposely offended him with her questions to see how he would react. She had seen compassion and understanding, rather than pity, in those deep green eyes of his. Of course, he would know what pity was like and must hate it, too.

If she could enlist his aid, she meant to teach that misguided brother of hers a lesson or two. Didn't she have enough to endure without putting up with Michael's machinations?

Feigning a short fit of coughing, she motioned across the room to where decanters were set out with brandy and sherry. As she knew he would, Michael dashed over to pour her a glass. Her father followed to get one of his own, another predictable occurrence.

While they were occupied, Amalie leaned closer to the captain, her hand hiding a whisper. "Play this out with me. Father will have Michael's head on a plate."

He gave her a doubtful look, then an infinitesimal nod.

Michael brought her brandy by mistake and she gulped it down, hissing delicately at the bite. She cleared her throat. "You will never guess what has happened!"

Her brother smiled in question, looking from her to the captain and back again.

Amalie reached over and held out her hand to their guest. There was nothing for him to do but take it in his. "Captain Napier has agreed to take me off the shelf."

Her father choked on his brandy. Michael looked non-plussed with the precipitous success of his scheme. The Scot held his smile. But she could hear his teeth grind. She bared her own teeth at him. "Isn't it wonderful? Love at first sight."

"Here now! What's this?" Her father had regained his voice. "He only got here a few moments ago. You don't even know the fellow!"

Amalie turned her lips down in a pout and made the lower one tremble. "But Michael brought him for me all the way from the peninsula. I like him and I want to keep him."

Her father blanched perfectly white and even Michael looked appalled at the swiftness of her decision.

She pressed on. "I've already promised him my whole inheritance from Grandmama, half the estate when we inherit, and—best of all—he's bringing me his three natural children to raise for my own. Their mothers won't mind, he says, for we can install them somewhere in the village."

Her father gaped.

She went on, fabricating to her heart's content. "Since

we can live right here with you, there should be plenty of help with little ones. Please, please, Father, don't say no. Mother will be delighted with grandchildren!"

In fact, Mother was so disinterested in children, she had paid only scant attention to her own. She was not even down here now, welcoming the one who had just survived a war.

The Scot squeezed her hand until she felt the knuckles grind together. Her father sputtered helplessly. Michael's eyes were wide, panicked, darting from her to their father. This was too entertaining.

Michael rushed to suggest, "Amie, perhaps you should consider—"

"What, brother? What's to mull over that you haven't thought out?" she demanded, trying to retain a cheerful tone. "Surely you considered every detail when choosing him? How much more suitable could he be, I ask you?" She flung out her free hand as if to present the man as the greatest prize imaginable. "Just look at him!"

"Just look at *us*," the Scot echoed, surprising her. "Matching bookends."

The underlying tone of his voice warned her to cease before he lost his temper completely. But Michael's face was a study in scarlet perplexity and their father was now eyeing her brother with an urge to throttle. She added one more little plea. "Please, Papa?"

At length, her father dragged his attention from the errant Michael and fastened it on her. Suddenly his face softened and his tight lips relaxed into a sad smile of sympathy. No, pure pity.

Oh, dear! Amalie's heart stuttered. *Don't say it, Father! Do not!* Her silent plea went unheard. She had overplayed her hand.

"Of course, my darling girl. You may have anything your heart desires. You deserve it."

The Scot leveled her with a glare that promised retribution for this attack of insanity. She bit her lip and wrinkled her nose at him, but she had a feeling a look of apology would not be sufficient in this case.

Michael dusted his hands together. "Well, glad that's settled! I shall go and fetch Mother."

Oh, no!

"Wait!" Amalie cried, throwing out her hand as if she could grasp his coat. He stopped and turned, eyebrows raised in innocent query.

She bit her lip, her glance skipping from him, to her father and finally to their guest. "Please." Her voice almost a whisper, she lowered her eyes and sighed. "This was only a jest meant to lesson you in meddling, Michael."

But that wasn't the worst of the matter. "Captain Napier, I do apologize for abusing your good nature in such an abominable way."

Her father's color returned. He rocked heel to toe for a few seconds, then hesitantly asked the captain, "Did she make up that part about the children and your... The mothers?"

The Scot lowered his face to his hand and pinched the bridge of his nose. He shook his head slowly as if at a loss in dealing with Bedlamites. "A fabrication, to be sure," he said. "I do have one son, but he's quite legitimate."

"Legitimate?" Michael croaked, clutching his chest. "Never say it! You're married?"

Captain Napier glanced up swiftly, still shaking his head. "No. My wife...passed away."

Widowed. Amalie felt terrible. "Do say you forgive me, sir. This was a horribly thoughtless thing for me to do. I had no idea..."

"I know," the captain said, not looking at her, but at the floor. "I'll have a brandy now if it's convenient."

They'd forgotten to offer him a drink! Michael and her father almost collided in their haste to reach the decanter.

Napier graced her with a dangerous look of warning as he spoke in a dark whisper, "If I were not confined to this chair, I would take you over my knee."

She bobbed her head up and down, noting how his deep green eyes glinted and his expressive lips turned up just a bit at the corners. It was in no way a smile. More like exasperation.

"I've confessed, sir," she told him earnestly. "What more could you ask of me?"

His lips firmed. His nostrils flared ever so slightly with an indrawn breath. Then he spoke. "I'd ask if you're lying about everything. I happened to notice you just moved your feet."

Alex had felt an overpowering need to lash out, to hurt someone, just because he'd been humiliated. Now, brandy in hand, his temper cooled somewhat, he hated whatever had possessed him.

She hadn't answered his cruel question, but he had not expected she would. If she was pretending, it was certainly no business of his. And if she wasn't, he had gained her enmity for life.

Just because she had moved her feet did not mean she was capable of walking. What had he been thinking? He could move his, too, but still could not depend on that left leg to support him.

Michael had taken a chair across from him and now appeared to be searching his mind for a way to explain his sister's strange behavior.

The baron had left the room—glad to get away, Alex imagined—and had gone to fetch the baroness. He wondered if she were as daft as the rest of the family.

"Has Dr. Raine been down from London recently, Amie? Is there any improvement in your condition?" Michael asked his sister.

"No change," she said, her tone defensive. "He should be here the day after tomorrow for his monthly visit."

Michael gave a resigned nod, then addressed Alex. "I should like him to see you, too, when he comes. See what he thinks. Raine is the best available. Father saw to that when Amie was injured."

That was all Alex needed, another opinion, when he was clinging so desperately to the only positive one thus far. His own. "Thank you, but—"

"Don't bother refusing," Michael warned. "You know I shall only wear you down."

Alex gave it up. He would talk to the doctor to placate Michael. Nothing more than a conversation. No examinations. No arguments.

"If you insist, I'll see him."

Michael jumped up and headed for the door. "Wonderful! I'll bring his letters of recommendation from Father's study."

"What's the worst Raine could tell you, hmm?" Amalie asked.

Alex turned on her, his anger flaring anew. "You've the devil of a tongue on you, you know that? If you've any feeling in that backside of yours, it ought to be made use of!"

"That's the second time you've suggested such," she retorted with a moue of feigned fright. "You'd cane a poor cripple?"

"Leave off," he growled. "This sniping serves no purpose."

She tossed him an insincere smile. "Oh, but it does, Captain. It serves to distract us."

He leveled her with a glare. "You are a spoiled, self-indulgent excuse for a lady if I ever met one. Is that all you do all day? Sit around throwing verbal darts at anyone who wanders by?"

She inclined her head as if considering the question in new light. "I suppose I do. It passes the time. That's bad of me, I know."

"Have you even tried to stand?" he asked, surprising himself with his own directness.

Her humor, black as it was, fled on the instant. "Yes, of course I have." Her voice sounded so small.

"You make me want to kick myself," he muttered.

"Now there's a picture!"

Alex smiled in spite of himself. He just didn't know what to make of this person. He began to suspect she harbored exactly the same frustrations he did, only she had endured them longer. And she seemed to have lost her hope, something he was terribly afraid of doing himself. He suddenly realized a deep-seated need to help this girl despite the fact that she nettled him so mercilessly.

"So, tell me of this doctor of yours," he said by way of turning the subject.

"Oh, Raine's pleasant enough when you say what he wants to hear, I suppose. He's not overly fond of me, as you might imagine."

"He expects too much of you, eh?" Alex guessed.

She slipped into a thoughtful mood, laying her brittleness aside for the nonce. "Yes, he does. He brought this Amazon with him not long after he began treating me. Magda, she's called. Frightful woman. She pummels and stretches my limbs unmercifully each day. Twice! It's quite painful."

"I see. Then you do have feeling in your…limbs." He smiled again. Legs were not mentioned in polite company. He should have remembered that earlier. Neither were backsides.

"Tremendous feeling," she admitted with a grimace. "Though no action at all." Her curiosity got the better of her. "You?"

"I work the muscles as often as I can now that the bone's healed. Hurts less now than it did."

"Truly?" Her interest aroused, she queried further. "How can you do that alone?"

"Have to," he explained patiently. "You see, if the muscles atrophy—and I suspect that's why your Amazon is so avid in her task—there's no chance you'll ever regain the strength to use them."

"Mine must have atrophied then," she said in a quiet voice, as though speaking to herself. "They're of no use whatsoever. Perhaps Dr. Raine and Magda began too late with me."

"Let me see," he demanded, his former training overruling any thought to impropriety.

Her eyes rounded with shock. "Sir! How dare you suggest such a thing?"

Alex scoffed. "Spare me the hysterics. I'm a trained physician. It's not as if I've never seen a woman's legs before. Lift your skirts." Meanwhile, he busied himself with the wheels of his chair, arcing them so that he faced her, knee to knee.

"You're a doctor?" she asked, frowning. "Seriously?"

Alex finished lifting her skirts halfway up her thighs, employing the swiftness and businesslike manner imperative in examining a female patient. "Not so seriously these days, but I trust I can still recognize a withered limb when I see one." His gaze traveled over the smooth ivory skin of her legs while his hands judged the amount of slackness of tendon and muscle beneath it.

"Quadriceps femoris seems firm," he muttered, reaching beneath her leg. She jumped and made a little sound. "That hurt?"

"No," she said breathlessly, then bit her lip.

"Good. Facia lata seems a bit lax to me. Flex it."

She gasped. "Flex what?"

"Your leg!" he ordered impatiently. "Try to lift it."

Suddenly she yelped and punched at his shoulder frantically with her fists.

"What's this?" Michael shouted. "What are you *doing?*"

Alex groaned, snatched his hands away and jerked down her skirts.

"He's a doctor!" Amalie cried. "He was only—"

"I know what he was doing!" Michael thundered. "Captain, if you were not…incapacitated, I should call you out on the instant!"

Alex grabbed the wheels of his chair and rolled himself backward, no small task given the thickness of the carpet. "Settle your feathers, Harlowe. You know I'm no threat to—" He broke off when he looked over at Michael and saw the baron standing beside him, sagging under the inert weight of a woman Alex supposed was the baroness. She had fainted dead away.

"He is a *doctor!*" Amalie wailed. Alex didn't blame her at all. He felt like wailing himself.

"They'll have to marry now," her father declared in a woebegone tone.

"Milord…" Alex let his words trail away, knowing it was no use. No matter that he couldn't manage a seduction right now if his life depended upon it or that the idea had not even occurred to him. He had thoroughly compromised Miss Amalie Harlowe beyond all redemption in the eyes of her parents and her brother. He'd been squarely caught with his hands up her skirts. And, since he had never confessed his former profession to Michael, any claim of purely medical interest under those ruffles would never be believed.

Even if he sent for his license to prove it, he still had no excuse. The lady had a physician already and no reason at all to be soliciting the opinion of one who had given up the practice.

He bit the bullet he knew he was expected to bite, and looked Amalie straight in the eye. "Miss Harlowe, I was just on the point of asking you. Would you kindly do me the honor of becoming my wife?"

She stared at him as if he'd grown horns. "You are mad, sir!"

Alex had to agree. "Assuredly, but I shouldn't think that would be an impediment you would notice much around here. So, will you, then?"

She dropped her gaze to her lap, then stared pointedly at his, her thoughts so apparent and well focused on any future attempt at consummation, she might as well have spoken them aloud.

Then she raised her head, looked him straight in the eye and shrugged one dispirited shoulder. "Why not?"

Chapter Three

Amalie had cursed her foolhardiness all through dinner and well into the night. Now, this morning, she suffered from lack of sleep that could very well make today even worse.

What in the world had come over her yesterday? Usually she maintained very tight control, both of her temper and the people around her. At the moment, she felt even more helpless than she had then.

"It has surely been half an hour! Stop!" She lay on her stomach on her bed while Magda tortured her, deliberately ignoring any demand to cease. This was nothing new, however. Amalie had grown used to it and accepted it as her ongoing punishment for past sins. But she didn't accept it silently or with good grace. Magda was used to that, too, and only dug harder into Amalie's calf with those beefy fingers.

Yesterday, Magda had plunked her in the library after she had finished and dressed her. There was nothing to do there but spend hours on end reading books already read a dozen times each. The limit of endurance had been fully reached when Michael arrived with the Scot.

"Now I'm doomed to his company for the rest of my natural life," she said aloud.

Magda grunted as she rolled Amalie over and began massaging the right foot. "Well, at least he will be someone different to look at, eh?"

"Um. I suppose." And that would be a welcome change for a while, Amalie thought. "He saved Michael's life, so they'd said, so I do owe him for that."

"*Ja.* Young sir is home safe." Magda rotated the ankle.

"There's nothing I can do to repay him but try to be pleasant," Amalie said, deciding she might as well try. How long that would last was anyone's guess, but she would make the effort.

"He does not want this marriage, but he's stuck with it now."

"Marriage is good," Magda commented.

"What a sad state of affairs that I welcome any change at all, good or ill, just to relieve the sameness of the days."

"Change is good."

Amalie ignored Magda as best she could, since she wasn't really talking to her.

"He mentioned a son. Perhaps it would be entertaining to have a child about the place. Someone to run and fetch and to watch play, if nothing else. I've never really known any children other than Michael when he was small. What a little demon he was, but funny all the same."

"You will be the mama." She lifted the right leg, eliciting a groan.

Amalie forced the pain from her mind though her words still emerged in small puffs. "It not as if…I shall become a real mother…to the child. Or a real wife to…the father."

"Hmph. We shall see. I like to get these hands on him!" Magda declared.

Amalie imagined she would. "No chance of that, Mags."

The memory of his hands upon her bared legs surfaced and gave Amalie a lilting little feeling in the pit of her stomach. His touch had been meant as impersonal, she knew, as efficient and medically inquisitive as Dr. Raine's or Magda's. Yet it had affected her in an entirely different way.

Captain Napier was no stodgy old Londoner with more than fifty years to his credit, nor was he a great strapping woman with hands like giant claws. He was somewhere near thirty, terrifically attractive, and had wonderfully agile hands.

Also, he could make her laugh. How long had it been since her laughter had not reeked with sarcasm or self-deprecation? Lord, she'd become a regular martinet, a thoroughly unpleasant companion to one and all.

Perhaps that was the reason everyone left her alone in the library so much of the time. She must somehow work harder to get past her anger at what had happened to her. Acceptance was the key, she knew. She had to accept her fate and be gracious.

Alex dressed himself. Not the easy task he had always taken for granted before he had been wounded. Except for removing his boots, he had refused the assistance of the footman early last evening after being rolled into the bed-chamber prepared for him. Thankfully the room was located on the ground floor, a vacant room meant to house a servant, of course, as all downstairs sleeping accommodations were.

Hopping on one foot, he nearly toppled before he managed to make it to the Bath chair. Maneuvering around the small front wheel and guidance lever took some doing, but he finally got into the damned thing.

He was just wondering what he would do about his

boots when Michael entered. "Good morning, Alex," he said, sounding a bit stiff.

"You're here to talk things out."

Michael sniffed, looking out the window, anywhere but at him. "I cannot believe you would abuse my hospitality in such a manner. I was so angry last evening, I could not bring myself to speak with you at supper." He flopped down on the unmade bed and clasped his hands between his knees. "Is it really true you're a doctor?"

"I *was*," Alex admitted. "And I swear to you, Michael, I had no intention of giving insult to you or your sister. We had been discussing our injuries and I thought perhaps—"

Michael's head jerked up and his eyes were bright. "Well, what? What do you think? Could she walk if she wanted?"

"I can't say. You should speak with her physician about it. He's coming today?"

"Yes. You still have to marry her, you know," Michael warned him. Idly he reached down, picked up one of Alex's Hessians and looked around for the other. "Father is adamant about it."

"As are you, I see."

Michael nodded emphatically and brought the pair of boots to him. "And you cannot take her off to Scotland. She must stay here." He crouched in front of Alex and acted the valet, as he had done many times on the journey from Spain.

Alex smiled. "Michael, your outrage isn't necessary. I'm perfectly willing to marry her." He sat forward in the Bath chair, leaning toward his friend. "And you needn't worry she'll be saddled with me permanently. If she does recover and wishes to make a better match, an annulment can be quite easily obtained. I want you or your father to call your solicitor and have papers drawn up to the effect that I require nothing in the way of a dowry. Everything hers, remains hers."

"But that's not how things are done."

"This time it is. However," he said, hoping to divert Michael to another topic, "I would ask a favor. Can you arrange transportation for me to Maidstone in a week or so?"

"To see a friend there?" Michael asked, frowning. "Is this friend a woman?"

How like Michael. He was jealous on behalf of his sister. "My mother-in-law. She is English. When her husband passed on last year, she went to live with her sister in Kent. She has the care of my son and I should like to see him."

Michael shook his head. "I swear I thought I knew you well, Alex, but you never said a word about a wife or child in all the time I've known you. I believed your only relative was the old uncle in Edinburgh. And you only mentioned him the once."

"My past is no pleasant subject."

Michael shrugged, then scurried around behind Alex and pushed him toward the open door. "Let's have breakfast. Father's waiting."

Alex wondered whether he would see Amalie this morning and what her frame of mind might be after mulling over their conundrum. She'd likely feel better once he assured her she would have a way out of the marriage whenever she wanted.

He felt a bit better about things himself, actually, after reassessing his finances. If he planned carefully, he could pay his way here at Balmsley so he wouldn't be a burden on Amalie's family. And he would be near enough Maidstone to visit his son now and again. It would also give him time to overcome his own injury while he decided what to do with the rest of his life.

If this Dr. Raine was of the firm opinion Amalie could walk again unassisted, then Alex meant to make it happen. She needed a firm hand and a bit of prodding to get her up and going. Leaving her to the tender mercies of a family that loved her too much would be doing her no favor. She'd remain just as she was.

Well over an hour passed as he and Michael and Lord Harlowe ate a hearty meal and retreated to the library. They discussed the newspaper reports of Wellington's retreat from Burgos, the progress of the campaign in general, and carefully avoided any further exchanges about the coming nuptials. If banns were to be cried the following Sunday, no one mentioned it.

The doctor arrived around eleven o'clock and was immediately shown upstairs. Alex had not yet met the man, but was anxious to speak with him about Amalie. He folded the newspaper and laid it aside when he heard voices on the stairs.

Michael made the introductions when Lady Harlowe herself brought Dr. Raine into the library where they were waiting. As might be expected, Amalie's mother cut up stiff, just as she had done the night before, after she'd recovered from her swoon. She left without even making an excuse.

"So you are the betrothed," Raine said with a merry grin. Short, rotund and energetic described him. Laugh lines creased his entire face and a smooth bald pate reflected the light from the window. Alex put him near fifty. "I must say Miss Amalie is all atwitter about the engagement."

"Yes, well," Alex growled. "We are all *atwitter,* sir."

Michael grabbed the back of Alex's chair and shoved him toward the door. "This way, Doc," he said. "We've a new patient for you today. Alex is also a medical man, y'know. Says those army surgeons are crack-brained know-nothings. Takes one to know one, I expect." He laughed, chattering on incessantly, making light of the diagnosis Alex had received.

Raine followed and they were soon ensconced in the modest little chamber just off the hallway to the kitchens. "Off with you, my boy," he ordered Michael, who left reluctantly.

"Now then," Raine said, turning serious. "Let's get those pantaloons off you and see what damage was done."

"Not necessary," Alex protested. "But I would like to speak with you about Miss Amalie since she is to be my wife."

"No secret there anyway. She's got the idea embedded in her mind that she can't walk since the bones healed. Or it may be fear of pain. Does hurt, I know, getting back up on her pins. Nothing wrong with 'em now." He tapped his head. "Mind over body but not in the good sense if you see what I mean. Now about you…"

"I'll be fine," Alex said. "That nurse you assigned Miss Amalie. She's to prevent atrophying?"

"Therapeutic manipulation of the musculature often does wonders. Let's see the leg, Captain."

"No."

The doctor stood there with his pudgy hands grasping his hips. "I'm waiting. Don't think you'll foist me off now. Curiosity and all that."

"I *will* walk," Alex said emphatically.

"We'll see." He helped Alex to stand and shed his pantaloons, then assisted him to the bed.

"Hmm," Raine said as he examined the scar, then moved the leg about as he expertly palpated tendons and ligaments. He wasn't quite so loquacious now, limiting his remarks to that same wordless sound all doctors make. Alex recalled making it himself more times than he could count. Usually when he didn't want to say what he was thinking.

After a few pertinent questions regarding the treatment, both by the doctors and what Alex had attempted since, Raine stood away. "Well, that's that."

"That's what?" He made himself ask, knowing the answer.

The doctor ran a hand over his balding pate and shook his head. "You have read all the ancient texts, I'll wager. And while some insist positive thoughts can affect the outcome of infirmities, no amount of wishful thinking will let you flex that knee at will. It'll buckle on you every time you put weight on it. I don't need to tell you that."

"I will walk," Alex said mulishly as he grabbed his pants to dress.

"Never said you wouldn't do that," Raine argued. "Only that the knee won't work. It is fair wrecked and nothing can fix it."

Alex managed to push himself to a standing position and held on to the metal footboard. "Thank you for the opinion," he said with no sincerity and held out his hand.

Raine shook it firmly. "Good luck to you, son." He hesitated a second, then asked, "Where were you trained?"

"Royal College of Physicians at Edinburgh."

"Excellent training then. War is hell, eh? May I ask why you went and why, when there is so much to be learned from battle wounds, you did not practice your art there?"

"Personal reasons."

"You Scots are a dour lot and that's a fact. You be good to that girl," he said, and waited for Alex to nod. Then he was gone.

Alex glared down at his leg. He supposed he had accepted the truth somewhere inside him long before now.

He spent the better part of half an hour struggling to get his boots back on. One success at a time, he decided. He sat there on the bed in sartorial splendor until Michael came to fetch him.

Alex refused to get in the chair. "Find me two forked tree limbs, anything to serve, will you? I have got to be on my feet." The compulsion was so great it wouldn't be denied.

Michael rushed out, so eager to please it made Alex dizzy. He was gone for quite a while and was running when he returned. "Look!" he exclaimed, holding out a pair of crutches. "Amalie's idea! I went to get her unused ones to make a pattern, but I think we can use these. See what she suggested? Won't they work for now?"

Alex considered the odd-looking things. They obviously were made for a woman. The fittings for the armpits were quite small and very heavily padded with soft pink fabric. On the bottom tip of each, Michael had extended the length at least a foot by forcing on two long metal pipes.

"I dismantled the waterflow from the roof cistern," Michael proudly informed him with a thump to one of the cylinders.

"I'm sure your father will thank you for that," Alex said with a wry frown.

"C'mon, try 'em out!"

Tentatively, Alex took them and placed them just so. After a few awkward attempts at balancing, he got the hang of it. The pads were too small, the handholds too narrow and his left leg swung uselessly, slightly bent at the knee. But as he took his first real steps around that small chamber without hopping and grabbing on to the furniture, Alex felt freer than he had for months. "I must see that sister of yours and thank her," he said with a huge grin.

"Aye, Cap'n!" Michael crowed. "Follow me!"

She was waiting in the hall beside the large curved staircase and was seated in a chair almost identical, save for size, to the one he had just abandoned, hopefully forever.

"You look patently ridiculous lunging about on those pipe-rigged contraptions, Napier," she said before he could even greet her.

"And you look entirely too comfortable riding around in that thing," he replied, frowning at her chair. "But not for long."

He swung the crutches forward and heaved himself closer. Then again, and once more until he reached her side.

"From my heart, I thank you." Bracing himself carefully, Alex leaned down, reached for her hand to kiss it. But she raised her face as he did it and kissed him soundly on the mouth. Such a sweet mouth it was, too. Eager and soft, tasting of berries and cream and...

Her chair rolled backward under his weight. Alex tumbled back and landed flat on the floor, spread-eagled and helpless as an upturned tortoise. The clang of metal pipe bouncing on marble echoed through the cavernous hall.

"Napier! Sir, are you hurt?" she cried, leaning sideways in an attempt to touch him.

He turned his head and groaned. "Ow, run fetch me a compress, quick!"

To his great surprise, she very nearly did. Elbows up and hands gripping the arms of her chair, she rose several inches from the seat before she remembered and dropped back with a groan.

Arms outstretched and flat on the floor, Alex laughed with delight. "You nearly did it!"

"Wretch!" she shouted down at him. And rolled right over his fingers.

"Ow!" he cried, this time for real, clutching his hand and curling up to a sitting position.

Michael and the doctor rushed to him and helped him up. But Amalie did nothing save sit there frozen, both hands covering her mouth, her bright eyes wide.

"Fat lot of good those sticks will do me one-handed!" he snapped.

She had the grace to look sorry even if she wouldn't speak. He let Michael and Dr. Raine help him back to the small room off the hall and sit him down again on the bed. He tried to flex his fingers, but they were already swelling.

Raine examined them carefully, bending them anyway. "Not broken, just bruised. Good thing the girl's not hefty!"

She was a small mite, thank goodness. He could only imagine the damage if she were of any greater size.

"Amie didn't mean to do it," Michael assured him.

"Mmm-hmm, the gentlest of souls, I know," Alex cracked. "Go and tell her I'll survive. Can't have her grieving over a minor injury."

Raine chuckled. "That chit will lead you a merry chase, on wheels or no, I'll wager. Better put your good foot down at the outset, m'boy."

"On her neck," Alex muttered, nodding.

Now he was back to the chair again, the makeshift crutches broken and useless, the fingers of one hand nearly so. "Go on. See about her," he told Raine. "I'll be fine."

Two hours later, he and Amalie found themselves alone again, trapped in their chairs within the library, staring at the fire.

"I hate this place," Amalie said finally. "Read every volume in here at least three times."

"Anything I despise, it's an overeducated woman," Alex said.

She glared at him. "You don't say!"

He smiled. "I did say, but I didn't really mean it. You should be happy your family's wealthy enough to afford books. What if this had happened to you and you were mired in some drafty cottage, knitting for pennies, wondering whether your next meal would be more than porridge?"

She shrugged one shoulder. "I am an ingrate, I know. And I had vowed to be more pleasant today. Now here I have damaged your fingers, given poor old Raine the back of my head and bemoaned my fate." Her sigh was forlorn. "Not a good beginning."

"Start again," Alex suggested.

She offered him a sweet smile that appeared sincere. "All right. Tell me about your life. No, about your son. Is he very bright?"

"I don't know," Alex admitted. "I only saw him as a babe. He won't know me, of course."

"He'll probably adore you right away," she told him. "Boys admire soldiers. He won't understand anything other than the romance of war, not the reality."

"And I suppose you think you do?"

She cocked her head and studied him. "Somewhat. War hardens men. It surely troubles boys like Michael. Then there is the useless loss of life on both sides of the conflict. None of that is good."

Alex thought she had a pretty good grasp on it. "Ideals aside, war is hell on everybody, even the side that wins."

"That's as may be, but he will admire you all the same. We should bring your son here," she suggested. "There is much to entertain him. I would like to know him and I expect you would, as well."

"I doubt that would be possible. His grandmother blames me for his mother's death so he's most likely set against me, too. It's true. I couldn't save my wife."

Sympathy shone from her remarkable eyes. "I'm certain you did all you could for her."

Alex nodded slowly. "But it was not enough, and at the time, my guilt and grief were so great, I could think of nothing else."

"So you went to war. Tell me, did you have a thought of dying to punish yourself?"

"Something of that sort, in the beginning, I suppose. Olivia was so dear to me. We grew up neighbors, shared so much, our parents were the best of friends. When mine passed during the influenza outbreak, I was only seventeen. The MacTavishes were a great consolation to me. It was always assumed that Olivia and I would marry, so as soon as I finished my studies, we did."

"You loved her," Amalie said softly.

"Of course. She died in childbirth. Her mother took the babe. Said I owed her the child because I let hers die. Her demand seemed justified to my muddled mind, but in the six years since, I've realized how wrongheaded we both were."

He cleared his throat and stared out the window. "Now it would be cruel to him, as well as her, to take him back and perhaps not a wise thing in any event. I want my son, but ask myself if I would ever be able to do him justice as a father."

He looked up at her then. "Raine agrees with the other doctors. I will have no use of the leg."

"So you believe it now?" she asked. "Then I'm sorry you saw him. The death of hope hurts as much as the injury, doesn't it?"

"Not quite. At least not in my case. Maybe in the back of my mind I had already accepted it to some degree. But crutches gave me a feeling of more control. In time, a cane should do. I can live with that."

"You believe me a slacker," she accused. "I have tried, Napier. Truly tried. I *wish* to walk."

"But for some reason you have convinced yourself you cannot. You almost did it, though," he reminded her. "You almost came out of that chair."

She didn't show anger as he expected. Instead, she offered him a steady look of warning. "Take me as I am or I won't have you. So there's your way out of this."

So she thought. Alex knew nothing short of his immediate death would cancel his obligation. It was highly probable that no one other than her brother and parents would ever hear of their inadvertent indiscretion, but servants gossiped. Word, especially scandal, spread like a case of plague. She could be ruined for life if the tale got out.

Like it or not, they would have to marry.

Chapter Four

Michael left the next day for London and had stayed away for a week. Alex tried to be patient, but all day, every day, he kept an ear tuned for the sound of the coach returning. After carefully measuring Alex's height and hands, the lad had set off, determined to acquire the best pair of crutches he could have made. Perhaps Michael felt that Alex's saving his life outweighed the fact that his sister had been compromised. In any event, Michael still seemed to feel obliged to help and Alex was grateful for that.

The weather had proved foul, cold and damp, keeping Alex and the rest of the family near the fire. The old manse looked grand indeed, but boasted numerous drafts round the windows and doors. Heat immediately sought the high ceilings and left the occupants hovering near the fire.

Amalie's parents sat with them in the front parlor this afternoon. Her mother sighed and put down her knitting. "Why not play for us, dear?" she asked Amalie.

"Reading," Amalie replied, lifting her novel a few inches off her lap for emphasis.

"Come now," the baron insisted. "Put that book away and show your intended how accomplished you are."

She gave an inelegant little snort and turned a page.

"Can you not play well?" Alex asked with mock sympathy, daring her to take up the challenge. "Tuneless, are you? Well, I suppose that makes no difference."

She rolled her eyes, sighed and tossed the book on a side table, not even bothering to mark her place. "Oh, very well. Give me a push," she said to her da.

The baron laughed as he hopped up and wheeled her to the pianoforte. She shot Alex a haughty look and put her fingers to the keys. After an ostentatious prelude and an operatic trill, she changed tempo, holding his gaze as she dropped her voice to a sultry contralto and sang.

"Young Cock Robin rode to Town,
His one intent to marry.
When he got there, his friend did swear
The ladies turned up wary.
He then commenced to jump a fence
And seek out one less scary,
Who gave him drink and with a winnnnkk...
Invited him to tarry!"

Alex tried to stifle his laughter as the baron leaped to yank her away from the pianoforte and her mother collapsed in her chair, fanning herself with a handkerchief.

Amidst their apologies to him and fervent remonstrances to their wayward offspring, Alex heard loudest of all Amalie's deep frustration and anger.

He believed her. She had tried. It was not stubbornness that prevented her recovery. It was not her parents' over-indulgence. Her only weapons against her helpless situation were contrariness and dark humor. He knew, because he used those very weapons himself.

He wanted to…what? Commiserate with her? But how, so that she wouldn't see it as sympathy? That was worse than taunting her, wasn't it? It would be to him. He started to applaud, but the sound of a carriage outside in the dooryard interrupted him.

The baron ran to the window. "Michael's back. Everyone stay where it's warm. I'll go out to meet him."

The wait seemed interminable. Alex kept exchanging looks with Amalie, both ignoring her mother who rattled on endlessly about her daughter's inappropriate behavior.

The door to the parlor opened, commanding immediate attention. Michael stood there holding out the new crutches, smiling like a cream-fed cat. And then he stepped aside.

"Father?" squeaked a small voice.

Alex's heart leaped to his throat, choking off any words that might have erupted. The lad who stood there could have been himself at six. Sturdy, auburn haired and round faced with a stubborn chin and large green eyes that widened as they took in the wheeled chair and the one who sat in it.

Alex cleared his throat and nodded. "Davie?"

"David, sir," the boy replied. "Now I'm not a baby, I'm *David*."

"Of course you are." Alex found himself grinning ear to ear. "Come here then, David. Let me see you better." He held out a hand, eager as anything to touch the child he hadn't seen since infancy.

"Go on, David. Greet your father properly," a stern voice commanded.

Alex looked up to see his mother-in-law. "Hello, Mother

MacTavish." He had never called her else since his marriage to Olivia and didn't think to change it before the words were out.

"Alexander," she replied, her lips tightening after the greeting.

He looked back to the boy who had drawn near and was executing a formal bow. "You've become a man since last we met," Alex said proudly. "Look at you! Your mother would be so—"

"My mother's dead," the lad stated baldly, without inflection.

"I know." Alex felt tears welling, but blinked them back, his voice hardly more than a whisper.

"Are you truly a soldier?"

He managed a smile and reached out a hand, feeling the lad's reluctance when he took it. "I was. No more, though."

"Did you race into battle, kilt flying and swinging your sword at the enemy?"

Michael piped in. "He did that, David. Bravest soldier on the field, I swear. Saw him myself!"

He had done no such thing, Alex thought. They had not even met until both were in hospital trying to survive their wounds. But he didn't call the lie. David's first smile was worth saving at any cost.

Michael was making introductions then and Alex reluctantly took his eyes off the boy to see how they were going. Hilda MacTavish and the baroness were exchanging greetings. He noted for the first time how much older his mother-in-law seemed. She had lost at least a stone in weight and her face was pinched and pale.

She smiled at Amalie's mother as they met and Alex felt a pang in his chest. She had her daughter's smile, not as sweet or sincere, but it brought Olivia to mind. And the guilt.

He turned back to David. "Has Mr. Michael told you that I am to wed Miss Amalie?"

The boy nodded and cocked his head. "Is she to be my mother then?"

Alex hardly knew what to say. David's grandmother answered for him. "She is to be your *stepmother*."

David's eyes widened. "Not like the wicked ones in the stories!"

"Certainly not!" Amalie exclaimed. "I shall only be wicked when we play draughts or war with your little soldiers! Then you must watch out, for I will trounce you soundly! Depend on it!" She grinned at David and winked.

The boy chewed his lip. "I haven't any little soldiers."

"Oh, but you shall," she promised. "Michael, you must take David up to the nursery and acquaint him with the troops." She leaned forward in her chair. "But not before he has his tea and biscuits. Cook Nan makes the best you have ever tasted. Word on it."

David had drifted closer to her, assessing her carefully. "Were you a soldier and shot, too? Can ladies be soldiers?"

"Lands, no! Except in play," she said. "A clumsy old horse unseated me and I fell right in the dirt! Can you feature that?" Before he could answer, she gestured to her mother. "We should feed our guests, Mother, don't you think?"

The baroness was already standing. "Come, Mrs. Mac-Tavish. I'm certain you'd prefer to freshen up whilst I arrange for tea." Belatedly, she remembered the child. "Uh, David. Would you come, too?"

"I shall stay here, thank you."

Alex marveled at the conviction in his son's voice, the

maturity and swiftness with which he made the decision. Here was no overcoddled lad, but a strong-minded young man.

His chest swelled with pride, no matter that he'd had nothing to do with making the boy so. He guessed he must credit Mother MacTavish.

Suddenly as that, Alex realized that he, David and Amalie were in the room alone. Michael had propped the new crutches beside the door as he left.

"Could you bring me those, David?" he asked. "I feel remiss not greeting you on my feet."

"Aye, sir." The boy retrieved the crutches, one by one, handing them to Alex.

"Now then, grab my knees and give me a shove against that wall to brace the chair."

David hesitated only a moment before complying. "I can hold those upright for you, sir, if you like."

"Excellent idea. There's a good man." He pushed himself up and settled the crutches beneath his arms. "Ah, just right." He looked down at his son and held out his hand. "How do you do, Master David Napier? It is indeed a pleasure to meet you again."

"The pleasure is mine, sir," the boy replied, grinning up at him and showing the blank space where his front teeth had been. "I have heard so much about you."

"All good I would hope."

The boy's smile dwindled. "Some."

Amalie drew their attention to her, shaking a finger at Alex. "I'll warrant David's head is filled with your boyhood antics! You shan't have a leg to stand on when he misbehaves."

David cocked his head and regarded her with a matching grin. "He has one leg to stand on, miss."

"Amie. My good friends call me Amie and so shall you."

"I'm not to address elderly persons so familiar, miss."

Alex laughed at her expression and chose to let them work it out together.

"Miss Amie, then," she said finally, and regained her smile. "I quite like you, David. Forthrightness is to be admired."

He nodded. "Grandmother advises it. She says if I don't come off strong, the older classmates will beat me when I go off to school."

"When?"

"Next year, I believe."

Amalie darted Alex a frightened look. "He's not to go so young, surely!"

Alex had the very same thought, but reconsidered before he spoke. He was in no way to raise a child and neither was Amalie. Mother MacTavish had obviously realized her limits did not extend past David's reaching seven. Small wonder, for he recalled what a raucous handful he had been at that age. And the poor woman had done more than enough already. Still, Alex remembered, too, what boarding school had been like.

"We shall see," he answered quietly, already dreading the next separation from his son, however it must come. "Shall we go in to tea?" he asked.

David moved behind Amalie's chair and offered to push without anyone suggesting it. Neither of them had thought to ask it, but she thanked the boy and nodded. Alex followed, maneuvering better than he expected to on his new apparatus.

So many surprises today, he could hardly register them all.

"The house seems much warmer, don't you think?" Amalie asked over her shoulder.

"Infinitely," Alex agreed, answering her smile. Yet in his

heart, he was already preparing himself for giving up again the person he loved most in the world.

It must have shown on his face, for she added, "Enjoy the *now,* Napier."

But he wasn't trained to do that, had no experience in it ever. All his happy moments existed only in retrospect. Even when Olivia was alive, he could never recall himself stopping in the midst of anything to think, much less say, "I am happy at this very instant." He had been happy then, many times, but realized it only in retrospect. Amalie had opened his eyes to celebrating the moment.

"I smell cimmanum!" David exclaimed. "Yum!"

At least his son had an appreciation of the moment.

Chapter Five

A full week passed and Amalie figured they had all endured enough of Hilda MacTavish's ill humor. When she was not hovering over young David like a wolf bitch with only one cub, she busied herself flinging ill-disguised accusations at Napier and making snide reference to Amalie's uselessness.

Napier needed a flogging for allowing the woman to carry on so. Where was the spirit he'd shown when he first came? Where was that humor with which he turned insults aside and made their speaker feel foolish? It was still within him, that was for certain, and neatly employed when the barbs came from her own mouth.

She supposed it fell to her to set the woman to rights. Finally, she found Mrs. MacTavish alone in the parlor embroidering whilst Michael had David outdoors, visiting the stables.

Amalie wheeled herself into the parlor, stopping when the edge of the plush Turkey carpet prevented her getting any nearer. Hilda wore unrelieved black as she always did, a color that in no way flattered her seamless complexion or the honeyed tint of her whitening hair. She was not so old as she tried to seem, probably only forty-five or thereabout. Amalie decided on flattery and distraction as the best approach.

"A word with you, Mrs. MacTavish?" she asked sweetly.

The woman put down her embroidery hoop and glared at Amalie with narrowed eyes. "Why?"

Amalie shrugged. "I thought we should become better acquainted." She paused. "Tell me, madame, since you have been widowed for nearly two years now, have you given any thought to returning to society?"

That met a short gust of disbelief.

"I mean to say, you are young yet and quite lovely. It seems a shame to deprive so many others of your company. And since you are living not far from London—"

Hilda sat forward, furious, as she interrupted. "How dare you presume so! And I resent your condescension regarding my appearance. I am *not* lovely and society can well do without yet another unattached female in its gaudy midst!"

Amalie smiled. "Forgive me for the suggestion. I but thought you must be dreadfully unhappy with matters as they stand. You certainly do seem so."

That took Hilda aback. She let go a heavy sigh and sat back again, roughly fiddling with her embroidery hoop and tangling the threads. "I am quite content and I shall thank you to leave me be."

"I must speak my mind on this," Amalie said gently. "Can you not see how your bitter vitriol could eventually affect your grandson? Not to mention how unfair it is to Alexander."

Hilda immediately rose and left the room without another word. Amalie watched her go, congratulating herself on holding her temper in check and not launching a pithy verbal attack. She might have done so if she had not sensed the fear in Hilda. Perhaps Napier should be told of that.

Or perhaps he already knew, Amalie thought suddenly. Why else would he meet Hilda's harsh words with such forbearance? If so, it did speak well of the man. That, added to the obvious love he had for his son, warmed Amalie to the core. Napier had a goodness in him she admired. And envied, she admitted.

Goodness, determination and a quick wit. And the ability to love deeply. How many of those qualities could she boast? Amalie wondered whether she even deserved the man a little! Fine one was she to cast stones at Hilda MacTavish for living a bitter-lipped existence that made people miserable.

She rested her chin on her palm and began to examine her own past behavior in earnest.

A good half hour passed before her brother burst in, followed by Napier and the boy. David had one hand firmly clamped on to Napier's right crutch.

"You should see our lad ride!" Michael exclaimed, turning to urge David forward. All three were grinning proudly, wind tossed, cheeks and noses reddened from the cold.

Amalie's heart lurched. How she wished she'd been with them out there in the late November sun. Her right leg ached for its position around the curved horn of her side-saddle, her hands itched for the feel of reins in them. Never to ride again seemed the most awful thing and one she had not allowed herself to dwell upon since her accident.

She forced a smile. "So, he has a good seat, does he? Then he must have a pony!" She shot Michael a worried look. "Surely you haven't set him up by himself on a full-size horse!"

"Yes, but on a lead. He managed very well." Napier's

large hand cupped the boy's shoulder for an affectionate squeeze. Then he maneuvered himself to the settee and offered the crutches to David. "Settle these for me, would you? Good man," he said, when the boy had stacked them neatly against the arm and within reach.

David beamed at the praise. He was such a sturdy little fellow and the absolute spit of his father. Amalie felt a surge of something strongly maternal whenever she looked at David. She shared a meaningful look with Napier that defied mere words.

"Well, I'm off for a quick wash before tea. Want to come, David?"

"Yes, sir. Riding's turrible dusty. Da?"

Napier waved him off. "I'll bide awhile. You're the one who reeks of horse." He added in a stage whisper. "Remember to bow."

David did so. "Excuse us, please, Miss Amie."

Amalie nodded and when they had gone, she turned to Napier. "His manners exceed yours."

"And yours," he retorted.

"And those of his grandmother! Frightful beast of a woman!"

He frowned at that. "Never speak ill of Mrs. MacTavish."

"Why? Her one goal in life seems to be making you out a villain of the worst order. And she's none too fond of me, that's for certain!"

"She believes I let her daughter die and now will take away the child who replaced her loss." He expelled a sigh. "And how am I to do that to her?"

"How can you *not?* She's sending him away to school next year! At *seven!*"

"Not *away.* I spoke to her about it. He's going to a school there in Maidstone."

Amalie regretted broaching the subject and decided to turn it since there was no point to the confrontation. "My back is breaking in this confounded chair." She tried to move it, but the wheels were stuck on the edge of the rug.

He grasped one of his crutches and hooked the handle over her front wheel, tugging her onto the carpet. Then he pulled her chair closer and beckoned for her to lean forward. When she did, he grasped her body and lifted her onto the cushion beside him. "There. Better?"

The strength of his arms amazed her. The sudden closeness of him overwhelmed her senses. He smelled of fresh air, leather and sandalwood soap. Perhaps a hint of evergreen. She breathed deeply and leaned closer, her shoulder and arm resting against his.

When she raised her eyes, he was looking down at her and the tempo of his breathing changed. His lips opened as if he would speak, but he said nothing. Instead he lowered his head and kissed her softly.

She felt his hand at her waist, the other cup her neck as his thumb caressed her chin. The kiss grew deeper, stealing her breath and her reason. Desire flowed through her veins like warm honey, sweet as the taste. Amalie shuddered, lost in the feelings she had only dreamed about.

He released her and peered into her eyes as if looking for something he desperately sought.

"What is it you want?" she gasped without thinking. "Tell me…show me."

Her question might have been a dash of cold water. He sat back immediately, releasing her and moving away as if she'd suddenly screamed for help.

"Nothing," he said, his voice curt. "For a moment, I lost

my head. I haven't kissed a woman in a very long time and here you were."

"Where you *put* me!" she snapped. "So *any* woman would have done, I suppose."

He cleared his throat and avoided looking at her.

"We kissed by the stairs. Have you forgotten that so soon?" She hadn't, that was for certain. The feel of his lips on hers had disturbed her sleep and a great portion of her waking moments.

He did look at her then. "I didn't forget it, but it was you who kissed me if you recall. This was *my* doing." His voice was soft with a touch of regret. "You're not entirely safe with me, you know. Everything about me works but one knee. It would be wise of us to have a care or we could find ourselves wed for good and all."

"What? How *else* could we be wed? Surely you are not suggesting a silly handfast marriage such as you have in Scotland! That's absurd! Not even legal here."

At that, he smiled. "The custom is a bit frowned upon these days, even north of the border. Nay, I'd thought that once you recover the use of your legs, we could arrange an annulment. Unless we...you know."

"Consummate the marriage?" Amalie asked bluntly.

He blushed. He actually blushed. Fancy that.

Oh, Lord. Amalie realized she was staring at him, shaking her head, giving him the impression she might want to...you know. Well, perhaps she did, but she would never admit as much to him.

It was only curiosity on her part, surely. She had only kissed two men before. Boys, really. She had never even entertained the thought of physical relations with them. But Napier had stirred something inside her that felt rather dangerous and very enticing. Damn him for it!

She tore her gaze from his. "Fine. If that is what you wish, so be it." How much plainer could he make the fact that he could never want her as a wife? "Would you leave?"

"Of course. I can be on my way directly after the wedding."

She rolled her eyes. "I meant *immediately*. Leave the *room*." If he did not, she feared she would grab the nearest heavy object, like the marble lamp on the side table, and brain him with it.

Alex snatched up his crutch and hopped over to retrieve the other one. If he had learned anything in his twenty-eight years, it was that a woman in a snit was best left alone. He couldn't figure what he had done to make her so angry. He was the one suffering for the restraint, not her.

Michael obviously hadn't discussed the idea of an annulment with her. Once she'd had time to digest it, she would see it was for the best.

He swung the crutches forward a step, loving the feel of being upright whenever and however long he wanted and not having to balance on one foot to do so. If only he could devise a brace of some kind to make his knee stable, he could probably manage a cane. "I'll find a way," he muttered under his breath.

Alex had just cleared the doorway of the parlor when he saw her.

"I daresay you will manage," Mother MacTavish said, her tone bitter. "But for her sake, you should not."

Alex was so shocked he couldn't speak.

"Yes, I saw you kiss her. And I just heard you declare you'd *find a way*," she declared. "If the girl is fool enough to wed you, she should know what to expect! You have no thought for anyone but yourself and your pleasure! She is a cripple, Alexander. Will you thoughtlessly get her with child?"

He saw the tears in her eyes and knew she spoke mostly out of grief for Olivia. She obviously had not overheard their conversation, only his last utterance and had misinterpreted that. But even so... "This is none of your affair, madame."

"No? You plan to marry this girl and take David from me to live with you. Of course it's my affair! I live for that child since you destroyed the only one I had!"

"I loved Olivia, too, you know."

"Yes, all *too* well, unfortunately!" she exclaimed. "And yet far too little." She turned on her heel and marched off down the hallway, leaving him alone to stew in his remorse.

He glanced back into the parlor. Amalie had turned, facing him with a look of compassion. "That was *so* unfair," she said. "So undeserved."

Alex couldn't answer. In his mind he knew he had done everything within his power to save his wife, but it had not been enough. The fact remained, he *had* been the cause of Olivia's travail. Without the stress of childbirth, she would still be alive. He had always loved and wanted Olivia, had adored her first as a friend, then as a husband and lover. Theirs had been a comfortable and expected union, a match both had welcomed and treasured. But his feelings for Amalie were keener, more intense. Somehow deeper despite their brevity.

And here was another young woman, one he desired even more than he had Olivia and deserved even less. Amalie was not ambulatory, her strength depleted by so many months of lassitude. She should not be put at risk of a pregnancy in her condition and he would see she was not.

He needed to think. Obviously, Amalie wanted to wed and expected a real marriage to ensue. Maybe she thought his was the only offer she would ever receive, given her belief that she'd never walk again. If he simply refused to marry her and left things as they were, who would change that belief? She would remain a cripple all her life and that would be his fault.

They must marry. And he must somehow convince her to keep their union platonic.

Amalie puffed out a breath of frustration. What was she to do about Napier and his dratted guilt? Mrs. MacTavish seemed determined to keep it at the forefront of his mind. For some reason, the woman had not yet poisoned his little son's opinion of the father, though. One would think she would have done so at every opportunity.

Her mother chose that moment to enter the parlor. She carried several swatches of fabric with her and sat down beside Amalie, plopping the samples in her lap. "Which do you think for your gown, my dear? Should it be the pale blue—a color that will surely enhance your eyes—or the yellow to highlight your hair?"

The dress didn't signify, Amalie thought impatiently. What did it matter whether she made a beautiful bride or not? Napier would probably not notice in any event. "It doesn't matter, Mama. Whatever you think."

"I like the blue." She glanced up from the swatches. "Are you afraid of him?"

The question jerked Amalie from her musing about Napier's regard. "Afraid? Why ever should I be afraid of him? He's a perfectly nice man!"

Her mother shrugged as she nervously fiddled with the fabrics. "For a Scot, I suppose. They are notorious for quick tempers. And Mrs. MacTavish has said he was overly…passionate. Before, you know, with her daughter. Your father and I shouldn't like you to be exposed to such."

Amalie coughed a short laugh of disbelief that her

mother would even broach such a subject. "You and Father discussed this?"

"Of course we did! And he is not so set on the marriage as you suppose. Michael is adamant we go forth, however. I think he fair worships Captain Napier."

Amalie figured it was time she asserted herself. For months now, she had decided on nothing for herself, letting the winds of life blow her whatever way they would. She had become the very kind of woman she had always pitied before. No more of that. If her life was to be her own, she must direct it.

"I will marry him, Mother, and you are not to worry." She plucked one of the samples. "I choose the blue, a simple empire style, no embellishment, save a white lace frill at the neckline."

Her mother frowned. "You are certain? About Napier, I mean."

"I am certain. He is the one."

That drew a small gasp. "I should have a talk with you before you're wed. Your father says I should."

Amalie patted her mother's hand. "Unnecessary, I assure you." Tempted as she was to see just how her mother would address the matters of the marriage bed, Amalie would spare her sensibilities. "I am well-read and observant, too." She leaned to kiss her mother's cheek. "And I will muddle through as all women do, I expect."

She noted her mother's frowning glance at her immobile legs and the slight shake of her head. Mama said nothing, but she was very obviously wondering how...

"Either we will manage or we won't. As it stands now, Napier wishes our marriage to be in name only."

And when that changes, Mama, Amalie thought to herself, *you need never know it.*

"In name only. My, what a relieving notion." Satisfied, her mother kissed her cheek and left, humming a little tune. Amalie belatedly recognized it as the off-color song she had played as a poor jest to discombobulate them soon after her betrothal.

Perhaps Mama knew her better than she thought.

Well, Amalie realized if she meant to take charge of her life, there was no time like the present to begin. She envied Napier his mobility. She envied his determination. And she dearly wanted to prove him right about her own ability to walk.

Could she have given up too soon? The truth was, she had never felt she deserved a normal life after the tragedy that was her fault. If only she had not been so set on riding Morgana, the mare Father had warned her not to attempt.

She had made friends with the roan, had her taking sugar lumps and apples out of hand without biting. Amalie had even sat astride Morgana's back without incident. It was only when she took her out of the enclosure that the poor thing had gone wild.

Then Jem, the stable lad she had known since their infancy, was trampled to death trying to keep the mare from attacking Amalie after she'd been thrown. And Father had ordered the beautiful Morgana put down.

Two needless deaths, Amalie thought with a sigh. Her fault entirely. Did she have the right to recover?

On the other hand, did she have the right *not* to make the most of her life in recompense for the loss of Jem's?

She made her decision.

Carefully, Amalie did a half turn, braced her hands firmly on the arm of the settee and pushed herself up. She balanced, stiff, tense, afraid to breathe. But she had barely straightened fully when the muscles in her legs trembled and then, as if her bones turned to liquid, gave way. She fell back to the cushions with a solid thunk.

"So much for will and effort," she grumbled under her breath. But in that all too brief second or two, she had felt almost whole again and she craved more.

Chapter Six

Plans marched forward for a wedding that would take place just after the holidays. The new year would mark the beginning of Amalie's new life as a married lady. Mrs. MacTavish would stay on for the ceremony. Little David had been the deciding factor there. She would not leave without him and knew that Napier would not let him go.

Whatever the reason, Amalie was delighted the boy would be there. She grew fonder of the child every day. He was noisy, overactive and into constant scrapes just as her younger brother had been at that age.

It would be such a joy to have a little one about for the holidays. And afterward, too. Perhaps for good if she could convince Napier that they could manage him better than the grandmother.

If only her secret attempts to stand on her own, to eventually walk again, were more successful. Then they could have some semblance of a normal family life to offer David. She knew she would keep trying.

Each time she tried, she managed to balance upright for a few seconds longer. Almost a full minute now, though she couldn't take a step to save her life. But one day she meant to go skipping about the meadows the way she used to, hopefully with a child or two in tow. The burgeoning hope certainly put her in a holiday mood.

Amalie always considered herself fortunate to live in the country where they celebrated the holidays. City folk hardly ever did, so she heard.

Thankfully, this house always spent the entire month of December festooned with greenery and berries. The mouthwatering smells of baking cakes and puddings filled each day as preparations got well under way.

No one reveled more in the expectations of good things to come than the younger Napier. This evening they would exchange gifts to mark the season. David crouched eagerly beside the fire as Michael helped him roast chestnuts.

"Do you think Grandmama will like these?" he asked her brother.

Michael raked a few from the coals and set them into the pile that was cooling on the hearth. "When you sack them up in that silky pouch you helped Amie to stitch, your grandmama will love it. Marvelous idea you had there, mate!"

David looked so serious as he gripped the bag they had made out of scraps and ribbon. His sooty little fingerprints only added to its charm as far as Amalie was concerned. Mrs. MacTavish had better think so, too.

Amalie thought of the jaunty cap she had made for the boy from a length of wool Napier had snipped from his Blackwatch plaid. A *braw bonnet,* Napier had called it as he voiced his approval. She had of necessity asked his opinion as to whether it resembled enough the tams that Scotsmen wore. She had added a pom of red yarn to the top and banded the cap with black grosgrain.

Napier had whittled a small wooden sword and carved

intricate designs upon it. Michael had driven Mrs. MacTavish to Maidstone earlier in the week on some errand. Amalie suspected the woman had gone to buy something for David. In any event, the boy should have a holiday to remember.

"Will those cool in time?" David was asking Michael.

"Oh, in plenty of time for the gifting. Here, these few are ready now, you see?"

David gingerly picked up the chestnuts and dropped them one by one into the pouch. His smile warmed Amalie's heart as it always did.

Napier swung into the room on his crutches, a bit more practiced and agile after frequent outings in the garden these past few days. "Good evening," he said, taking a seat beside her on the settee. "Quite warm out for the time of year."

She smiled. "It is freezing and you know it, but I doubt a blizzard would keep you inside." She leaned sideways and surprised him with a kiss on his cheek.

He smiled in response, but the kiss did seem to discomfit him. So much so that he didn't comment on it.

Her parents entered just then, her father bearing a basket of gaily wrapped gifts. Moments later, Mrs. MacTavish made her entrance with one large gift. When all were greeted and seated, Michael took charge.

"We haven't a huge yule log, but Father, David and I have provided one that should keep us warm through the festivities." The two proceeded to dump the oversize section of a tree trunk onto the smoldering ashes in which they'd roasted the chestnuts. He stoked it to a flame, then turned to the boy. "Now, my man, it is time for you to present our gifties whilst I provide music!"

David's little chest puffed out with pride as he waited for Michael to reach the pianoforte and begin playing softly. "Grandmama, you first, for you are the oldest!"

Mrs. MacTavish quickly erased her frown.

"This is for you from me," David said, presenting the rather grubby pouch of warm chestnuts. She accepted them with sincerest thanks, commenting on how good they smelled.

Then he reached into a box beside the hearth and turned to her parents. "Milord and Lady Harlowe, new nib pens from Mr. Michael and me. I found the feathers and he trimmed 'em." Her mother and father applauded and smiled, accepting their gift.

"Miss Amie, for you," David said, handing Amalie a small packet of sachets, purchased no doubt from one of the local ladies in the village. She sniffed them appreciatively. "Lavender! My very favorite!"

"And Father," David said at last. "I made you a picture with watercolors." He tore off the wrapping himself before Napier could take hold of it. "See, Da? It's Scotland!"

"Indeed it is. Old Ben Muir," Napier said, eyeing the bare, purplish mountain with gorse and heather stippled over it in a childish hand. "Well done, David," he added, his voice thick with pride. "Very well done."

Amalie saw the tears gathered in his eyes, though he never let them fall. She offered him a smile and he returned it with a sheepish quirk of his lips. She thought she had never loved him more and the very idea shocked her.

She *loved* Napier. Alexander. The Scot. When had that happened? From the first meeting? No. Later, perhaps, when he met her every insult with humor and equanimity? Did it even matter when? She loved him now with a mixture of such longing, exasperation and need to give that she could barely stand it.

She had only meant to make him like her and to learn to like him. Love was not what she'd always thought it was. Not an easy thing at all. He almost surely had no such feelings for her, and why should he? She had not given him a single reason to feel so. He probably didn't even like her very much. But he *did* want her and that was a fact. And it was a start.

He gave her a silver trinket box lined with silk that held a delicate brooch set with amethyst stones. Amalie thanked him rather more formally than she would have liked, then produced her gift to him, handkerchiefs embroidered with his initials. He smiled and complimented her needlework. How proper they were with each other after such an improper beginning.

"Your turn, I believe," Napier was saying to his son. He presented the beautifully carved wooden sword and Amalie added the tam she had made. Michael and her parents gave David a mechanical bank, a metal monkey that snatched a penny as he raised his hat.

The boy delighted in everything. His manners were impeccable when he remembered them. When he forgot was when he was most adorable, Amalie thought with a grin. Away from his grandmother's watchful eye, he was a rambunctious little rascal. This evening he was an angel.

She pictured Alexander as being very like him at that age. That made her wonder what his daughters would be like when he had some. She dearly wanted them looking somewhat like her. Little hellions, most likely. At the fantasy, her grin grew wider still.

And then Mrs. MacTavish produced the skates.

David's mouth dropped open in absolute wonder as he ran his small fingers reverently over the highly polished blades attached to shiny leather boots. He threw himself into his grandmother's arms. "Oh, Granny! Skates! Thank you, thank you! You knew what I most wished for in the whole world. You always do!"

Mrs. MacTavish tossed Napier a gloating look of superiority over her grandson's shoulder. Amalie wanted to smack her for it. The woman never let an opportunity pass to remind them that David was better off in her care than he ever would be in theirs. But one had to admit, the skates were a brilliant move to secure David's undivided affection.

Amalie leaned closer to Napier and said behind her hand, "I knew we should have gotten the pony."

"His birthday's next month," Napier replied in a whisper. "And I've a saddle on order."

Amalie placed her hand over his and gave it a squeeze. "Well, then, let her top *that* if she thinks she can!" She smiled back at Mrs. MacTavish, granting the woman today's small victory.

Amalie realized that at some time during David's visit, she had begun to lay a motherly claim upon him. And while she did not approve of spoiling children in general, she wanted to make this boy happy, to show him how much a real family with two loving parents could do for him as he grew to manhood. She felt responsible for making that happen and she would, no matter what.

When all the gifts were given, they went into a late dinner of roast beef and plum pudding. Amalie hardly tasted the food, so busy was she in planning her future. Nothing could go wrong, she kept telling herself. The wedding was set, only a week away. David would stay. She would have all the time in the world to regain her ability to walk. Then, in realizing she was not a slackard, Napier would like her, perhaps even come to love her in time. She would work to that end with all the energy and determination she could muster.

Chapter Seven

The next morning, after a restless night, Alex dressed and took up his crutches, intending to head for the breakfast room, but David almost ran him down in the hallway. "Father, come and watch me skate! Granny says I may on the shallow fishpond! Will you come?"

"Absolutely! Wouldn't miss it. Do you know how it's done?"

"Aye. I've skated a bit with borrowed ones, but it's hardly ever cold enough to freeze," he declared, grasping on to one of Alex's crutches as was his custom.

His son thought he was helping and Alex didn't even think of disabusing him of the notion. It was as close to holding the lad's hand as he could get while walking together.

"Where are you off to? Aren't you two hungry?" Michael asked as he wheeled Amalie toward the breakfast room.

"A skating expedition," Alex explained. "Apparently it won't wait until after we eat."

"Come watch me!" David chirped, grinning as his grandmother also approached to accompany them.

Alex offered her a smile and said good morning, wishing they could mend fences. It did not look likely and he did understand. She would be lost without David, but then, so would he. And a boy needed a father.

Michael fetched Amalie a blanket and wrapped her against the cold, but she argued him out of the weather shield that attached to the front of the chair. Michael pushed as Alex lurched along beside her, David hanging on to his far crutch, gaily impeding his progress. Alex could not recall a time since his injury when he had felt such contentment.

I am happy now, he thought with wonder. This very moment.

Suddenly, unable to wait, David let go and made a dash for the little frozen pond at the edge of the garden. It was a man-made pool used in warmer weather to hold fish caught for the kitchens until they were ready to be cooked.

David plopped down near it, kicked off his shoes and began donning his new skates. Just beyond the pond lay the lake crusted with ice. The entire tableau, including his son, was beautiful beyond words, Alex thought. As life should be.

Michael parked Amalie within five feet of the pond, near a stone bench where his mother-in-law had taken a seat. Alex sat on the other end, propping his stacked crutches between them.

They watched as David stood, ankles wobbling, and cut his way to the ice of the fishpond. Amalie applauded when the lad achieved his balance and took a few hesitant slides.

Within minutes, he had the hang of it and was gliding around in a circle on the solid sheet of ice. Alex called encouragement and Amalie's soft laughter warmed the event. His mother-in-law issued hums of approval and actually returned Alex's proud grin. Maybe the boy would bring peace between them eventually.

Michael excused himself to return to the house for a heavier coat. The sun shone brightly, but it was frightfully cold. Alex wished he had opted for something more substantial, and nodded as Michael offered to fetch his woolen cape for him.

Unfortunately, David used the distraction of Michael's leaving to search out a greater arena. When Alex looked back at his son, the lad had crossed the short stretch of lawn that separated the pond from the lake. He was at the edge already.

"David!" he cried, and fumbled for his crutches, but Hilda had knocked them to the ground in her rush to get up.

Alex hopped frantically toward the lake. A rush of rose-coloured fabric swished past him and he nearly fell down in shock. Amalie was on her feet. And running right past Hilda, too!

She dashed straight for David just as he disappeared beneath the broken ice. Without hesitation, she jumped in and followed the boy down. Her skirts billowed, then vanished into the freezing waters.

"They'll both be lost!" Alex cried, and fell to his knees, scrambling to the shattered crust of ice at the edge. It gave way and he submerged.

The water was only chest deep, he realized as he got his feet under him. He began tearing at the ice, breaking away chunks, making a larger opening, hoping against hope that Amalie and David could find their way back up to the surface.

Amalie's head emerged. "I have him! Help me!" she gasped.

Alex clutched her wrist and tugged. Her other hand held fast to David's coat. Together they struggled out of the water, dragged the boy out and laid him on the bank.

Hilda was screaming at the top of her lungs.

"Shut up!" Amalie commanded. "Get Michael and my father! Anyone you can find! Now! *Go!*"

Alex had rolled David to his stomach and was trying to press water from his body so he could take in air, but the boy wasn't responding. He continued to work, treading a fine line to keep from breaking the lad's ribs and yet applying enough pressure to empty the lungs.

Michael and Lord Harlowe had arrived and stood close by with Hilda. No one spoke as Alex turned David to his side and kept pressing and releasing. Suddenly, a gurgle sounded and David expelled a gush of liquid, gagging and coughing spasmodically. Then he began to cry.

Alex grabbed the boy off the ground and held him close, weeping unashamedly, burying his face in the crook of David's shoulder.

"Amalie!" Michael shouted. When Alex turned, he saw his intended lying on the dry grass.

"I'm all right. Only resting," Alex heard her rasp. Her brother scooped her up and headed for the house.

"I'll take the boy," Lord Harlowe offered. "He's breathing all right now, simply frightened." And howling because he'd lost one of his skates. Harlowe reached for the squirming child. "We should get him warm right away. Let go of him, Captain."

"Here, Alexander," Hilda said, sniffling loudly. "Your crutches."

He let Amalie's father take David from him. Hilda started to follow, then turned back, looking at Alex oddly, fingers pressing against her lips. Then she hurried back to his side and stayed by him, helping him get to his feet and position his crutches so that he could follow the others.

"Thank you," he said once he'd gotten his balance.

"You saved our boy," she said, her voice teary. "He'd be dead if not for you."

"It was Amalie who dove in for him. I'd never have managed by myself."

"Oh, I know. That brave girl, how can we ever thank her? I'm so sorry, Alex," she cried, burying her face in her hands.

"No need," he assured her. "You couldn't have known David would try for the lake. He told me you gave permission only to skate the fishpond. And he didn't know the lake was too deep to have frozen solid as the shallow pond."

"That...that's not what I mean. You...you were so good to let me have David when..."

He picked up the pace. "I wasn't *good,* Hilda. I was selfish in my grief. There was no chance I could have been a proper father at the time. I know how you feel about giving him back. We'll work things out somehow. Now stop this weeping and hurry on without me. See he's thawed out and comforted until I can get there, will you?"

She nodded, lifted her skirts and ran as fast as she could. Alex stumped along after her, hoping with all his heart that lung fever wouldn't take his son and that Amalie would not suffer for her heroic rescue. He couldn't bear to think what would have happened if she had not found that burst of will to get to his son in time when he could not.

Of course, this meant Alex must lose her. There was no way she could deny the use of her legs now. He did not know what course of events had caused her to do so before, but it was surely a thing of the past. Amalie could walk. She could run. What woman in her right mind would want to attach herself to a man who could not?

If she had been his wife before or even a betrothed who loved him, then she would be obligated to follow through and take care of him. But they had not even known each other. She certainly deserved a better opportunity, a better match.

Michael would be the only one to object to breaking the engagement. For Amalie's sake, he would simply have to understand.

A sadness he had seldom experienced enveloped him, warring with the elation over his son's escape from a watery death.

He was exhausted and wet to the core. He'd be lucky to make it to the steps of the house in his condition. Maybe he should simply collapse in the garden and freeze to death. That would solve everyone's problems, even his own. That problem being how he was to give up gracefully his recent taste of contentment and happiness. But death was no answer. If he'd ever thought it was, he would never have made it home from the peninsula.

Two footmen reached him just then and all but carried him inside between them. After being reassured that both David and Amalie had quite recovered and were resting comfortably, Alex was treated to a hot bath and put to bed like a child. His leg ached abominably and he felt chilled right down to his soul, unable to stop shivering. Hilda entered then, dosed him with laudanum despite his objection and proceeded to tuck him in. Hilda herself tucked him in.

"Like old times," she said, smiling down at him as she adjusted his covers. Much to his surprise, she laid a soft kiss on his forehead. "You were such a dear little boy. Remember when your parents went on their trip to Italy and you stayed with us?"

Of course he remembered. Hilda had been a different person then, laughing, happy. "I was what? About six?"

"Yes, just David's age now, wasn't it? La, he reminds me

so of you then. Gets up to such tricks. You recall when you and Olivia found that hedgehog and put it in my jewel box?"

He smiled at the memory. "You threatened to thrash us both and should have done. I'd quite forgot."

He noticed tears streaming down her face. "Please don't cry. I expect you've wept enough for both of us, especially for Olivia. You know I loved her with my whole heart, surely? I did all in my power to save her."

She nodded. "I know. I think I've always known that, but I needed someone to blame and there was only you."

"It's all right. I understood."

She fussed with his covers again. "And now you love this girl, Amalie." Her sigh was long and loud. "I don't begrudge you, Alex. You should be happy. Olivia would want it and Amalie will be a good and loving mother to our boy. It's only that I'll miss David so dreadfully when you take him from me. I fear I shan't be able to bear it."

Alex patted the hand she rested on his arm. "Don't worry. I'll see that you and David will be together often."

She obviously wasn't convinced as she turned to leave. "Mother Hilda?"

She looked back at him, her eyes red and her mouth pressed tight.

"I've missed you," he said, wanting to say more when he realized he was being perfectly honest, not just attempting to lighten her sadness. "And I thank you for being a parent to David in my absence. I wish I could repay you."

"It was my pleasure. My only joy." She shrugged and left him alone to think how he could save her more grief. Anything but giving up his son to her again, he decided. He could not do that.

But unless he went through with the marriage to Amalie, sacrificed his pride and lived off her wealth, how could he provide any kind of home for David? If he did go ahead with the wedding, how grandly would that reward Amalie for her selfless rescue of his son? The questions followed him into a restless sleep.

Amalie could not be still. From the time she regained her wits and body warmth, she had been on her feet. The entire family followed her about as if she'd fall on her face at every turn. She was tired, her muscles aching and trembling like mad, but it felt so wonderful!

"Why don't you come away and leave him alone?" Michael asked in a loud whisper. "He's bare as newborn and you can see his naked back! It's not proper, Amie."

"Prude! It's only a back." But what a back it was, skin smooth, stretched tightly over great muscles she wanted to knead, to feel and stroke. Ah, she was in lust with the man. And in love with him, too.

Love had not turned out to be what she'd once thought it, a blending of desire and admiration. It was that, too, of course, but also a driving need to put someone else before yourself, to trust completely, to protect, to console, to inspire, to adore. Gad, she was in over her head here as surely as she had been out there in the lake. Would Alex ever come to feel this way about her?

At Michael's urging, Amalie closed the door to Napier's room after checking him for the twentieth time that day. Hours had passed and he still slept, but it looked to be the sleep of the damned the way he had tossed the covers. If only she could hold him in her arms right now and calm him. Imagining his shocked expression made her smile wryly.

She could hardly wait for him to wake, for him to see how she could walk almost normally. What would he say about that? She wondered if he would praise her and like her now. Or would he feel the same envy that she had felt, seeing him upright on crutches?

Michael took her arm and led her firmly back into the library where her parents were sitting. They looked on anxiously while her brother practically forced her onto the settee. Perhaps they feared she would not be able to get up again, that her walking today was a fluke that would reverse itself if she didn't keep at it. Truth told, she had worried about that possibility herself.

"So what will you do about the captain?" Michael asked, trying hard to sound merely conversational.

She could see how important her answer was to him, however. Michael was never one to mask his feelings well. Neither was she. "Do you mean whether I intend to break off the engagement now that I've regained the ability to walk? Do you really think me that shallow, Michael? I shall marry the man, of course."

"He'll want you to end it," Michael warned. "He said as much to me, that when you recovered, he'd seek an annulment."

"Perhaps you *should* cry off," her mother suggested. Her father was nodding in agreement.

"Not if he should be bedridden the rest of his life!" Amalie declared. "If he refuses to marry me, I shall bring suit against him for breach of promise, see if I don't!"

Michael rolled his eyes. "One would think you were in love with the man!"

Amalie smiled evenly. "One would think so, wouldn't one?"

His mouth dropped open. "Are you?"

"No doubt," Amalie said, meeting his and her parents' identical looks of surprise. "All that remains is to convince him of it." And she knew how.

Chapter Eight

Alex woke with a start, uncertain whether he had dreamed David's near drowning, Amalie's run for the lake, Hilda's sudden devotion. All of it seemed too real to have been a dream, but it seemed so unlikely to have happened, he had to wonder.

Slowly, he sat up, swung his legs over the side of the bed and saw his boots by the chair. The leather was dark, water soaked. No dream, then.

David and Amalie might need him. He hopped to the small cupboard, gathered clothing and dressed as quickly as he could. There was nothing for it but to venture forth in his stocking feet since his boots were wet and he had no other footwear.

He heard voices in the dining room and headed there. The whole family was seated and in the midst of a meal. Since they only ate there in the evenings, he reckoned he had slept most of the day.

"Ah, here's our good captain!" Harlowe announced, seeing him first.

"Good evening," Alex replied, heading for the empty

chair next to Amalie. He passed David on the way and stopped to brush a hand over the lad's head. "Are you feeling well, son?"

"Aye, Da," David said through a mouthful of food. "But I lost my skate. Will you fish it out for me?"

"We'll get you another," Alex promised. "You're certain you feel all right?" He pressed a hand to David's forehead to check for fever. David smiled up at him, looking the rosy-cheeked picture of health for one who had been so near death only hours ago. Alex gently tweaked an ear. "I think you'll do."

Amalie greeted him as he awkwardly took his seat, laying his crutches on the floor. "And how are you?" she asked, taking up her fork again as if nothing out of the ordinary had happened.

"I feel like a slugabed, sleeping half the day. Have you rested?"

"No, she has not!" Michael exclaimed. "We couldn't hold her down once she found she could walk. She has driven us mad, skirting around the day long. Tell her she should not overtax herself, would you?"

Alex placed his napkin in his lap and regarded Amalie with a serious look. "You should not overtax yourself."

She laughed, that merry sound he feared he'd not be able to live without. "Thank you, Dr. Napier."

Alex made no reply. Her words, though uttered in jest, settled in his head like a blessing. It was the first time he had been addressed as doctor in six years. And somehow, it felt quite right. He met Hilda's steady and approving gaze across the table. She had forgiven him. And surprisingly, he found he had almost forgiven himself.

He sat back a bit as a footman served his plate and he suddenly felt ravenous. Alex had figured out what he would do and turmoil was a thing of the past. He would set up to practice in Maidstone, living near Hilda and her sister so that she could be with David every day and Alex would have him in the evening. A perfect solution.

Except that he would be too near Amalie for comfort. She would marry eventually, of course, and he would have to hear of it, perhaps see her and her new husband now and again as they came into town to shop. Somehow, he would have to live with that.

"Hurry and eat, Da, so we can have the pudding!" David demanded.

Alex tried to dismiss the thought of losing Amalie, but it would not leave him alone. He drank more of the wine than he ought, trying to dull the edges of the emotions that warred within him. Elation that David had survived, that Amalie could walk, that Hilda had forgiven him, that his decision had been made. And the soul-deep sadness that he felt at the thought of relinquishing this family and the spirited young woman he had come to care for so deeply.

He realized that he also was mourning the loss of hope he had tried so hard to keep alive. He would always be looked upon as a crippled man and could never run or ride or do so many of the things he had prided himself on before.

But self-pity solved nothing. He must set a good example for his son and put a good face on his acceptance. What must be, must be, and that was that. Life was not what one made it, as he had once thought, but what you made *of* it.

When everyone began to retire for the night, he did not seek a moment alone with Amalie to speak of breaking their betrothal. She was too enthralled with the newness of her astounding recovery and he did not want to spoil that with what she might view as a rejection.

He would never be able to sleep. Aside from his chaotic emotions, he had slept most of the day. A good book should help. He asked Michael to choose one for him, then went to his room.

The Serious Reflections of Robinson Crusoe, a rather dull sequel to one of Alex's favorite novels, and perhaps the wine he'd consumed at supper, had his eyelids drooping before the first chapter ended. Sleep proved the great escape from all things, he supposed. He laid the moralistic tome aside and gave in.

Amalie felt empowered, energized and able to do anything but rest on her laurels. She had not missed that expression of regret on Napier's strong countenance all evening. He must be planning how he would set aside their agreement without causing a rift with her brother. No chance of that, she decided.

Her old confidence had returned, doubled by determination. She must take matters into her own hands. He did not feel as strongly as she, but she loved enough for the both of them. She would see he never regretted their match.

Several hours passed before the house grew quiet and everyone was asleep. Then she opened her bride's chest and donned a night rail of sheerest batiste trimmed with webs of fine Brussels lace. Beneath it she wore nothing. She brushed her hair until it shone, her best feature a waterfall of pale gold that flowed over her shoulders and down her back.

Carefully, she daubed spots of lavender water over her wrists, behind her ears and, in an added naughty afterthought, at the backs of her knees. Her reflection in the vanity mirror gave her a much needed boost of courage and returned her saucy grin.

Amalie pulled on a robe and quietly stole out of her room and padded barefoot down the stairs to seduce her future husband. There would be no backing out of this match if she could help it. She moved slowly, mindful of how her leg muscles complained, resisting the day's overuse. Determination drove her on.

She checked whether light emanated from beneath his door. It did not. Good. He must be asleep for this to work, she thought.

Her heart beat as rapidly as that of a trapped bird and her hand trembled as she opened his door, slipped inside and shut it behind her. Would he protest? Toss her out on her ear? Laugh at her inexperience?

The bed on which he slept was small, too narrow for her to climb in and lie beside him. For several moments, she simply stood and watched him sleep. Moonlight from the window blanketed him with a glow of exaggerated light and shadow, an old master's painting depicting the beauty of the male species. She could only see his upper half, hard muscles relaxed in slumber and pale smooth skin that beckoned her touch. His lips were slightly parted, his lashes lying like dark little fans, a lock of straight hair obscuring his wide forehead.

As much as she hated to disturb his rest, she yearned to do so. Coupling would be new to her, a curious thing she wasn't quite sure would be to her liking. But there was a heated need deep inside her that urged her to make it happen. What if he was unable? Oh, dear, she hadn't considered that before now!

Ridiculous thought. It was only his knee affected, she reminded herself. Hadn't he warned her that was the only thing about him that didn't work?

She inhaled deeply, drawing in the heady scent of

leather, her own lavender and the faint underlying touch of his particular essence. Smoothly as a wraith, she glided to the bed and gently lowered herself on top of him. Her lips found his, softly tracing them with the tip of her tongue.

He groaned and sought more, his mouth opening to the kiss, his body moving sinuously beneath hers. He tasted of wine and passion, fueling her thirst for more.

Her hands were flat against the mattress, bracing her upper body above his. She relaxed, bringing her breasts flat against the expanse of his chest. Goodness, that felt nice! She brushed her palms lightly over his face, down the strong column of his neck and over his wide shoulders. His muscles tensed under her touch.

"Amalie?" he whispered, sounding rather choked. His palms slid up the sides of her hips and grasped her firmly. She could feel the ridge of his manhood, hard against her.

She writhed slowly, allowing her legs to encompass his. "Love me," she whispered near his ear.

His sigh shuddered out as his fingers gathered the soft, thin cotton of her night rail to her waist, then higher. She raised her arms and he swept it off. She watched it drift to a moonlit heap on the floor. One of his hands slid between them, palm flat against her abdomen, lifting her slightly as the other dragged the blanket from between them, the only impediment to their lying skin to skin. Instead of removing his hand, he slid it lower, touching her intimately.

Amalie closed her eyes and moaned with pleasure. All thoughts of plying her wiles on him dissipated in a fog of heat. He needed no encouragement, she needed no expertise. This was magic with a life of its own.

The caresses were all too brief and she almost cried out her protest when he withdrew his hand and reached for her knee. The other was already lifting. She felt him draw her higher and the part of him she wanted most nudged her intimately. Then she pushed down. A moment's pain gained infinite pleasure.

Then, deeply inside her, he finally spoke. "No dream."

"Oh, yes," she replied, all but crying out the words. "Yes, it is."

He moved, as if to withdraw, but she held fast with her legs, her arms, her body, clinging as if her life depended upon it. He returned, a gentle thrust, then one not so gentle, moving in and almost out.

Sounds emerged from her throat that might have been pleas, protests or intentions that had no words. Nothing mattered but the feelings he gave and took. She knew he was caught up as surely as she. The intensity of his movements heightened, as did hers, until she felt unable to bear it. Suddenly he rose under her with a deep, almost impaling thrust and a burst of heat flooded inside her. Her body shuddered violently with a pleasure so encompassing, she could not stop shaking. Again and again she undulated, clenching, pressing, grasping. And then it was over. Subtle echoes rippled through her, her breath catching at each occurrence.

"Why?" he whispered, his fingers trailing lightly along her spine all the way to the base of it, triggering yet another spasm of ecstasy.

She couldn't speak. She couldn't think. She could only feel.

He nuzzled her neck and laid a soft kiss there. "Will you ever believe me now when I say I love you, not because you came to me in the night, or because you saved my son's life? Can you trust that I felt so before this day and night ever happened?"

Amalie groaned softly. "At the moment, I'd believe the earth flat as a baker's paddle if you said so."

His laughter shook her gently as she lay inanimate as a blanket over him. "What a treasure you are." His big hand squeezed one nether cheek. "But you'll appear a tarnished treasure to your family if anyone finds you here. Whilst I'm not complaining you came, this was *not* your wisest move."

"I know, but I love you dreadfully, however you might feel about me. I love your son. I even love your cantankerous mother-in-law. How wise is that?"

He kissed her soundly and held her close as could be. When his lips left hers, he scored a path of kisses to her ear and nipped the lobe gently. "Save me from wise women, then. I can never let you go now, Amalie."

"I should hope not. Why should you?" She planted her elbows on either side of him and played with the lock of hair that fanned over his brow. "Because of your leg?"

He nodded. "I admit now that I'll never run or ride or do many of the things I used to, things that made me a whole man."

"Whole, indeed!" She smiled down at his earnest frown and kissed the tip of his nose. "Run? I cannot imagine any instance in which you would run from anything, Napier! And ride? Well, why shouldn't you?"

"One commands a horse with the knees, Amalie."

"Not so. I've ridden sidesaddle all my life, and while I am not suggesting you use my trappings and try that trick, you should do quite well if I teach you other ways to guide a mount."

His dark eyebrows met. "Well, of course there are other ways, but I hadn't thought—"

"Then *think!* And as for those other things—whatever those might be—I'm certain we'll devise enough that you *can* do to keep you busy and out of the whisky bottle."

It was his turn to smile then and he did so as he lifted

her and sat up. "Get your gown and go back to your bed. Michael will shoot me for certain if he suspects we've anticipated our vows."

She obediently swept up her night rail and slid it back on. "At least there will *be* vows. No more cock-brained notions of crying off or annulling me." She sat down on the edge of his bed and placed a hand over his heart. "You love me. You cannot let me go."

"And you wouldn't allow it even if I could."

"Of course not. You have saved me from myself, believed in me when even I did not. Even if I didn't love you so abominably and you did not love me, I would insist we keep our bargain."

"Why is that?" he asked, grinning, probably fishing for compliments.

She slapped his chest lightly and got up. "Because you are so damned entertaining, of course!"

He grabbed her hand and kissed her palm. "Then you'd best leave whilst you can before I *entertain* you again," he warned. "Good sleep, my sweet."

Amalie sighed, held her hand to her breast when he released it and left him without another word. Her throat was so tight with tears, she could not say anything, even to repeat how dearly she loved him. But surely he knew, and perhaps he loved her, as well.

At least he thought he did or felt obliged to say so. And that had been her goal in coming to him.

Six happy days later, Alex stood beside Michael and watched Amalie, on the arm of her father, glide slowly to the altar of the little stone church in Balmsley village. How angelic she looked in her ice-blue gown with its modest tucking of white lace. Her blond curls had been caught up with another lace frill and the pearls Michael had purchased for him in London graced her lovely neck.

Briefly, he recalled his first wedding and the vows to Olivia. Then he saw her smile reflected in her mother's features, a blessing from both, a wish for his happiness. Love should be remembered and treasured, not wrapped with sorrow.

He beamed down at his son, who grinned back, gap-toothed and endearing. They shared a wink at their good fortune. Alex felt that his future seemed exceptionally bright at the moment and his love for Amalie unparalleled. Thank goodness he had come with Michael to Balmsley.

Alex faced this stage of his life with infinite hope, propped as he was on his new silver-and-malacca cane. His bum knee felt comfortably steady laced tightly in Amalie's unique groom's gift, a finely boned, scarlet satin knee brace she had cut and fashioned from her favorite corset.

The matching laces reminded him of the scarlet ribbons in Amalie's fair hair the first time he had seen her, glowing ethereally in the firelight like an angel.

An angel she was not, he thought as he reached out for her hand, but she was his saving grace nonetheless.

As the minister began with "Dearly Beloved," Alex looked down at Amalie and mouthed the words, *I love you*.

The tiny residue of doubt still there in those wide blue eyes would vanish soon enough. He could hardly wait to erase it completely. "I *will*," he vowed, hoping his timing of the words was appropriate.

"So will I," Amalie declared, not waiting for the minister to repeat his questions.

She didn't wait for him to grant Alex leave to kiss the bride, either.

"Save me from hesitant women," he whispered when they broke the kiss.

She laughed, that lovely musical sound he never wanted to live without. "I believe I just did, Napier!"

* * * * *

CHRISTMAS PROMISE
Carla Kelly

Dear Reader,

I love to write Christmas stories. Technically, I consider them an exercise in restraint, rather like a poem. The shorter length demands concentration of ideas, which appeals to me. Mainly, though, I like to write Christmas stories because they are a personal "gift" to the season.

"Christmas Promise" is a logical story for me to write, considering my recent series on the men of the Channel Fleet during the Napoleonic Wars, and the women who loved them and waited for them.

The story poses an interesting dilemma for a career naval officer who sailed and fought during some of England's darkest decades: What does a frigate commander do when peace breaks out?

That is Captain Faulk's dilemma. Christmas seems like an appropriate time to resolve it. I promise.

Merrily yours,

Carla

To Scott and Jody Barrett of Fargo,
who took in three refugees when the Sheyenne River
rose and we were homeless.

Prologue

The long war was over. Napoleon, under protest, had set up housekeeping in his central-Atlantic change of venue. Surely it was high time for Parliament, free from war's alarms, to attempt some social legislation, namely, a law about procrastination.

I cannot be the only procrastinator in England, Ianthe Mears thought as she sat on her bed, staring at her open wardrobe and bureau drawers stuffed with ten years of accumulation. Never mind that she was far from a wealthy widow. She had acquired too much stuff, and she had put off disposing of it until now, when she had informed her solicitor to put her home on the market.

She had to move. Trouble was, she had also put off explaining to Jem why she had just recently placed a deposit on rented rooms over one of Torquay's unpretentious eating places. True, he was only ten and saw the matter as an adventure, which made him puzzled when she swore him to secrecy.

"When you go to Plymouth to escort Diana home, don't say a word about what I have done," she had insisted when she put him on the coastal carrier, warmly dressed against December, and warmly admonished to avoid all sailors and other shady-looking characters. Better she told Diana herself. Selling the house went hand in glove with the not-so-minor detail that economic retrenchment at home also meant no more tuition for her beloved daughter at Miss Pym's Female Academy in Bath.

Of course, when she had both children together under the same roof, she could tell them why she was uprooting them from the only home they had known, and ending Diana's academic career, or at least, her studies of Italian, embroidery and approved world literature.

Frustrated with herself, Ianthe flopped back on the bed and stared at the ceiling, wishing for the umpteenth time she could think of another way to set by enough money for a dowry for Diana—fifteen now—and leave enough to entice a merchant in Torquay or Plymouth to take on Jem as a shop apprentice. There would be no future for either of her darlings if they did not sacrifice now.

She took several dresses stylish in earlier times and tossed them into the giveaway box until they covered her late husband's old uniforms. Ten years it was since Trafalgar and his death, and she still had not the heart to look at the navy blue uniforms or discard them. Better to cover them with another layer of clothing. A casual observer would have pitied Ianthe Mears's devotion to her dead naval hero—wasn't everyone at Trafalgar a hero?—but never have understood her own conflict.

Ten years had been enough time for the raw pain of James's death to evolve into the occasional sigh. Immediately after his death, it had taken all her will not to express the anger she felt at her husband leaving her impoverished and with a baby growing inside her. She had hated Jim briefly, until sorrow took over, grief that would have survived any sharp-eyed matron's scrutiny because it was genuine.

The mundane business of save and discard soothed her. She was setting aside the box of Jim's letters when she noticed the letter underneath the box, the one Jeremiah Faulk had sent to her after Trafalgar, and which contained Jim's last, half-finished letter. She opened the letter box to place it with the others and was closing the lid when she saw another letter.

She sat down on her bed again, turning it over in her hands, trying to decide whether to keep the letter, which was only the barest scrawl from Miah, dated six months after Trafalgar, telling her he had been given leave to send her Jim's portion of the prize money awarded for Trafalgar.

"Liar," she said softly. "You sent me *your* prize money."

Even after ten years, his generosity in the face of his own slim resources made her dab at her eyes with her apron. When she received the bank draft, she knew she should send it back, but she had used the money to buy the house up for sale now. She had sent a thank-you note, care of the Channel Fleet, but never heard from him again. She had wanted to write, but knew how improper that would have been.

Ianthe decided she couldn't throw away the scrap, and added it to the letter box. She looked out the window at Tor Bay, wintry and sterile. Her mother had never understood why she had not moved with her to Northumberland after her father's death. Mama would have been shocked if her proper daughter had confessed she was staying in Torquay because Captain Faulk might someday appear on her doorstep.

He never did. She knew he was alive somewhere in the world, because she asked her vicar to check the *Naval Chronicle* regularly, not approved reading material for

ladies. Maybe just knowing he was alive was her only consolation. After all, she was a practical woman, and a better
widow than most.

Chapter One

In twenty-two years of war at sea, Captain Jeremiah Faulk had only indulged in introspection when he had time to write in his journal. As he walked through the nearly empty HMS *Spartan,* his frigate and home for eight of those years, he began to indulge: Was peace to be the worst event in his naval career? Jeremiah wondered as he stood for the last time on his quarterdeck and watched the skeleton crew sway off the big guns. *My ship is no longer mine and I am homeless,* he thought.

He did something unthinkable then, and leaned his forearms on the quarterdeck railing, watching the guns rise from the deck. He knew he was a hard captain, but he also knew his indomitable will had kept his ship and crew on the water on many fraught occasions, when other leaders would have faltered. Still, he hadn't been prepared for what had happened earlier in the day, before his men took jolly boats and gigs to shore and an alien world.

He hadn't been prepared for them to gather around him for a hip hip hooray, and for his bosun to come forward with a timepiece from his crew. God knows where they had found the money for such a gift, or even the opportunity to buy it. He would treasure that token as he treasured nothing else in his life. It came from men he had flogged, and chivied and dressed down, and also commended and cajoled and encouraged. He knew they called him The Old Man. Maybe they suspected he regarded them as a father would his sons. At least they had been kind enough to overlook the tears in his eyes, as he had been to overlook the same in theirs.

"Captain?"

Arms still on the railing, he turned to look at his sailing master. The man sounded uncertain, and Faulk wondered if he was ill. Then he noticed the direction of his master's eyes, and straightened up. "Yes, Mr. Benedict?" he asked, trying to sound frosty enough to discourage any comment on his precedent-shattering posture.

"I just wondered, sir," the master began, then stopped because the world must have ground to a halt to see his captain let down his discipline to such an extent.

"I am fine, Mr. Benedict." Could he admit to a qualm? Perhaps. "Well, I own to a feeling of dismay. It's hard to leave her."

His master nodded.

"We're supposed to be happy, you know," Faulk said, and risked his credit with his senior warrant officer by resuming his casual pose at the railing. "This will be your first Christmas with your family in how many years?"

"Too many to recollect, Captain," Benedict said. "My wife sent me a letter yesterday." He sighed. "She said our house will be full of relatives bent upon seeing me."

He sighed again, more gusty, and Faulk had to turn his head to hide his smile. He had a kindred spirit in his crusty sailing master.

"You're not overjoyed, I take it?" Faulk asked.

The men looked at each other in perfect understanding. Still, Faulk thought, there would come a moment when all the company was gone or abed, and it would be Benedict and Mrs. Benedict. Faulk silently wished them joy of each other and a happy coupling. As for himself, he would take himself to the Drake in Plymouth. After that, he had no idea. He could easily find for hire what Benedict got for free, but he was not willing—at the moment, at least—to lay down his blunt for a prostitute. It had been more than a year since his last bedding, and heaven knows he had thought about it, but he doubted he could perform to anyone's satisfaction, not the way he was feeling now.

"You'll be at the Drake, sir?"

"Aye."

"And then?"

"Not sure, Mr. Benedict."

Suddenly he wished his sailing master would leave, because he knew what was coming. *Brace yourself, Miah,* he thought.

"Sir, you'd be welcome at my house for Christmas dinner."

He knew it was true; the Benedicts were kindness itself. Still, there would come that moment when the goodbyes were said, and he would be outside in the street, walking back to a hotel or—in former days—his frigate. All it served was to remind him how alone he was, and now, how homeless.

"Please thank Mrs. Benedict for her kindness to me, but I think I will just stay at the Drake this time," he said.

"Very well, Captain," Benedict said. Still he stood there on the quarterdeck. He cleared his throat. "I'll take my leave, sir."

Faulk knew it would startle his sailing master, but he went to the man and held out his hand. "Let us shake,

David," he said, further breaching all naval etiquette by a Christian name. "You have been as fine a master as ever served a ship."

It was easier to say than he would have thought, probably because he meant every word. Neither man chose to look the other in the eye.

An hour later it was Faulk's turn to leave the *Spartan;* a captain was unnecessary now. There were no guns to serve, no need to pace the deck, no French and Spanish ports to blockade anymore. The *Spartan's* small crew would keep wood rot away, and burn sulphur in the hold to drive out rats. Possibly the *Spartan* would be refitted, or sold to a merchant, or even broken up as scrap. If it was the first, he would only be jealous of her new captain; if the last, he didn't want to know about it.

His dunnage had already been taken ashore to the Drake. Better to get the whole thing over with, Jeremiah thought, especially now that night was coming so early. His log tucked under his arm, Faulk took a last look around, then let his bosun pipe him over the side of the *Spartan* into a gig bobbing below, ready for the short pull into Devonport. When he put his feet on dry land, there was no returning to the sea that had been home.

He received his first jolt of the new order of things on land when he peered into the game room at the Drake, scene for the past two decades of what every officer called "the perpetual whist game." The room was empty. He didn't linger, because it felt amazingly like a tomb.

He had feared dinner that night at the Drake would be gall and wormwood, considering his bleak state of mind, but Mrs. Fillion had exerted herself. The roast was tender, the potatoes cooked just the way he liked them.

He ate alone and silent, which was nothing out of the

ordinary. Although the room was nearly empty, he had time to observe two young ones in the dining room, probably a brother and sister, but looking on the outs with each other. For want of anything better to do, he watched them.

The young lady was a pretty chit, with guinea-gold hair swept up in what he reckoned was the latest fashion, but which hung bedraggled now. He could only surmise that she had been traveling recently, and her hair had suffered the slings and arrows of the mail coach. He thought she might be fourteen or fifteen.

His attention was caught more by what must have been her younger brother, because he looked vaguely familiar. That couldn't be, though; how would he know a boy that young? Still, there was something about the way he wore his brown hair, and the way he was frowning at his sister that made Faulk wonder.

Not for long, though. Mrs. Fillion herself brought out the cheap navy cheese that she knew he preferred to fancier Stilton and plunked herself down with it, ready to eat a slice of it with him.

"Captain Faulk, will you be staying with us long this time?"

It was a question she had asked off and on through two decades. Usually his answer was a shake of the head, and the request that she have her laundress wash all his clothes in fresh water as soon as she could, because he was outward bound soon. Beyond that, all he ever required of her was fresh water to drink, and a place to store a few more of his journals.

"I'll be here through Christmas," he told her, slicing off a sliver of cheese. "Maybe through New Year's."

"Where away then?" she asked, allowing their familiarity as hotelier and guest to give her privilege not even his first and second mates had dared.

"I'm not precisely certain," he said, then said no more.

She was too shrewd to inquire further, or possibly too kind. They ate cheese together companionably, maybe because she was softhearted enough to not want him sitting alone. Or so he thought, until she finally came to the point.

"Captain Faulk, I wonder if you would do me a favor, at some time during your stay here."

"Ask away," he said, willing to be useful to someone.

"That storeroom where you keep your journals," she began, accepting another slice of cheese from him. "I'm certain you have noticed all the other things tucked away in there."

He had. For years, Mrs. Fillion had allowed officers based in Plymouth and Devonport to leave their extra dunnage in an unused room off the scullery. It never ceased to amaze him what world travelers could collect, although he admitted to a shiver down his backbone at shrunken heads and pouches made of parts that would have made the ladies blush.

"What I ask you to do is take a look at what is named and labeled," she said. She couldn't quite meet his gaze then. "I'm certain there are items stored and their owners are no longer alive. If you could mark those, I would have them sold at auction, or put in the ash bin."

"That's grim duty," he told her.

"That is why I have never asked it of anyone before," she said, equally forthright. "Now that there is peace..." She let the thought dangle.

"I can do that," he said, not because he wanted to, but because he had never shied from unpleasant tasks in a career of unpleasant tasks on a worldwide scale. "You'd probably like me to move my journals, too."

"There is no hurry," she said, and he could not overlook

the sympathy in her voice. She knew he had nowhere to go except the Drake. "Do you know, I almost read one once."

"You would have been welcome," he replied, flattered that she had almost done something no one had ever been interested in before. Some of what he wrote might give a lady the blushes, but Mrs. Fillion was no lady. She would probably only have smiled at his descriptions of women bedded in foreign ports, right down to distinguishing characteristics. He had written less of that later, either because the novelty had worn off, or because a captain had less time for fornication.

Or so he thought, even as he admitted to some warmth under his collar at some of his more spectacular recollections. Time for a massive change of subject. With the cheese knife, he indicated the two young persons across the dining room.

"There seems to be a quarrel going on," he said in a low voice.

Mrs. Fillion looked where he gestured. "I think the boy has been sent to escort his sister home from school in Bath." She shrugged. "They can't stiff me for their lodging, because I have already collected it. As for dinner, they only ordered tea."

Mrs. Fillion spent a few more minutes in pleasantries and then took the cheese with her and left the table.

He took himself from the dining room before the remaining inmates, who by now were looking at each other with expressions he could only classify as mulish. The thought crossed his mind that they may have needed a loan to get the rest of the way home, wherever home was. *You needn't take care of the entire world, Captain Faulk,* he reminded himself. If they still looked concerned in the morning, he could step in and help, if they would permit him.

He spent the next hour walking, enjoying the freedom of stretching his legs and moving in a direction larger than his quarterdeck, which he had paced with regularity for so many years: So many steps this way, then that way.

He passed St. Andrew's Church, stood a moment, then went inside. Faulk would have protested had any man accused him of being religious, but he was. He knew only divine intervention had kept his ship from more than one lee shore. As captain of his flock, he had buried many a man at sea, and meant every word he read from the Book of Common Prayer, every scripture that sent his lads into the welcoming arms of the deep.

It was a small matter to light a candle, then kneel in a pew, his forehead down on his hands as they rested on the pew in front, as he thanked the Lord for a final safe voyage. He prayed for the souls of all the dead whose faces he still saw in his dreams, and wished he could have done better for them.

He sat back finally, stared at the altar, then went to his knees again. "And bless those two foolish children," he whispered.

There was no particular rush in the morning to rise, because he had nowhere to go. Still, he was up early as usual, half listening for four bells to indicate six o'clock and his time to rise. He fancied he heard bells far away, on some lucky ship anchored in the sound with a full crew yet.

There were more people in the dining room when Faulk came downstairs, which surprised him, until he remembered the Drake was one stop for the Royal Mail and the coastal carriage that supplied service to Torquay and other small towns.

He didn't deliberately sit closer to the two young ones this time, but there were no free tables farther away. If he overheard any drama from the boy or his sister, he could intervene on the side of the angels.

Mrs. Fillion knew what he wanted, and her dining room girl delivered eggs, sausage, toast and black pudding to his table. He noted with some consternation that the boy glanced at his food, then looked down at his own empty place setting. Faulk also caught the fishy glare the boy's sister fixed on him for coveting a lodger's breakfast. She has good manners, Faulk thought, as he broke his fast and tried not to think about starvation at the next table. He'd gone without a meal or two more than once in his youth, and more in the past twenty-two years. He knew the boy wouldn't perish before he reached his home, wherever that was.

The food was excellent as usual. He tried to turn his full attention to the plate in front of him, but he couldn't help overhearing the quietly voiced tempest at the adjoining table.

"What on earth will Mama think when we're not on the carrier this afternoon?"

"I didn't mean to lose it," the boy protested wearily.

That was all the captain needed. *I can't ignore them,* he thought, putting down his knife and fork. He wasn't sure who to address first. The young lady was obviously older, but a man was a man, after all, no matter how young. He chose to address the boy, simply because he had oceans more experience with his own gender.

"Lad, pardon my impertinence and a pair of sharp ears. I can't help but wonder—are things at low tide with you?"

The look the boy gave him was one of infinite relief. Not so his sister, if that's who she was.

"We are quite well, Admiral," the girl replied, which made him smile.

"I'm but a post captain, and I think you're hungry," he replied. "What's more, I think your pockets are to let. If that's not a lee shore, then I don't know what is. How can I help you?"

He wasn't sure what he expected, but the boy leaned across the table to his sister. "Diana, don't be a nod. You know Mama says we can always trust men with gold on their shoulders."

"She is absolutely right," he said, touched that not everyone in England considered the navy lacking in couth, culture and concern. "What happened, and how can I help you?"

He didn't think there was anything about his crinkled and wind-whipped face to inspire confidence, but a whore in Piraeus had once told him he had the kindest eyes. Or that's what he thought she said. His Greek wasn't as good as his Spanish.

The story seemed to pour out of the little boy. Faulk stopped the flow long enough to speak for two more breakfasts. Neither wasted a moment in digging in, although he could see the young lady was suffering from acute embarrassment. He turned back to his own eggs to spare her any more humiliation. He could wait until they weren't so hungry.

The boy finished first. He turned a frank and honest face to Faulk. "Thank you, Captain. I was gut-foundered."

Faulk smiled, even as the boy's sister—did he call her Diana?—pursed her lips at her brother's cant. "I know what it feels like to be hungry and ill-used." Did he ever. Spanish prisons would never Claridge's make. "Tell me what is going on."

Diana Whoever-she-was took up the narrative. "My brother—" she gave him a look that would have blistered paint "—was supposed to escort me from Plymouth to Torquay. I've been at school in Bath, and came this far on the Royal Mail."

So far, so good. She was obviously gently reared, to understand the niceties of an escort, even from a young brother. Too bad their father did not accompany him, Faulk thought.

"And you?" Faulk asked, turning to the brother, who was returning an equally blistering look to his sister. "Spill your budget. Nothing's so bad that it can't be confessed."

The captain knew he could have been gentler in comment, but the boy didn't take his sharpness in bad odor. "After I spoke our room here, I lost the coach fare," he said, not mincing his words or mumbling them. "Mama gave me the exact amount, but this is what happened."

He reached inside his short coat, pulled out a purse, and wiggled his forefinger through the hole at the bottom. "I don't know where it happened. I've looked all over Plymouth."

"This isn't the most honest town in England," Faulk said. "I've lost money here, too." No need to tell the lad he had lost it over whist and amour. "How much do you need for the fare?"

They looked at each other this time, need warring against propriety. Need won, and Diana murmured a small sum, which Faulk promptly took from his own purse—one with no hole—and laid it on their table.

"That was a simple matter," he said, smiling to put them at ease.

The girl blushed becomingly. "We are grateful to you and in your debt."

As far as Faulk was concerned, that was that. "No debt of mine," he assured her cheerfully. "Call it a Christmas present from someone who doesn't want children stranded in Plymouth."

"Captain, my mother would be in the boughs if she could not repay you. Could you write your direction for me?" Diana asked.

He shrugged. "Just here at the Drake, care of Captain Faulk."

He wasn't prepared for the look both children gave him, then each other, then him again.

"Captain Faulk?" the boy asked.

"The very one." They were still looking at him, eyes wide. "Should I know you?"

The young lady shook her head. "I'm not... I don't know. Maybe there are several Captain Faulks in the navy."

"In addition to me, it happens there are an Alexander, an Edward, a Martin and someone rejoicing in the name of Octavian. Claims his father was a Latin scholar. We call him Caesar."

The boy smiled at that, but not his sister. What happened next touched him. Astounded, he watched as tears started in the young lady's eyes. "Never tell me you are staying at an inn for Christmas," she said, as though daring him to repeat what he had just said.

"I am. I'm just off the *Spartan* and have nowhere else to go. Look here, now, it's not a tragedy. Please don't do that!"

She was crying in earnest. Hastily, he reached for a handkerchief, hoping it wasn't the one he had used to wipe his chin where he had cut himself shaving. "My God, don't do this!" he exclaimed, keeping his voice low. It wouldn't do for some sharp-eye to think he was abusing these children.

She dried her eyes quickly, squinting at her brother, as if daring him to make any comment. "It is this way, Captain," she said, striving for dignity beyond her years, but not entirely out of reach. "Everyone should be home for Christmas."

"I agree completely. I promise that next year I will have a place to go."

"Promise?" she asked.

"Cross my heart, if that will help," Faulk vowed, thinking that someday she would be an excellent mother of sons. Heaven knows he was cowed.

He was only saved from babbling by the arrival of the coastal carrier. The boy got to his feet at once.

"Come on, Diana. I'll get you a seat inside, but I want to sit on top."

"He'll catch his death, too, and Mama will be exercised," Diana muttered. "One moment!" With real style, she curtsied to Faulk, and glared at her brother until he managed a sketchy bow.

Faulk bowed in return. "Very well, then. I wish you Merry Christmas. By the way, I told you I am Captain Faulk, but you have never enlightened me."

"Oh!" she said, putting her hand to her mouth at her social misdemeanor, and becoming much younger in the process. "I am Diana Mears and this is my brother, Jem."

"Jim!" He couldn't help himself. It came out too loud, almost as though he still stood on his quarterdeck. The coach riders impatient at the back of the line looked around in surprise.

The boy turned around to hear his name, a smile on his face, and Faulk knew precisely where he had seen him before. Thank God Ianthe had named her son James, and not William, after the boy's pompous grandfather.

"Jim Mears," the captain said. "Miss Mears. Jim. I knew your father well."

Diana Mears smiled, and he suddenly knew that look, too. "You know more than we do, Captain," she said. "Jem never knew him, of course, and I have but the barest memory."

"I know. I know. You were only five years old," he replied, unable to keep the longing from his own voice.

She didn't know what to say and there wasn't time to

explain, not with the line moving now. He walked beside the Mears children, determined now to see them onto the conveyance, unwilling, almost, to let them out of his sight, now that he knew who they were. He saw their dunnage stowed, then handed Miss Mears into the vehicle, while Jem climbed on top.

"Do this for me. Tell your mother hello from Captain Faulk, will you?"

She nodded. "Thank you for your kindness to us, Captain."

He watched the coastal boneshaker until it was out of sight around the bend of the Barbican. She did have her mother's look.

He stood there a long while. The sleet forced him in finally, where he followed Mrs. Fillion to the storage room to fulfill the unpleasant task she had set for him. He went first to the row where Mrs. Fillion had stored his journals. He knew he was a no-hoper once he picked up a journal, but he hadn't promised to inventory the whole storage room in one day.

He turned first to October 21, 1805, as he had known he would, especially since all he could think of right now was Jim Mears. More properly, he turned to October 31. Ten days had passed before he'd had more than a moment to snatch some writing time after that titanic struggle. Trafalgar had been the fight of a lifetime, a battle to be refought for the rest of the new century. As the only surviving lieutenant on the *Conqueror,* Faulk remembered Trafalgar as a blur of noise and death.

Jim Mears had died in his arms on the quarterdeck, pierced through by a splinter from the railing. From that moment to October 31, Faulk had scarcely slept as he did the work of three and tried not to think about his friend, dead and consigned to the deep.

He was one of several lieutenants to profit from Trafalgar with a promotion to captain and his first command, a saucy sloop of war named *Nancy.* As an officer at Trafalgar, Faulk had received £269 from a grateful government, which he had promptly sent to Ianthe Mears. He had mailed Jim's personal effects to her, including Jim's final, half-written letter, and added another £100 from his own then-meager savings. He knew she was entitled to a minuscule pension, and was grateful she had parents who would help her. Besides that, she was beautiful. She would find another husband.

He had worried no more about Ianthe Mears. The *Nancy* had been followed in sweet succession by a frigate, and then the beautiful *Spartan.* Napoleon ruled his life as surely as if the Corsican Tyrant had been a puppet master. For ten more years, he had sailed and fought and blockaded until it all ended in Plymouth where it began, twenty-two years earlier.

He woke in the middle of the night, alert to the creaks and groans of the old hotel, and thinking of Ianthe Mears. Knowing he wouldn't go back to sleep, he reached deep into his duffel bag and felt around until he found the packet of letters. He took them to the chair by the fire, and poked a little heat back into it.

There weren't as many as he would have liked, mainly because some were at the bottom of the ocean, and others had disappeared, the way paper does. Considering that he had written all those love letters at Jim Mears's request, he wondered why he had kept them.

His father had been Sir William Mears's steward. There had been four hopeful Faulk offspring but never much money, because Sir William never overpaid anyone. The major irony of the whole thing was that of all the children, only Faulk remained alive, the one in England's most dangerous profession.

He had grown up with James Mears, a younger son. When Jim was fourteen, Sir William had called on a family connection to see his son onto the *Agamemnon* as a midshipman. As an afterthought, Sir William included the son of his steward in the bargain. So began Faulk's naval career.

Faulk read two of the letters, as he wondered just when it was they had both fallen in love with Ianthe Snow, a daughter of Sir William's vicar and someone he saw frequently enough while Jim was away at school. *I think I had the prior claim,* Faulk told himself. *A fat lot of good that ever did me.* There had been a lull in 1802, when peace—if one could call it that—broke out briefly, and the midshipmen were put ashore. That was the precise moment when Ianthe Snow, younger than both Jim and himself, but so beautiful now, had charmed them both.

Alone in his room, he didn't even try to stop that marvelous stirring he felt whenever he considered his early love. *I wonder if she still has hair the color of dull gold,* he thought. *I am certain her eyes are still as blue as Tor Bay.*

When the dread midshipman years ended, he and Jim had parted company to separate ships, not to reunite until the *Beech,* a cranky, leaky, stinky ship of the line where he was first mate, and Jim second. Jim was in love now, struck dumb with admiration for Ianthe Snow, after another visit home. Perhaps that excused his occasional lapses in quarterdeck judgment.

If he lived to be seventy, Faulk knew he would never forget the night Jim shoehorned himself into his tiny cabin and asked for help. "Miah, you're by far the better writer. Would you… Dare I ask… Would you write letters for me to Ianthe?"

Lieutenant Jim Mears was shy beyond belief, and for no particular reason, considering that he had good breeding and handsome, dark Devonshire looks on his side. There was family money, too, or at least enough to render him respectable. Faulk had none of that. A widow he had courted briefly in Naples once commented on his excellent shoulders and build, and he had indeed posed naked for that duchess in Livorno who thought she was a sculptor, but only when the duke was elsewhere. Still, Jim Mears had the look, if not the body.

Shy. There was Jim, face aflame, pleading with him and flattering, too, because Faulk knew he could write better than Sir William's seagoing son. Besides, they were in the Orient, where life was humid and boring. He agreed to write Jim's letters for him—marvelous bits of prose expressing his undying love for Ianthe Snow. It was the easiest thing he ever did, because he meant every word.

Jim was none the wiser. When Faulk finished each masterpiece of adoration, Jim copied it in his own hand, and gave the original back to its frustrated owner. The result was an engagement through the post, and then a wedding in Torquay, when Faulk was number one on a bigger ship of the line and roasting near India now.

He didn't want to see Jim after that, mainly because they had been in each other's confidences for years. Faulk was a strong man, but he also knew he could not bear any description of married felicity with Ianthe Mears, not when he wanted her so badly for himself. Better not to meet at sea the husband who was the unwitting author of his unhappiness.

They were three years apart that time, until both were posted to the *Conqueror*, Jim as first this time (Sir William knew the captain), and Faulk as second. Faulk's duties on the upper gun deck at Trafalgar kept him fully occupied until he had seen Jim falter on the bridge. It was a simple error; maybe Jim was rattled. This was Trafalgar, after all. Leaving his excellent gun crew for a moment, Faulk had raced up a deck and countermanded Jim's order, only because Captain Israel Pellew was engaged elsewhere.

Faulk put down the letters, trapped by an unwilling memory this time. Recalled to his senses, Jim had thanked him, turned away to another duty, and been skewered by that exploding splinter. His last words were, "Watch over Ianthe. She's increasing again."

And now, at the Drake Inn, Faulk had met the product of that coupling, a ten-year-old boy with Jim's look, but something of Ianthe in him, too. Life is strange, he thought. The nondescript son of a steward rose in rank and ships, and Jim ended up shrouded in his sleeping cot in cold waters off the Spanish coast. Faulk spent the rest of the night dozing in the armchair by the fireplace, his letters clutched unread in his hand.

Chapter Two

"My stars, Diana, Captain *Faulk?* You're certain it was Faulk?"

"Mama, I told you. That is what he said."

Jem made a face at his sister. "I told you he was *our* Captain Faulk, Diana. It was nice to finally see what he looked like, Mama."

Ianthe Mears had more questions, but knew when it was time to stop quizzing her offspring. No fifteen-year-old alive had much patience with a mother who seemed suddenly not to be her usual calm and biddable self. Still, she wanted more.

"Diana, or you, Jem. What did he look like? I haven't seen him in more than twenty years, and he was an old friend...of your father."

Hmm. Ianthe was not certain she trusted that look Diana was giving her. What were they teaching young ladies at female academies in Bath nowadays? "I am just curious," she finished, knowing how lame it sounded. She couldn't help it that the words were spilling out of her like a giddy chit. *Steady, Ianthe,* she told herself. *What will Diana think? More to the point, what are you thinking?*

Jem, bless his heart, hadn't yet reached the age of suspicion. "Mama, he looked hard."

Then Diana leaped into the discussion, reminding Ianthe that fifteen-year-olds sometimes forget they are fifteen. "Jem, you nod, people don't look hard! Mama, he had gray hair and it was clipped really short. And my goodness, he was *old*."

Jem nodded in agreement. "Really old, Mama."

Ianthe put down the sock she was mending. "I'll have you both know Captain Faulk is only three years older than I am. Don't look at me like that! I am only thirty-five! The sea tends to age men, my dears," she told them. *That's a crock,* she thought. Jeremiah Faulk was blessed with the broadest shoulders. That could hardly have changed.

"He did have a lot of wrinkles around his eyes, Mama," Diana said.

Her children, the traitors, seemed perfectly satisfied to drop the subject entirely. "He was probably fleshy, wasn't he?" she prodded, picking up the sock again, as well as the conversational thread.

"Oh, no. He was lean and looked quite excellent in his uniform," Diana said. "Probably like Lord Nelson himself. Except he was taller. And he had both eyes."

All saints and the Lord Almighty Himself seemed to smile then, and use Diana as their willing messenger. "Mama, I really think you should invite him here for Christmas. He has nowhere to go." Diana leaned closer, as though it was a deep secret. "Mama, he looked quite shabby."

"That is a sad thing to contemplate," Ianthe said, harrowed with guilt as she remembered who had sent his prize money, which he obviously could have used.

"I liked him, Mama," her son said. "He didn't scold me because my money was gone, but said something about how he had lost money enough in Plymouth himself."

Probably on whist and women, she thought, amused. "No, Captain Faulk was never one to belabor an issue." She put down the sock for the last time, knowing she had no wish to darn, not when she wanted to walk down to the quay and back, her usual remedy when the ache of her widowhood clamped down in her loins and allowed her no church-sanctioned release.

"We will invite Captain Faulk to spend Christmas with us," she said decisively. "I must reimburse him for the money he gave you, and why not invite him? Shoo, now. I'll write a letter and walk it down to the quay."

"Mama, can we afford a guest?" Diana asked, hesitant. "I know you don't want to worry us, but…"

"It will be fine," Ianthe said, churning inside because of the letter she had written to the school in Bath, some lie about wanting Diana closer to home, and therefore she would not be returning to the academy after the holiday. Having Miah here would mean she could postpone breaking the bad news to Diana for a few days.

But what will my darlings say when the house goes up for sale in the new year? Ianthe asked herself as she walked to the quay that afternoon, head down against the wind that had blown several warships into anchorage. *What yarn can I spin about lodging in rented rooms now?* Maybe Jem was still young enough to think it great fun, but Diana would know how low the tide was with the Mears family.

She stood a long time on the jetty, watching the frigates at anchor. From what she had gleaned from the *Naval Chronicle,* most ships were headed for home ports to be put in ordinary, now that the endless war had ended. No wonder Miah was homeless. How ironic that she would be homeless soon, as well.

* * *

Not even as a favor to Mrs. Fillion could Faulk force himself back into the storeroom, except to cart his twelve journals upstairs. The whole time in the storeroom, his skin crawled with so much death around him: Abercrombie, Ainslie, Baker, Bridewell, Bothell, Carruthers, Dixon, Edgeley, Etheridge. Mrs. Fillion had stored everyone's effects alphabetically. He only felt relief when Faulk was no longer among them. He could carry his journals with him in a canvas bag until he figured out what he was going to do with his life.

The weather was raw, but he spent the next two days walking from Plymouth to Devonport and back, drawn to where the *Spartan* swung on her anchor, sails furled, guns gone. He envied the ships still manned, taking on supplies and headed back to duty.

Mrs. Fillion stopped him when he returned from one lengthy walk with the news that he had three pieces of mail at the desk, an event in itself. The first one he expected—his quarterly statement from Brustein and Carter, indicating that all was well in the world of banking. No worries there.

His heart beat faster at the next letter, more of a document, with its prominent seal so well-known to him. He spread out the document, hardly daring to hope.

Praise God. The Sea Lord was offering him another ship. He was "requested and required" to report to Admiralty House at four bells in the forenoon watch, January 15, 1816.

They were offering him another frigate, this one a fortyfour with the mellifluous name of *Golightly*. The *Golightly* was bound as escort to Australia for a convoy of convict ships. "That is one place I have not sailed in recent years," he murmured out loud. As rain turned to sleet outside the window, he could almost feel the warmth of the antipodal sun on his back.

The last letter was in a hand he did not know. He could feel coins inside, though, so he could guess. *Ianthe, you didn't need to reimburse me,* he thought, as he spread out the letter on his leg.

> *Dear Miah,*
> *Imagine my surprise when I learned you had come to the rescue of my foolish children. Starting as soon as you can get yourself here to Torquay, you are invited to spend Christmas with us. We are all of the same mind on this, so don't try to weasel out. We are the white house with the light blue shutters on Claremont Street.*
>
> > *Yours sincerely,*
> > *Ianthe Mears.*

He hadn't expected she would still be Mears, not at all. What is the matter with the men of the Devon Coast? he wondered. He remembered Claremont Street, too, and frowned. It was a modest address, where the families of ships' carpenters, gunners and surgeons' mates lived. He read the letter again, but it divulged no more secrets.

Content, he read through all three letters again, happy about his quarterly statement, ecstatic about the *Golightly,* and philosophical about the missive from Torquay. It had been so many years since he had seen Ianthe Snow—far too long to still be in love, especially since during some of those years, he hadn't thought of her more than a handful of times a month. Still, he had been a poor shepherd, where she was concerned. Maybe he could actually do Jim the favor he had promised him on the slimy deck of the *Conqueror.* Maybe Ianthe did need some sort of watching over.

Torquay was much as Faulk remembered it, a lovely town in a beautiful bay. His courage, never an issue when under fire, seemed to take a direct hit as he walked down Claremont Street toward the only house with light blue shutters. He frowned to see how small the house was, and shabby, too, in need of paint. He couldn't fault Ianthe's tidy yard, or the pot of hopeful Johnny-jump-ups still protected by the house from winter's prevailing wind. There was something endearingly brave about the flowers that made him nod in recognition.

He was still smiling when Ianthe Mears opened the door. He hadn't even knocked yet; perhaps she had been watching from the window.

He reckoned she could have done anything then. What she did was clasp her hands together across her breasts as though he was the greatest treat she had ever seen. He resisted the urge to look over his shoulder and see if perhaps the Lord Mayor of London, or the great Sarah Siddons herself stood behind him on the walk, jockeying for position.

"It's the same Miah Faulk," he said. "Just older."

She frowned then, or he thought at first she frowned, until he saw how tightly her lips were pressed together, as though she was forcing herself not to burst into tears.

"Ianthe, you were never a watering pot, were you?"

That was all it took. She burst into tears, then holding out her hand to him, practically hauled him into her house. His astonishment increased as she swiped at her eyes then reached up to unbutton his overcoat. He put his hands over hers.

"I can still take off my own overcoat, silly widgeon," he told her, which only made her dab at her eyes with her apron, then turn around and run up the stairs, her hand to her face. He stared after her, unable to decide where he had gone wrong.

He wasn't the only one staring. Jem and Diana watched him from the door to what must be the sitting room. Their looks were just accusatory enough to make him realize that Ianthe Mears had two fierce champions. He had better plead innocent.

"Look you here, all I did was say hello," he told them, not sure whether to take off his overcoat or put about. "Does she do that often?"

"I have never ever seen her cry," Jem said, his tone only a shade short of belligerent.

"I have," Diana said softly. "It was when she received a letter saying Papa was dead. I barely remember."

"I sent that letter," he told her. *I remember it all too well,* he thought. "Miss Mears, what should I do? Is it better if I just leave?"

Diana gave it some thought, then shook her head. "I think that might make her even more sad." She looked at her brother, as if for reassurance, then back at him. "After all, Captain Faulk, we have been saying a prayer for you every night for the past ten years."

This was apparently to be a season of surprises, Faulk thought, as he slowly unbuttoned his overcoat. Jim took it from him without a word, practically staggering under the weight of it, and hung it on a peg in the hall. "You're serious?" he asked.

"Captain Faulk, Mama is not the daughter of a vicar for nothing," Diana informed him. "Every night, we pray for poor King George, the Regent, the army, the navy, the marines sometimes and Captain Faulk always."

"Mama says, 'God bless Captain Faulk, wherever he sails,'" Jem chimed in.

"I'll be damned," he said, then felt his face go warm. "I mean…"

Jem was generous. "No fears, Captain. Mama's warned us about the navy."

"Wise of her! What should I do?"

Diana had made up her mind. "I think you should go upstairs, knock on her door, and tell her I'm not certain when to turn the roast. Second door on the right."

"Aye, aye, sir," he said.

In the ten years she had lived in her house, Ianthe had never heard a man's steps on her stairs. Jem had been born on the Mears's estate, because her father was dead by then, and her mother living in Northumberland with her sister's family. There were nights she wished for the sound of footsteps. She got up quickly and dabbed at her eyes with her apron as he knocked.

She knew she couldn't ask him to come in. Her bedchamber was as small as the other rooms, and certainly no place for a man. Still, she wasn't prepared to go downstairs and face her children.

He knew what to do, which shouldn't have surprised her. Of the three of them, Jeremiah Faulk had always known what to do. He opened the door wider, then elaborately ushered her out and pointed to the stairs, where he sat himself down.

Shy still, but less so, she sat beside him. She looked down the stairs at her children, who were wide-eyed with amazement.

"You must not sit on your stairs too often," he whispered, barely moving his lips.

"Never."

He nudged her ever so slightly. "Diana has a culinary question."

Ianthe leaned forward over the step, and found herself almost too startled to say anything when the captain clamped his hand on her apron strings. She blushed, but he didn't release her. "See here, Captain," she whispered out of the corner of her mouth.

"Habit, Ianthe. Captains look after everything."

She offered no more protest. "Yes, my dear? You have a question?"

Diana recovered faster than Ianthe would have imagined. She even seemed to be trying not to laugh. "Mama, should I turn the roast?"

"Certainly. Jem, you may set the table now."

She thought there might be objection, considering that nothing this interesting had ever happened before in their house, but her children scurried away without a fight. She sat back, and Jeremiah released her apron.

How on earth could both Jem and Diana have overlooked his best feature? she asked herself, remembering her quizzing earlier in the week. Well, his best feature after his broad shoulders, which had changed not a bit. His hair was certainly gray, but how could Diana have overlooked how finely chiseled Captain Faulk's lips were? The years had done nothing to change that. She gave him another sidelong look, and had to agree with Jem. He did look a trifle hard. More than a trifle. And he wore a shabby uniform.

"No, not the same old me," he assured her. "I creak in the mornings like a coal ship from Newcastle, and I barely remember what color my hair was."

"Auburn," she said immediately.

"It went gray after Trafalgar."

"You were only twenty-eight then," she said, dismayed.

"Blame Bonaparte," he replied, then leaned back on one arm on the stairs. "Ianthe, you haven't changed at all."

"Oh, I have," she contradicted, although pleased. If he chose to overlook that her figure was that of a mother of two children, she could overlook it, as well. Suddenly she wished she had done more with her hair than twist it into a knot on the top of her head. She had planned to do something better before he arrived, but time got away.

His steady look remained the same, but reminded her she should change the subject. Maybe she should just get up. No, it was too nice to sit on the steps with Captain Faulk. She could remember her manners, though.

"Miah, thank you for helping my children." His old nickname just slipped out. "Oh, I should perhaps call you—"

"Miah will do," he said. "Ianthe, no one ever calls me by my first name, let alone your nickname."

How sad, she thought. How sad. Then she blushed and thought, *It was my nickname, wasn't it? I had forgotten.*

"Should I call you Mrs. Mears? I don't want your children to think I am a ne'er-do-well with rag manners."

"It would be proper," she said. "No. Call me Ianthe. It is my name and…" She was struck by something. "Come to think of it, no one ever calls me by my first name, either. I am Mama, or Ma-am, if Jem is peckish, or *Mama*, if Diana feels like putting on Bath airs."

She knew she had an unruly tongue and an independent mind. In the years since Jim's death, it had caused her monumental trouble with the Mears family. She had to ask him, "Why did you never come to see me, Miah?"

He had been watching her face as though trying to memorize it, but when she asked that, he looked away. "There was a war, Ianthe. I've been run ragged for twenty-two years."

It was no answer and he seemed to know it, because he still did not look at her. *I suppose men have their reasons,* she thought, as she got to her feet and touched his arm.

"I had better see to that roast. It's been a while since I have splurged, and Jem will be sorely disappointed if I muff it. You're welcome to grace my stairs, but the sofa in the sitting room is much more comfortable." She touched him again lightly, unable to help herself. "In fact, I recommend it to someone who has been run ragged."

Chapter Three

She was right about the sofa. Faulk took off his shoes and made himself comfortable. So a roast of beef is a rare thing, he told himself. Is it *that* low tide with the Mears family? Surely Jim's eldest brother and head of the family hadn't forsaken Ianthe and her brood. He could tell there was more to the story than he knew, but his eyes were closing then.

He didn't sleep long; it was one of his catnaps famous throughout the fleet. Still, his nap had been long enough, deep enough for someone to cover him with a light blanket and even loosen his neckcloth. She had light fingers.

He was wide-awake when he opened his eyes, but not inclined to move. No officer needed him; no emergency loomed. The weather gauge didn't matter because the war was over. He could lie there, comfortable, and listen to Ianthe and her children singing in the kitchen. My God, how pleasant, he thought. Poor Jim never heard it. Damn Napoleon anyway.

Now they were laughing about something. He had no idea what it was, but he smiled anyway, enjoying the sound of women. They smelled better than men, too. Ianthe's house had the pleasant odor of roses, even in December. Still lying there so comfortable, he looked around the sitting room for some sign of Jim, but he saw no portrait, not even a miniature. The thought made him melancholy. After their marriage, Jim was never in port long enough to pose. And what lieutenant would waste that much time, when he had a wife to visit and a daughter to become acquainted with? Perhaps she kept a miniature of him beside her bed.

He was up, shod again and trying to tighten his neckcloth in the mirror over the fireplace when Ianthe came into the sitting room. She stood beside him so he could see her reflection in the mirror. How was it she did not age? he asked himself again. *And I didn't realize she was so short.*

"I remember you as taller," he said. It was so inane he winced inside, but Ianthe only laughed.

"You were the tall one," she replied, looking at his face in the mirror.

"None of that! I'm barely past middle height," he protested.

"Well, then, you always acted tall." She turned then to look at him and not his reflection. "Is that the secret to leadership in the navy?"

He knew she was teasing. "Aye, that. Never tell anyone this, Ianthe, because I'll deny it, but it helps to love them, too, and scold them when they need it, and bury them when they die." He could have slapped himself. "I'm sorry. I didn't mean to say that."

She seemed not to be ruffled. "Don't apologize. I don't doubt for a moment that it is true. But tell me, did your rough crews have any idea you loved them?"

"Lord, no," he replied, relieved he had not caused her pain. "There are some things you dare not tell people."

"Fearing they will think you soft?"

He hadn't even considered the matter before. One didn't just tell a gang of hardened men—criminals, some of them—of his love for them. He knew they knew, though, and he had no idea how to explain that to a woman who lived a quiet life in a peaceful place.

"Maybe it's this way, Ianthe. From my powder monkeys to my number one—my first lieutenant—we were all brothers in arms. I made sure even that powder monkey knew he was vital to our success in Europe."

"How on earth?"

He did know now, even if it was something he had never even divulged in his journal. "After each engagement, and sometimes for no reason at all, I wandered around my— our—ship and thanked them for their service." He touched Ianthe's shoulder. "Thank you for asking. I never put it into words before."

"Or wrote it?"

"I should, shouldn't I? How do you know I write?"

"Jim told me you kept a journal, in addition to your log." Ianthe laughed. "Jim wrote me it was all he could ever do just to keep his log, and there you were, scratching away, when everyone else slept."

He smiled at the memory. "A time or two when we served together, I let him copy parts of my log." He didn't know it happened, but he was standing there, probably even leaning a bit on Ianthe, his arm on her shoulder, not just his hand. "Always before we finished a voyage. Log-keeping. That's how we are paid, you know."

"No, actually, I didn't."

"All logs went to Admiralty House and pay chits were issued." He hugged her then, barely conscious of it. "Let us pray Admiralty never examined the Lieutenants Faulk and Mears's logs in the same sitting!"

He thought later that he could have stood that way for hours, except someone knocked on the door and Ianthe gracefully ducked from under his arm.

"Our dinner guest. Don't be so puffed up thinking you were the only one."

Don't let it be a suitor, he thought suddenly, as if that mattered. Probably no one in Torquay needed a suitor more than Ianthe, if times were tough. After a few murmured words in the house's small entryway, she led a familiar person into the sitting room.

"Captain Faulk, do you remember Mr. Everly?"

With the name put to him, he did. Faulk came forward with a bow, but was met with a handshake. He took the old man's hand gently, noting how his knuckles were twisted in arthritis.

"My vicar and tutor, sir! I was never your best pupil, eh?"

The gentleman's eyes were filmy, but they crinkled in good nature. "I think you would have been, Jeremiah, if only your father had not needed your help on the estate."

"It was the world I was born to, Mr. Everly." He felt ten years old then, still holding the vicar's hand.

"The world you seem to have escaped, sir! You're a post captain. You've done well."

"Thankee, sor," he said, knuckling his forehead in perfect imitation of one of his own crew. If he recalled aright, Mr. Everly's congregations used to be full of the common sailors of Torquay.

"You can still laugh at yourself, Captain," the vicar said. "A notable quality! Perhaps you even listened to a sermon or two of mine."

"Aye, sir."

Diana must have turned the roast beef in time, because dinner was delicious. He didn't know how it happened—

he could blame Ianthe later—but his companions at table seemed to want to know about his exploits at sea. Glossing over the worst parts was easy enough. No need for them to know the terrors. Even Diana, who wasn't nearly as interested as Jim, laughed when he told how seagulls would sometimes land on a seaman's head and snatch food from the unsuspecting man's hand, then fly off.

"Happened to me once in the South Pacific," he said. "Pesky critters."

Perfect hostess that she was, Ianthe allowed everyone their turn at conversation. Mr. Everly told of other boys he had taught. "As you well know, Captain, I didn't have the parish with the Mears living," he reminded Faulk. "That was why I had to eke it out teaching ruffians like you!"

"I never thought you minded, sir."

"I never did, lad," the vicar said, giving Faulk a gentle glance. "It was the world *I* was born to."

I know that modest world, Faulk told himself. *It was what I was born to, as well.* He looked around at Ianthe's home. *I could grow to like it here,* Faulk told himself, *if only the floor moved up and down occasionally.* He glanced at Jem—positively burning to ask more questions—then back at the vicar. "Mr. Everly, pardon me for asking, but your wife…"

"Gone these four years, lad. I miss her," he said simply.

"I seem to remember the best cinnamon buns, whether we deserved them or not."

From the look of real pleasure on the vicar's face, he hadn't been wrong to mention the late Mrs. Everly. Jem's questions could wait until tomorrow. Maybe Ianthe would let him borrow her son for conversation of a seafaring nature.

"Captain. Mrs. Mears. I remember something my good wife said about the three of you once," the vicar said.

We were three, weren't we? Faulk thought, glancing at Ianthe, who happened to be looking at him. *You're reading my mind, lovely lady.*

"She had the gift, you know, or thought she did," Mr. Everly said. "Second sight, lad!" he said, to answer Jem's questioning look. "I remember one time when she looked at the three of you and told me, 'Jim will go, but Ianthe and Miah will stay.'"

"Jim and I both went," Faulk said. "After all, we were at war."

"I never said my dear companion was accurate."

"Mama could have left once," Jem said suddenly.

"Whatever do you mean, dearest?" Ianthe asked, plainly puzzled.

Jem looked at his sister. "When I was really small, Diana said there was a solicitor from Paignton."

"Long distance to travel, Ianthe," Faulk teased, wondering why she had obviously not accepted an offer of marriage. Solicitors were certainly respectable enough, even those from three miles west in Paignton.

She gave him a smoldering look that seared right through his vitals. "I'm sorry. I should not quiz you," he murmured, instantly chastened.

Ianthe's look vanished quickly enough, when Jem leaned toward him, his voice perfectly serious. "Captain, Diana told me Mama said he would not suit, whatever that means."

Mr. Everly chuckled and Diana only sighed and glared at her little brother.

"And that was the end of that," Ianthe concluded, even as she pinked up like a schoolroom miss.

She adroitly turned the subject again, and it was Diana's turn to tell of school in Bath and her friends there. Faulk relaxed and actually allowed his spine to touch his chair back, content to listen to Diana, who, now that he regarded her, had her mother's coloring but her father's face. He wondered if that caused pleasure or pain for Ianthe. What must it be like to see your dead husband and lover mirrored in your child? *At least I never knew that anguish, if it is anguish,* he thought.

The meal ended. He knew Ianthe would not take herself and the children away so he could jaw with the vicar, man to man at the dinner table, but what she did surprised him. After she and the children cleared the table, she brought back sherry and glasses.

"Don't you salts always toast at the end of a meal? Jim told me that once."

"Indeed we do, my dear," he replied without thinking. "It's your house, though. You lead."

She smiled and poured sherry all around, even for Jem, although she added water to his glass. "Smuggler's sherry," she said. "I've had this bottle for years. It's for special occasions."

He could see it had never been opened. Obviously there weren't too many special occasions in the Mears household.

"All rise, then," she said, and turned to face him. "Let us drink to peace and absent friends returning."

He smiled at her over the rim of the glass. "Thank you, Ianthe."

"I've heard navy toasts are colorful," she said, while they were still on their feet. "Your turn, Captain Faulk."

"Let's see now. It's Wednesday, is it not?" He grinned at Jem. "Lad, if it were Saturday, we would toast, 'To our wives and sweethearts. May they never meet.'"

Diana giggled, but Jem only looked puzzled and glanced at his mother. Oh, no, Faulk realized, now she'd probably have to explain that to him.

Ianthe was way ahead. "Jem, Captain Faulk will be happy to explain that later!"

"Fair enough, madam." He raised his glass. "Since it is Wednesday, Jem, this is what we would say at sea—'To ourselves.' And someone would chime in, 'Because no one else remembers us.'"

"That's not true," Jem said quickly. "We always remembered you."

"I, too, lad," Mr. Everly said. "Every night."

Faulk couldn't help himself. He swallowed several times and the others were kind enough not to make an issue of a grown man, hardened in the service of his country, taking a moment to recover himself.

"Nevertheless, dear boy, that is the toast. Since you are the youngest crew present at table, it is your task to give it. We're waiting. Lively now."

Jem regarded him seriously for a moment. "'To ourselves, because no one else remembers us.'" He sipped and put down his glass. "Might you ask the navy to change it?"

"Tradition is hard to buck, lad, but I'll entertain that proposal and advance it through proper channels."

Everyone chuckled, even Jem, as he hoped they would. They adjourned to the sitting room for some chat, but it became quickly obvious that the vicar was tiring. *I shall offer to walk him home,* Faulk thought, but again, Ianthe was way ahead.

"Diana and Jem, would you kindly walk our dear friend home? I intend to put Captain Faulk to work over dishes."

He must have been the only one surprised, until it occurred to him that Diana and Jem were probably given that assignment every time the old gentleman came to eat. Jem held out his overcoat while Diana fussed over his muffler. Faulk smiled to watch them, so careful of the vicar. *Jim, you would be proud the way your dear wife has raised your children,* he thought. *They are fine in ways I wish you knew about.*

When they were gone, he joined Ianthe in the kitchen, taking off his uniform coat and looking around for an apron.

"Heavens, you needn't become my scullery," Ianthe scolded, her hands deep in dishwater. "I just wanted a moment's conversation with someone older than ten years, and not moody and fifteen."

He found a large enough dishcloth and tied it around his middle. "That's another measure of a leader, Ianthe. Never ask crew to do something you wouldn't do." That didn't sound right. "Not that I am implying you are my crew, but I can do every man's job on ship, right down to stuffing oakum in cannon shot below the waterline." He could have slapped himself for sounding so wistful.

Soapy hands and all, she turned around. "You miss your ship."

"Like chunks out of my heart. Let me wash, because you know where things go."

He took over at the sink, happy to be busy, and already restless because he was not. He did not know how he would survive the two weeks before he was to report to Admiralty House and learn more about his new command. And yet, washing dishes with Ianthe Mears was a memory he would treasure always, mundane as it was. Maybe that was life on land: small moments of purest pleasure, rather than world-changing battles and hours of terror. He glanced at Ianthe, who seemed to be drying the same plate over and over.

"Ianthe, a solicitor wouldn't suit?"

"Not if I didn't love him. What would be the point?"

It was blunt and honest, stripped of all frills, rather more like a comment from his mates.

"I think that one is dry, Ianthe," he said gently, wishing he hadn't mentioned the damned solicitor.

Her face rosy now, she put it down and picked up another.

"I suppose I alone in the world knew how much Jim loved you." It seemed the right thing to say, but he had no idea how to comfort her, beyond taking her in his arms and holding her as close as a man could hold a woman, until she could feel the buttons of his shirt clear through to her spine.

She astonished him by laughing, a heartfelt belly laugh that he didn't know women could make. "You knuckle-head," she said, and it sounded like an endearment. "You should know, of all people, considering that you wrote all those letters!"

If she had suddenly dealt him a body blow that tumbled him into the sink headfirst, he couldn't have been more surprised. "You *knew?*" he asked, dismayed when his voice cracked like a midshipman's.

"Of course I knew," she told him. "Jim was a wooden letter writer. The first few letters he ever wrote me were so stilted, bless his heart." She took his hands, dried them off on his apron, and pointed to the chair at the kitchen table. "Sit down. You're going pale under your tan, and I am not strong enough to pick you up off the floor if you faint."

He did as she ordered, hardly daring to look at her. She sat down across the table from him, her eyes merry. He almost thought she was enjoying this.

"In his last letter—at least the last one before they started sounding really polished and loverlike—he mentioned that you had come on board as third mate."

"The *Clarion*," he said, happy enough, at least, that the words didn't come out in an undignified squeak this time.

"Am I wrong about the letters?" she asked, not looking hurt or injured, or in any way melancholy.

"Not at all. We shared a cabin, and he didn't waste a minute in telling me how desperately in love he was. He said he wanted to do everything right, and if he had to court you through the post using his feeble words, he was doomed."

Ianthe laughed and clapped her hands. "Doomed," she repeated. "What a darling he was."

Faulk had to laugh, too. She was making his subterfuge so easy. "You know Jim. He was persuasive and utterly sincere, and I could not turn him down. And I do like to write."

She propped her elbows on the table in a most unladylike way and rested her chin in her palms. "Did he tell you exactly what to write?"

She had him there. He could lie and say yes, or tell the truth and say no. He chose discretion and lied, and she saw right through him.

"Jeremiah, you must be the worst liar in the fleet," she told him, reaching across the table to give him a little shake. "You forget. I knew Jim almost as well as you did. He probably told you how much he loved me, then kind of waved his hands the way he did when he was at a loss, and said something like, 'Miah, fill in the rest.' And you looked after him the way you looked after me, when you sent me your prize money after Trafalgar."

"That…that was Jim's share," he said, forgetting she had just told him how transparent he was.

"No, it wasn't, you big liar," she said softly, and it sounded almost like an endearment. "All I was entitled to was a pension, not a bonus of two hundred sixty-nine pounds, plus the additional hundred pounds you sent me. Miah! You were poor as Job's turkey then and could have used the money yourself."

"Do I look like I suffered because of a spot of kindness?"

"Not now." She put her hand on his arm again. "I bought this house with your gift to me, and had money left over to help my own family when Papa died and Mama fell on hard times. Miah, those letters you wrote for Jim were the most wonderful letters in the history of the universe."

He knew there was no sense in trying to bamboozle this female. "I was proud of them. I wrote them for Jim and he copied them in his own handwriting. Rest assured, though—he did not share your replies."

She blushed then. "Good for Jim." She tightened her grip on his arm and gave him another look, similar to the one that had sliced through him at dinner like a cutlass. "Know this, Miah—I loved my husband. You watched over me there, too, with your letters, and steered me into a safe harbor. Oh, this war. Our time was so short. After we were married, I know you saw him more than I did."

He nodded, miserable.

"Miah, we cannot undo the war. I had a good husband who went to sea, and we have two excellent children."

He knew she wanted to say more, but the front door opened then, and in another minute, Diana and Jem were in the kitchen, too, insisting that he sit at the table while they finished the dishes. All he could do was watch them, almost overwhelmed with the sorrow that Jim would never know how wonderful his family was.

Ianthe apologized profusely, but he didn't mind sharing Jem's room. He did draw the line at taking Jem's bed and insisted the cot was probably more comfortable than his sleeping cot at sea. It was, mainly because the pillow smelled of roses. If he had been a romantic sort of fellow, he probably could have dreamed that Ianthe slept beside him. As it was, he lay there—comfortable, hands behind his head—and thought of the unnatural state of all those men in all those ships, lying alone through decades of war, when most of them probably wished to be in the gentle grasp of wives or lovers.

The irony of the Mearses' situation was not lost on him. True enough, Jim may have been married to Ianthe, but he spent more actual time in Faulk's company. All those letters, he thought, as he started to drift off. And the whole time, she knew he had written them. He wondered if she suspected that even the best writer in the world, which he was not, could hardly have written them if he had not felt the sentiment himself.

He was nearly asleep when Jem spoke to him.

"Captain Faulk?"

"Aye, lad."

"I'm glad I lost that money. If I hadn't, we never would have met you."

Faulk could almost feel his heart twisting with those drowsy words from the son of a man he admired and still missed. Sometimes events did pass like ships in the night. Thank God this one didn't.

"My sentiments precisely, Jim. Jim? Sleep tight."

Chapter Four

Ianthe lay awake a long time that night. The house was quiet, and she yearned to do what she always did, but knew how improper it would be, since Captain Faulk shared a room with her son. Still, not a night had ever gone by since the boy was born that she hadn't checked on him and his sister.

She got out of bed, finding her robe this time, and putting it on while she went to Diana's room first. It was such a pleasure to have her daughter home that she stood a long moment beside her bed, looking down at her. She dreaded having to be the bearer of bad news later.

I hope you understand, my love, she thought, as she twitched the blanket higher and admired her child's lovely face. She looked so much like her father, a softer version, of course, but Jim had never been a resolute, hard sort of man, not like Jeremiah. She had never been able to shake the idea that if he had not died at Trafalgar, her husband would still not have survived the brutal grind required of men on the blockade.

The sea had been Jim's idea, and Jeremiah had followed. He had told her once before they shipped out as midshipmen how grateful he was to Sir William for finding him a berth with Jim and giving him an opportunity his own father, good man that he was, could never have provided. *Miah, you were always the more ambitious one,* Ianthe thought, as she looked at her sleeping daughter. *If I am not being disloyal to your father, Diana, I would hope you would find a man more like Jeremiah.*

She left her daughter's room and stood for the longest time outside the door to Jem's room, wanting to enter and look at him, even as she knew how unnecessary it was. Maybe looking at her sleeping children was her talisman, her lucky charm. It was a habit she felt uneasy about breaking. Perhaps Miah was a sound sleeper.

"Ianthe?"

She hadn't even put her hand on the doorknob yet. Miah Faulk must be the lightest sleeper in the universe. *Of course he is, you nod,* she scolded herself. *He is probably still tuned to instant response.* She sighed and opened the door, sorry to disturb him.

He was on his cot, but propped up on his elbow, alert. "Is everything shipshape and aboveboard?" he whispered. "All's well in here."

"Every night since they were tiny, I have always looked in on my children. You must think me so forward, but I have never missed a night."

"No bother. I've been known to walk around belowdeck, just to see how my crew is. I do understand you." He looked at her in perfect comprehension. "Maybe we are more alike than you ever thought." He chuckled. "Post captain and mother."

She couldn't help but smile as she went to Jem's bed and stood there her usual moment, watching her son's peaceful slumber. *And what is your future, my son?* she asked herself. Lately she had wondered that more and more often. Not for the first time, she mentally chided herself for not taking that solicitor seriously. No other offers had come her way. Ah, well. She pulled Jem's blanket a little higher, kissed his forehead and turned to leave the room.

While she was looking at Jem, Miah had composed himself for sleep again, hands folded peacefully across his stomach. Impulsively, she went to him, pulled his blanket higher and kissed his forehead, too. In the morning, that would perhaps seem like the most brazen thing she had ever done. In the moonlight, it wasn't.

She turned to leave, but he took her hand, held it and kissed it in turn. "Thank you for watching over me in your prayers," he whispered, and released her.

"How could I not?" she told him quietly. "Good night, Jeremiah."

Her own bed was cold. She seemed to take forever to get warm enough to sleep. At least the room was dark and she was alone, so no one could see her blush as she thought of how nice it would be to put her cold feet on someone's warm legs.

Faulk woke before Jem, but lay there enjoying the deep breathing of another human. The house was so quiet at night that he had only dozed fitfully until he heard Ianthe outside the door. As he had watched her tend to her son, he was again struck by sadness at what Jim was never to know. Her kiss, so surprising, but so right, had been as tender as a benediction, and he slept more peacefully than he had in years.

The mood was on him this morning, though. He lay there wanting Ianthe as much as he had ever wanted her in his entire life. Maybe it was wishful thinking, but he had a strong suspicion that if he were to go to her room right now, she would pull back the blanket and let him inside. God help him, when he was with the widow in Naples and later, the duchess in Livorno, he had pretended they were Ianthe.

Maybe it was his male vanity, but on later reflection—amazing how the mind could run during a midnight watch—he did not think Ianthe would make impossible demands like the duchess, or pretend her own climax, like the widow. Other women in other ports were bought for a price. He could have called them Ianthe, for all they cared. He knew better than to do that, however. That kind of thinking could make a man crazy.

Carnal, sensual and devilish as he knew he was—Mr. Everly's sermons had penetrated—he couldn't help but marvel at the strength of love, even after so many years. He was older now, wiser maybe, but it still humbled him. Time, distance and grinding toil had done nothing to extinguish the flame of his love and devotion.

Breakfast was cinnamon buns and porridge, and Ianthe watching as everyone ate. He couldn't overlook the real pleasure on her face from seeing them all enjoying her cooking. She even put her hand on his shoulder once when going out of the room for more buns. He was in heaven.

When everyone was full, she finally sat down to her own breakfast. She issued her orders for the day over a cup of tea, including his own duties, which amused him. "Jem, you are to take Captain Faulk into the wild for greenery for a wreath and garlands."

"Lad, I distinctly remember a holly patch on your father's family land," Faulk said. "Shall we go there?"

"Oh, no," Ianthe said hastily, then blushed and corrected herself. "That is, we don't need to go all that way for mere greenery. Jem knows a good place not far from St. Mary Church."

There it was again. Maybe Jem would tell him why his mother seemed not to associate with the Mearses. He had questions maybe the boy could answer, if he could work around to the subject without causing suspicion.

As it turned out, nothing was simpler, which was fortunate, because Faulk never had been the best friend of subterfuge. He never had found a substitute for the direct question, and as post captain, had never needed to. He did wait until they were on the street by St. Mary Church.

"Jem, doesn't your mother want anything to do with the Mears family?"

Jem didn't seem surprised by a relative stranger wanting to know family skeletons. Maybe he didn't see him as a stranger anymore, Faulk dared to think.

"Captain, Diana remembers when she and Mama used to be invited to eat at the estate, and even stay, but they didn't do that after I was born." He shrugged. "Maybe the Mearses on the hill don't like boys."

The more fool they, Faulk thought, as he watched Jim's son. He put a tentative hand on the boy's shoulder and was rewarded with a smile. "It's their loss, lad," he said.

They found holly behind the church, and then bay leaves, still fragrant in the cold. Soon the bag was full enough to decorate a house much larger than the modest Mears home on Claremont Street. Jem said there was red ribbon and wire somewhere, enough for a wreath, so the business was concluded.

Still, there should be some reward for greenery gathered, Faulk decided as they walked down the street toward the quay, not turning on Clarement. Jem looked at him, a question in his eyes.

"I think you and I need to visit that little dining place

over there, and see what they have in the way of pasties," he told Jem. "If we leave this bag outside the door, I don't think we need to worry about holly thieves. You know your town better than I do, though. You tell me."

Jem grinned at the notion of holly thieves, but he was as careful as his mother.

"This is nice of you, Captain, but Mama would rather I was not a financial burden."

It was Faulk's turn to laugh. "Did she tell you that?"

He nodded. "Mama says I should never place anyone under obligation." He sniffed the air. "It does smell good in there."

Jem polished off two pasties without a pause, then slowed down over a sausage and turnips, while Faulk drank his coffee and watched his best friend's child. He didn't know how to broach his next question, but it turned out he didn't have to.

Jem leaned back in his chair, thoroughly satisfied. He looked around. "I could live here."

"Thank your stars you have a home, lad," he said, thinking of the Drake and all the years he had slung his hammock there between postings. "Besides, it's probably noisy at night."

"Mama is planning to rent us rooms here, so it can't be too noisy," Jem said, as he picked up his fork again to capture the last bit of sausage.

"What?"

He hadn't meant it to startle Jem, who cast a guilty look his way. "Don't tell Mama, but I overheard her talking to Mr. Everly about it."

Be patient, Faulk counseled himself. *Casual would be good, too, and not brusque, as though you are grilling a midshipman.* "I don't understand."

"Mama is planning to sell the house after Christmas and move us into rented rooms."

Faulk took a deep breath and blew it out slowly, the better to contain his patience. *What on earth is going on?* he wanted to bellow, but knew better. "Why would she do that? I'm confused."

Jem wrinkled his forehead. "That is what confuses me, too. She told Mr. Everly she wants to put something aside for a dowry for Diana, and we can rent rooms and live on the rest." He leaned closer to Faulk. "Why does she have to pay someone to marry Diana?"

"Custom, lad," Faulk said, desperate to know more, but cautious.

"Maybe I understand. There are times when I would gladly pay someone to take Diana off my hands. Why couldn't someone want Diana for free? Would you want money to marry someone?"

"I don't need the money."

"I don't understand adults," Jem said, shaking his head.

"If it's any comfort, I don't understand people on land," Faulk replied, touched with how willing Jem was to do whatever his mother requested. What other choice would he have? he asked himself sourly. My God, Ianthe and her children in rented rooms, just so she could make a future for them, and there sat the Mearses higher up the hill.

He hoped his face wasn't betraying his uneasiness, but Jem was frowning now and looking uneasy. Faulk leaned closer to him. "What does your mother have in mind for you?"

Jem shrugged. "I think she wants to educate me to balance ledgers, or maybe persecute people as a barrister. She doesn't want me to go to sea."

"Wise of her. I think you mean 'prosecute.'"

"I wouldn't like doing that to people."

"Even the ones who deserve it?" Faulk asked, touched. *Jim, you sound more and more like your father,* he thought. *I wish I could tell you how many times I wished he had never gone to sea. It was not his life.* "What do you want to be, lad?"

Jem looked at him shyly, reluctant to speak.

"Tell me, lad," Faulk said, in a voice so gentle his crew would never have believed it.

"I want to help people. I want to be a surgeon. Maybe a physician, but Mama can't afford such a thing, not if we have to sell our house." The words tumbled out of him as Jem put down his burden.

Faulk let out his breath slowly, wondering how long Jem had been stewing about the potential disruption to what had been an ordered, quiet life. The boy was trying to make the best of the situation of rented rooms, and kicking his own dreams into a corner, all not to worry his mother. *You're a son to be proud of,* he thought. *You're also too young to worry about adult problems.*

He regarded the boy with what he prayed was a benevolent look. He must have succeeded, because Jem leaned toward him. Faulk moved a little closer, until his arm touched Jem's shoulder. He felt his own cup run over as the boy let out the smallest sigh. Maybe it was relief. Maybe he was going to watch over this boy, his father's dying wish.

"Two things, lad. First, you have an excellent goal. Your father and I both saw many surgeons hard at work in the fleet. I know he respected them as much as I do. Second, I don't want you to worry one more minute about this. I'm going to see that things are made right. That's a promise."

Jem looked at him, and Faulk knew he was committed, even more than he had been committed on the bloody deck of the *Conqueror,* because now he fully understood how much he had promised his dying friend. "You have to trust me completely. Can you do that?"

"Aye," Jem whispered.

"I mean it," Faulk said.

"I know," Jem whispered, his eyes filling with tears.

He was just a little boy with too much on his plate. Faulk put his arm around his shoulder and held him tight, making no comment and doing nothing more than holding him and then offering his handkerchief.

Jem blew his nose heartily, then folded the handkerchief, frowned at it and put it in his own pocket. "You'll get it back later, sir," he said.

The captain smiled. "I'll be around." He released the boy, but kept his arm across the back of Jem's chair. "Here's what I need from you, lad—the name of your mother's solicitor. Do you know it? Is he here in Torquay?"

"His name is 'Tre-something.'"

"Good enough. You've done the right thing, Jim. Here's what will happen. I have to return to Plymouth and— Oh, lad, I'll be back!"

The handkerchief was out again. This time Jem just pressed it against his forehead until he was calm. Faulk's hand was on his head now. "I have some arrangements to make in Plymouth that I can't make here. I'll be back by Christmas Eve."

"I wish you wouldn't go at all," Jem said.

Faulk winced inside, wondering what would happen when he informed the Mearses he had received another ship, bound for Australia. *Pray God Jim won't think I didn't mean it,* he thought, as he gave the boy's head a little shake, then patted his shoulder. "Let's go home. Someone may be eyeing our holly outside the door, and we can't be guilty of tempting good churchgoers so close to Christmas."

It was feeble, but Jem laughed and stood up, putting on his watch cap again and skipping ahead to look out the door, just in case. Faulk had a few words for the publican, who identified Tre-something as William Trelawney. "He can make a will so leak-free even Jonah would float," the man declared.

He sent Jem ahead with the greenery, giving himself time to find Trelawney on the High Street and make arrangements for the coasting vessel to wait for him. Even after years of relative affluence, Faulk was still amazed how the application of money could smooth over every bump in the road. Of course, he had been at sea most of those years, with little opportunity to touch all the prize funds resting at ease with Brustein and Carter in Plymouth. Time to put those soldiers to work, he thought.

He knew he was transparency itself, where Ianthe was involved, but he thought he could invent a lie plausible enough to get him to Plymouth without suspicion.

As he knocked on the door to Trelawney and Majors, he suddenly felt less sanguine about the ship, the one he had hoped and prayed for. He glanced back up the hill toward Claremont Street, wondering what it felt like to stay in a house.

Ianthe had put Diana and Jem to work at the kitchen table with wire and red ribbon. Jem was more cheerful than she had seen him in several weeks.

"Mama, the captain just said he had some business on High Street and that he'd be along directly," Jem said calmly, keeping his eyes on the growing wreath. "Diana, please pass the wire cutters. He's not the sort of man I want to question."

Ianthe rubbed his head absentmindedly. "Nor I, really. He *is* coming back?"

"Mama, he didn't take his duffel bag along to hunt the greenery," Jem said patiently.

Well, if you can be calm, I daren't be otherwise, Ianthe thought, cross with herself and out of sorts for worrying about Jeremiah Faulk. Obviously the captain had been taking care of himself through two decades of war. Any man so skilled or lucky could surely navigate the perils of the High Street and return to Claremont unscathed.

He returned half an hour later, looking cheerful, too. She had an irrational urge to pummel him about the head, but she kept her hands to herself. That was certainly no way to treat a Christmas guest. There he was, smiling at her from the doorway in a perfectly maddening way. One would think life couldn't be better.

To make matters worse, he came to her side, put his arm around her and coaxed her out of the room. She looked back to see Jem grinning at them both. He led her into the sitting room, sat her down and seated himself in chair opposite her.

"I trust our greenery hunt met all your expectations," he said, crossing his legs and making himself comfortable.

"Yes, of course," she said impatiently. "Miah, what is going on?"

"Not a thing," he said. "I must tell you, though, that I have to return to Plymouth immediately."

There was no way she could disguise her disappointment. She put her hands to her mouth and pressed hard against her upper lip. Sometimes it worked to prevent tears.

"Hey, none of that," he admonished gently. "I'll be back."

"In a year? Two years?" She couldn't help it that her voice was rising. In another minute she would sound like one of the fishwives on the quay.

"On Christmas Eve," he said. He uncrossed his legs and looked directly at her. "You need to know this—Admiralty has offered me a frigate, part of the convict convoy to Australia. It leaves in March, I believe. I have to go to Plymouth and inform the port admiral of my acceptance, which he will forward to London."

She didn't want to hear any more. She returned her hand to her lip and pressed harder. She took a deep breath because she felt herself getting light-headed. *Don't go, don't leave me,* she thought. There was no sense in telling him that, not with him looking so pleased. He probably couldn't wait to get back to sea. *What did you expect, Ianthe?* she scolded herself. *He came here for Christmas.*

She waited a long moment until she had control of herself, and found herself further unsettled by the look in his eyes. She didn't know if she had ever seen another human being so sad.

"That's good news," she managed. "I know you wanted another ship."

"Excellent news," he assured her. "When peace breaks out, it's hard to know the future."

Don't tell me about the future, she thought. *I am terrified of mine and now you are leaving.* "At least you will be here for Christmas."

He stood up. "That I will, but I must be going now. I'll pack my duffel."

Her face must have looked as bleak as she felt, because he looked down at her, then crouched beside her chair, which was a relief, because she had no strength to rise.

"I'll be back Christmas Eve," he reminded her. He touched her cheek. "Hey, now. Should I take along Jim as a surety?"

"Never!" she exclaimed, startled, then took a closer look at him. "You're quizzing me."

"A little. Ianthe, I'll do what I said I would. I'll even leave my journals here. You know I'll be back for those."

She clutched his arm. "Did you write in there how Jim really died? I…I want to know, Miah. It's my right."

He stood up then, too quick for her comfort. "I'll never tell you."

She rose too, shaky, but on her feet. "That was the only letter I ever received from you, and I did not believe it. You said he went quickly and was in no pain. Is that the letter you sent to all those who died? Was it?"

He was backing toward the door now, holding up his hand as if to ward her off. "He did go quickly. Beyond that, I'll not tell you. I have to go now, Ianthe, if I'm to make the coaster." He left her then, to go upstairs and throw a few things in his duffel while she sank back into the chair, disturbed beyond measure by the look in his eyes again.

I do want to know, she thought, miserable, *but why did I ask?* She was still sitting in the chair when he came downstairs. He set his duffel at the foot of the stairs and went into the kitchen, where she heard Diana and Jem wish him goodbye, and then laugh at something he said.

He came into the sitting room next to kiss her head. "I left my journals on your bed. I haven't exactly been a saint for twenty-two years."

"I never expected that," she said softly. After he closed the door, she leaned back in her chair, so tired.

Chapter Five

⁓⁓⁓⁓⁓

Ianthe knew it wasn't anything she said to her children that caused them to walk quietly about the house for the next two days. Maybe it was the look on her face; maybe it was her own distraction when they spoke to her that turned them less lively than usual. For a moment, with Jem at least, she had a suspicion her son was missing Captain Faulk. Heaven knows he had sucked the air out of the room when he left.

He lingered there in an interesting way. The next day she received a visit from the grocers with everything she needed for a Christmas dinner such as they had not enjoyed in years. The butcher came next, lugging a beef roast of kingly proportions and a goose large enough for banqueting purposes. The gifts were anonymous, but she had no doubt of their originator.

With more cooperation than she was accustomed to, Diana and Jem decorated the house, and then found excuse to take their leftover greenery and continue their work at Mr. Everly's vicarage. While they were gone, Ianthe made herself comfortable on the sofa and looked through the journals Miah had left.

She began immediately with the 1805 journal, turning to October 21. The captain had written nothing of the battle that took her husband's life, which disappointed her until she read the closest entry, dated October 31. *No need for me to write what happened off the coast of Spain,* she read. *This engagement will be long-remembered, and others will tell it better. I promised Jim I would look after Ianthe and their daughter, and the child unborn. Why did I do that?*

It was question a for the ages. "Because for all your common upbringing, you are as honorable a gentleman as I have ever known, that's why, you idiot," she murmured, then rested the journal on her stomach. Considering how busy he and other commanders had found themselves during far too many desperate days of war, Jeremiah Faulk had taken the trouble to send her enough money to buy the house and allow her to help out her own mother. It had never occurred to her then that he should have done any more; it never occurred to her now. What he did was enough.

She thumbed through the volumes. Most entries—he tried to write every few days—were a deepwater man's comments on the trim, the sail, the course, the duty of his career. She didn't understand much of it, but she did appreciate the beauty of his style. She relished those moments when he took the time and space to describe his world of war, the domain of men.

Before Trafalgar, and then most recently, she knew he had been posted to the Mediterranean. She smiled at his comments about women he had bedded—particularly a duchess and a widow—too much wine drunk, and card games won and lost. It was a man's life, told by a man with real skill in writing. Too much skill, she decided, when she felt herself getting warm with his descriptions of his amours, and realizing she wished herself in their place.

He never mentioned her at all, but she did pause over one entry both ambiguous and tantalizing. It was April of 1809, and he was at Basque Roads during that sharp and controversial fight. He had written numbers beside his entry as he had with other battles. These must be the dead and wounded, she decided. This time he concluded his entry with this sentence that got her on her feet and digging in her cask of letters. *I've read through the letters again. On days like this, when we fight and die, they give me heart, even though...* The thought was unfinished, as though he had been called away. There was not another entry until a week later.

She took Jim's old letters to her from their rosewood box, a gift from him on their last day together. With an eye toward the street below, the better to see her children return, she wrapped a blanket around her and tucked the letters beside her. She read them again, not as Jim's letters this time, but as Jeremiah's letters to her.

He had begun "their" correspondence formally enough: *Dear Ianthe.* After ten months, he wrote only *Dearest.* Each one was a gem of declaration and commitment to her from Jeremiah Faulk, steward's son, if she chose to read them that way. For the first time, seriously, she saw all the love that was there, as he wrote to her for his friend.

Years of widowhood had conspired to convince Ianthe she saw things only as they were, and not as she wanted them to be. She tried to put the idea out of her mind that Jeremiah Faulk, childhood friend, was anything beyond a sorely pressed man doing a favor for a dying friend.

He had never made any push to see her, or even to write, but how could she have given him any encouragement? Newly widowed or otherwise, ladies did not write unsolicited letters to men. And where during war was there much time for contemplation? Did love need time and space, or could it grow in hidden places, untouched when the larger firestorm of war passed over, searing everything?

If she was reading too much into letters, so be it. She could say nothing, do nothing, and nothing would happen. She could also take a chance. There was also the smallest suspicion, growing hourly, that he needed her, too. The blank in his journal after Trafalgar, and the way he recoiled when she asked to know how Jim had died told her volumes beyond his written words.

With these thoughts in her mind, buoyed by the food he had sent, and his insistence that he would return, she resolved to pass the next two days at peace with herself. If he chose not to return or respond, she would at least enjoy this final season in her home before she sold it to further her dreams for her children.

Faulk almost found himself short-tempered with Mrs. Fillion during his brief stay at the Drake. They were not on a first-name basis, but he had assumed an easy attitude toward her, during all those years the Channel Fleet called Plymouth home port. Still, he wished she would not pummel him for information about his stay in Torquay. He preferred to keep his business to himself.

His business was straightforward enough. He visited Brustein and Carter first thing in the morning, handing over the document of sale from Trelawney and Majors and requesting that amount in a bank draft.

"You are buying a house in Torquay?" Brustein asked, looking at him over his spectacles.

"I am, indeed."

"Settling down?"

Why did everyone on the Devonshire Coast want to know

his business? "No, sir, I am not." He answered the unanswered question, not because he liked Brustein or Carter, but because—possibly—he wanted to convince himself that his decision to sail again was the only one. "I have been offered another frigate and will leave in early spring."

But Mr. Isaiah Brustein would ferret about, damn the man. "I hope you will not be leaving it empty, Captain. Empty houses seldom prosper."

"It will not be empty."

Nosy man, meddling man! "May I wish you happy then, Captain?"

"What you may wish is that I do not lose my temper while you waste my time," Faulk said, addressing his banker and solicitor in the same low tone that had terrified years and years of midshipmen. With no small glee, he discovered it was just as effective on bankers.

Faulk put on so quelling a face that Brustein did not dare question him when he established a trust fund for Diana Mears, to be applied for upon her marriage, and left in the control of Ianthe Mears. He set up a larger fund for James Mears, simply because he had no idea how much medical school cost, and Diana's pretty face wouldn't require much larding in a dowry. Both trusts contained a clause that more funds could be requisitioned as necessary. He left both Brustein and Carter to the task of drawing up the documents while he accomplished a few more errands about town.

With advice from a helpful hatmaker, he bought a bonnet for Diana, one adventurous enough to appeal to a young lady on the verge of womanhood, but not something to alarm said young lady's mother.

Ianthe was trickier to buy for. The rogue in him—never too far below the surface, else what's a navy man for?—wanted to buy a silk nightgown. He decided instead on a pair of kid gloves, understated and hugely expensive. He cased the crowded shop until he found a lady about Ianthe's size, bowed, and requested her hand for a moment, so he could choose the pair. Maybe no woman can really resist a man in uniform. He had no trouble soliciting help.

Jem's present was the easiest of all. Since Trafalgar, Faulk had saved his friend's telescope, dented from use. The lens had broken when it fell to the *Conqueror's* deck in Jim's last moments, but Faulk had seen to its repair. Mrs. Fillion found him a box. Not feeling up to any Star Chamber questions, he never showed her his other purchases. He wrapped burlap around the hatbox and Ianthe's gloves fit tidily over his heart in his inside breast pocket.

When the documents and draft were secured from Brustein, Faulk took a moment to visit the port admiral, just so he could make true his lie to Ianthe. Over a glass of rum, Faulk accepted the man's congratulations and best wishes for a new year of peaceful sailing. It all sounded like a dreadful bore to Faulk.

His skepticism must have registered on his face because the admiral shrugged his shoulders. "Peace. What can we do about that?"

He had to hurry to make the coaster for Paignton and Torquay, running because he had returned to the shop with the expensive ready-mades and bought that nightgown for Ianthe. He tucked it in the bottom of his duffel bag, already regretting the purchase. There was barely time to make the sloop.

As it was, the winds were unfavorable; it took considerable tacking to leave the harbor. He stowed his dunnage carefully below and went on deck. He was ready to offer all kinds of advice on trimming the sails just so, but no one asked. The whole experience made him yearn for his own quarterdeck, even as he felt a growing discomfort over leaving Ianthe and her children.

You're a fool, Miah, he told himself mildly. *You haven't even arrived yet, and you're already missing them when you leave.* He wasn't totally sure of his reception, considering that he had left on an abrupt note, with her asking how Jim had died. His answer had been more brusque a tone than he wanted to use with Ianthe, but surely she did not need to know everything.

Braced by the cold mist coming off the sea, he had to be honest, reminding himself that he did not wish to recall the event, either, even though it still haunted him occasionally as he slept. It was one of several fraught moments he knew he would take to his deathbed, but it remained the most vivid. He knew he could summon it before his eyes right now, but he did not wish to. Better to concentrate on the lee shore and remind himself that owners of coasting vessels had considerable skill.

It was full dark when they tied up at Torquay's jetty. No one lingered on the vessel. It was Christmas Eve, and everyone had somewhere to go. "Even I," Faulk said under his breath. "This is a novelty."

He approached the house with the blue shutters that belonged to him now, at least until he handed the deed back to Ianthe tomorrow morning, and the money. She was standing at the window, hugging herself, looking for him. He stayed in the shadows, watching her.

It came over him like a benediction, because he knew how much he loved her. Until it was taken from him during his Spanish imprisonment, he had carried the letter he had written with Jim's proposal. He had thought it would have been wrenching to write, but he had only done what his heart dictated. He had always wanted Ianthe for himself.

* * *

He would never come if she stood at the window, Ianthe scolded herself. Besides, the coastal carrier had come and gone, and it was too late for any coasting vessels. He had changed his mind.

She was determined not to show her disappointment to the children, who would be disappointed enough, especially Jem. She would paste on her usual cheerful face, the same one that had seen her through years of young widowhood, disappointment and that peculiar ache from too many years spent craving a man's love. Her only consolation was that England was full of war widows who knew exactly how she felt.

She could have fallen to the floor in relief when Miah knocked on the door. Jem got there first, opening it wide and then amazing her by enveloping the captain in a hug. Miah dropped his duffel and returned the embrace, looking at her over the boy in his arms, his face so serious at first, and then so happy. She had not seen that look on his face since he left for sea with Jim many years ago.

"Heavens, Jeremiah, let him be," she said.

"I'm doing my best," Miah said, at the same time her son said, "But Mama, he's back."

"No. I mean…" she began, then stopped. The captain obviously didn't know. My stars, she thought. He doesn't know. He thinks I named Jem after his father.

She pulled them both into the room and shut the door. Jem had released his grasp now, which allowed her to move into his place. With not a thought to propriety, she unbuttoned the captain's overcoat then wrapped herself around him inside the folds of the garment.

She hoped he would kiss her, and he didn't disappoint, even though his hat fell off. His arms went around her and his embrace was entirely proprietary, as though she belonged to him.

To make things even more pleasant—after all, the entry hallway was prone to drafts—he wrapped his open overcoat around both of them, cocooning them against everything. She had never felt safer in her entire life, even if he did smell of brine.

Surely not much time had passed, considering that kissing requires some air. She was not so totty-headed a romantic to think that time stood still on such occasions. It was the thick silence behind her back that made her pull away finally.

Miah must have had the same thought. He released her, but not by much, and surely not enough for her to be free of his overcoat. He merely looked over her head at Diana and Jem, standing in dumb-faced wonder, she didn't doubt.

"Jim. Diana. It's like this—I am extraordinarily fond of your mother. Come to think of it, I'm a bit besotted with all of you."

He opened his arms wider then, and there was room for Jem immediately, and then Diana, who tucked quite tidily under his arm. Ianthe closed her eyes in the basest sort of pleasure when the captain rested his chin on her head.

After a long pause, he said, "Thank God no one is crying," which made them all laugh, and Ianthe and Diana reach for handkerchiefs.

When they all finally separated, he noticed the children were wearing coats and cloaks. "We were just about to leave for evening services," she told him. "Unless you're an old heathen, you'll join us, won't you?"

"No heathen, Ianthe! Every Sunday I stand like God Almighty on my quarterdeck, read the Articles of War, and a few appropriate scriptures relating to war and general tumult. I refer you to the Book of Exodus and many passages in Kings and Chronicles. Now and then a psalm. Job when we feel cast-off."

He retrieved his hat and helped her into her own cloak. "At what time in the Mears household do we open presents?"

"After church, Captain," Jem said.

"That's another relief. I feared we would have to wait until morning."

"It's never too grandiose, Miah," she warned him, gratified with the way he immediately took her hand in his when they walked outdoors. "Still, I have always preferred late-night presents, which earns me more early-morning sleep. There now—you know the worst about me. I am a case-hardened layabout."

He merely smiled and tucked her hand close to his side.

Since it was Christmas Eve, Ianthe Mears knew the service, if some sharp-eyed parishioner had decided to quiz her about it afterward. There was a reading from St. Luke, to be sure. The vicar must have said something about Christ Jesus born to save all mankind, or at least he should have. As it was, Ianthe could only guess, because she spent a major portion of the service just staring down at her hand in Captain Faulk's pleasant but firm grip. His arm went around her at some point, which only made Diana smile and whisper something to her little brother. Jem giggled, which caused Ianthe to suspect it had nothing to do with mangers or wise men.

She wasn't sure how it happened, but the children managed to run far ahead of them on the way home. The captain seemed quite content to measure his longer stride to her shorter one. He appeared to be in no hurry, which suited her. It would give her enough time to correct a misapprehension she had only discovered.

"Miah, I don't think you're aware that Jem's name is Jeremiah."

He stopped walking and stared at her, amazement on his face. "But you've been calling him Jim."

"No. No. *Jem.* Can you not hear the difference between Jem and Jim?"

He shook his head and his expression changed to rue. "That's too delicate a difference for a man twenty-two years before the guns. But why name him after me?"

"That last letter from Jim—the one you enclosed in the letter you sent me on October 31. It was folded, but not in an envelope. I wonder you did not read it."

They had started walking again. He stopped. "Please believe I never had anything to do with your correspondence, once you and Jim married." He took her hand more firmly. "I have to tell you, though. There was an envelope. He had been carrying it in his uniform pocket. I...uh...oh, Ianthe...it..."

"...was bloody?" she finished calmly.

He nodded. "I couldn't send you that envelope," he said, when he could speak. "But I didn't read the letter."

"I wish you had. In the letter, Jim asked me to name our child after you, the author of his success at courting me through the post."

"My God," was all the captain could say. He bowed his head, which gave her ability and permission to kiss his cheek, now that it was within reach.

He was not slow. In another moment he grasped her shoulders. "Jim's family must have been shocked when you did that."

"Indeed they were," she said, amazed at her own calmness. "Sir William called me terrible names and made accusations that were, as we know, completely baseless. He cut all connection."

"Ianthe, you should have named him James!"

"Never. It was Jim's last wish to me, as his was to you. So you see, you've always been with me."

She shouldn't have said that. It was more than a battle-tested and well-regarded post captain could manage. She made him sit down on the stone wall that traced the street up from the harbor, holding his hand while he sobbed. She dried his face with her handkerchief, then moved closer into his embrace.

"I think you should also tell me how Jim died. You need to let go of that."

She had him in a vulnerable place. Whatever Jim had suffered, it was long over. Maybe he didn't understand that as well as she did, she who had waited but not witnessed.

"I could write it in my journal, couldn't I?"

"You could. Would you rather do that?"

He nodded, in command of himself again. "Those scamps have left us far behind. Was it by design? Are your children so devious?"

"I fear they are, Miah."

He kissed her again, one hand gentle on her throat this time, and the other farther south, reminding her acutely that he was—and always would be—a deepwater man. A bit of a rogue.

Chapter Six

When they finally arrived at home, Diana and Jem were already in the sitting room, their few presents around them. Ianthe glanced at the captain, seeing the compassion in his eyes at their meagerness, then smiling at their utter unconsciousness of how little they had, when they had so much.

There wasn't much furniture in the sitting room, but Diana indicated the captain should take the remaining chair, then gestured to the ottoman in front of it. "Mama, that's for you. You're always one to let us take the biggest piece of beef or the nicest bolt of fabric." She sighed elaborately. "I suppose this means you must use the captain's ottoman, if he will share."

To Ianthe's utter bliss, Miah laughed, and reached over to ruffle Diana's carefully coiffed hair. She looked at him indignantly, then pinked up nicely.

"Very well. If I must," Ianthe said, seating herself on the ottoman, so close to the captain's legs.

He got up then, and went back into the entryway, rummaged in his duffel and returned with gifts of his own.

He sat down again, this time with his legs on either side of Ianthe. Diana nodded her approval, then glanced at Ianthe with a look of woman to woman and not daughter to mother, which warmed Ianthe almost more than sitting so close to Captain Faulk.

Their presents to each other were the usual: fabric for a new dress for Diana, a book for Jem and a lace collar from both of them to her. Ianthe gave the captain mittens she had managed to finish before his return.

"Since you are bound for Australia, I doubt you need these now," she said.

"No fears. If I get blown off course and fetch Antarctica, I'll be the happiest man alive," he joked, as Jem laughed.

Diana and Jem gave the captain two steel pen nibs. "I suppose you mean me to continue my journal," he said to the children. "I can use these. Thank you, my dears."

Ianthe tried to rise then, to send everyone off to bed with Christmas biscuits and milk, but Miah put a hand on her shoulder.

"It's my turn," he said. "Why do you think I went to Plymouth?"

"To see the port admiral?"

"Well, that, and a few other things. Here, Diana, catch."

He pulled a hatbox from out of a burlap sack and lofted it her way. Eyes wide, Diana untied the ribbon, then gasped with delight as she took out the bonnet.

"Mama!" she exclaimed.

"I had some help selecting it," Miah said. "The milliner said it would be all the rage at Bath."

Ianthe felt a snag of conscience. *It serves me right for putting off giving Diana the bad news in that quarter,* she thought. Well, it can wait. "That is a splendid bonnet, Diana."

The next present was Jem's, but the captain held the box

in his hand for a moment, looking down at it, getting control of himself. Ianthe hoped the children wouldn't notice, but she leaned against Miah's knee, simply because he seemed to need the comfort. Her answer was a touch on her head, as he confirmed her effort.

"This is yours, Jem," he said. "It's the right time."

She watched her son as he opened the box, and saw his face soften and then his lips come tight together. When he lifted out the telescope, she couldn't help her own intake of breath.

"Your grandfather gave us each one. They're made in Edinburgh, where all good telescopes come from. Your father used it well."

Jem put the instrument to his cheek, and Ianthe felt Miah's leg tense and then relax, as the rightness of it seemed to comfort him, too.

"Was he a good officer, Captain?"

"One of the best, lad. I've never found his equal in a mate."

Miah must have felt things were getting too serious, because a moment later she felt the soft slap of leather on her shoulder. "Couldn't find a box the right size," he said, his voice gruff. "I think they'll fit, though."

They did. She wished her fingers weren't shaking as she pulled on the most exquisite pair of kid gloves she had ever seen. "My word, Miah, these will put you in the poor-house," she murmured.

"No, I assure you. Now, where are you going?" His hand was on her shoulder again.

"I still have some refreshments in the kitchen."

"I can get them, Mama," Diana said, already on her feet. "And maybe Jem can help me."

"Belay that," Miah said, in a voice of command that dropped both children in their chairs again. "I'm not finished. If Jim could be here, he'd remind me I have a number of Christmases to make up for."

That should have warned her, but nothing could have prepared her for what happened next. His hand was still on her shoulder. In fact, his thumb was caressing her neck in a way she was finding disturbingly pleasant. Hopefully, Diana wasn't watching. Heaven knows Jem wouldn't care.

He handed her a document and what looked like a bank draft. He leaned closer to speak more in her ear. "You probably know how seamen are when they make port. They spend their blunt on the strangest things. Merry Christmas, Ianthe."

It was the deed to her house, and a bank draft for the sum she had suggested Mr. Trelawney place on her house. *He bought my house,* she thought. *The dear man is giving me back my deed.* She glanced at the bank draft. *And the crazy darling is turning over the sum he paid, too.*

Speechless, she turned around to look at him, then back at her son. "Jem, you didn't tell him…"

The hand on her shoulder was firmer. "I weaseled it out of him. You'd better look at this, too." He handed her another document. "I don't know what a good dowry runs these days, but Mr. Brustein nearly choked on his collar button when I suggested this figure. Dearest, don't cry."

What could she do but cry harder? And then Diana was in her lap, demanding to know what was going on, and Jem seemed to balance easily enough on Miah's leg. She couldn't talk, but took Miah's handkerchief from him again while he grumbled good-naturedly about not having enough handkerchiefs for the Mears family. She hugged Diana, who was crying, too, and protesting about so much dowry money, and insisting that she needn't return to Bath because it was an awful expense, and she didn't much care for the headmistress, anyway.

"I've never met such a family of watering pots," Miah said finally. "Diana, rally your brother and fetch those refreshments from the kitchen, if you don't think they'll get soggy. Take your time. Handsomely now."

After they left the room, and with no fanfare, Ianthe curled up on his lap for a good cry. In a moment he was crooning to her as if she were a child, and not a widow thirty-five years old with too many responsibilities and not enough resources. When her tears subsided, she couldn't help noticing how comfortable he was, for a hard man in a harder profession. She circled an experimental arm around his back, which made him sigh.

She could feel him laughing, even though it was soundless. "What now?" she asked.

"I'm afraid to show you the next document."

"I know it's not an eviction notice, because I have the deed here," she teased.

He handed her another document, this one for James Mears, her son. "I'll have the name corrected to Jeremiah when I'm next in Plymouth," he said. He opened the document because her fingers were beginning to shake again. "Jem told me he is interested in the medical profession. He is only ten, though, so whatever he decides upon will do just as well."

"How can I ever repay you for all this kindness?" she whispered, when she could speak.

"You could marry me," he said. "That way I wouldn't have to be jealous of solicitors in Paignton, or anyone else, should the men of Devon grow brains and realize what an utter nonpareil you are. Ianthe, I have loved you for years. I know how devoted you were to Jim, and if I'm out of order..."

She put her hand to his lips. "Shh, Miah. You're right. I loved Jim. Would you think me very odd if I told you I turned my attention to Jim because I knew you would never offer for me?"

"Heavens, Ianthe."

It was his turn to be dumbstruck. She closed her eyes against the sound of him struggling to control himself again. It was her turn to make those crooning sounds of comfort.

He collected himself, borrowing back his sodden handkerchief. "Of course I wouldn't have made you an offer, my love. I was the son of Sir William Mears's steward, with nothing to recommend me. You're still beyond my league, but times have changed. You really love me, Ianthe?"

He sounded like a lovestruck mooncalf, and not a dignified post captain of experience and wealth. She nodded, then rested her head against his chest.

"I came to love Jim, because I couldn't love you," she told him. "I hope you're not disappointed in me."

He kissed the top of her head and held her closer. "No. That's the way the world works. If Jim had lived, you and your little family would have been happy with each other, and I would have been, well, what I am now. Or was." He kissed her again, and rested his cheek close to hers. "It was a near run thing, Ianthe. If Jem hadn't lost that money in Plymouth, I'd be at the Drake tonight."

She shivered. "Let's not think about that, not ever again."

"We won't." He kissed her long and deep.

It was well after midnight before everything was sorted out. When Faulk asked, Ianthe brought his 1805 journal downstairs and left him alone with it at the kitchen table. He would spend Christmas Day with them, then take a post chaise to London and the Court of Faculties and Dispensations for a special license. He had neither time nor patience for banns, nor even a parish of his own to cry them in.

He wrote his account of Jim's death slowly, not because he had forgotten any of it, but because he remembered it all in such vivid detail that he had to wait between words practically, for his hand to stop shaking. He cried all the tears he had not cried at the time, because he was too busy and the war had no patience for grief.

When it was done to his satisfaction, he doused the lights in the kitchen and carried the journal upstairs. Maybe someday he'd let Jem read his account, but not now. The house was dark and quiet, but he was beginning to know it, and he had no trouble navigating. He stood a long time at the top of the stairs, completely unwilling to go into the room he shared with Jem. He went to Ianthe's room instead.

She was awake. Maybe she was even waiting for him. Wordlessly, he set down the journal and all his burdens, too. She helped him off with his clothing and into her bed, where he clung to her, savoring the sweetness of her body, much as he had in his dreams throughout all sea lanes in the known world. He felt as though he had had a lifetime of practice in making love to Ianthe because she had never been far from his thoughts, particularly when the cruelty of the blockade often meant watch and watch about, with only brief moments of actual sleep. He had dreamed of her awake then; only Ianthe could ever totally banish the terrors he had lived in the middle of for so many years. Maybe someday he would tell her of the hundreds of letters he had written, but never sent.

Still, he hesitated, until she took his hand and placed it on her breast, which he began to knead gently. She kissed his forehead. "Miah, you have my permission. Don't think for one moment I haven't been imagining this." She took his other hand, raised it to her lips, and to his great humility, kissed it. "I don't pretend to understand my heart, dearest," she whispered, her lips moving against his hand.

He freed his hand and ran it down her body. "I swear you have the softest skin," he whispered back. "Especially here." He stroked her inner thigh and then higher, smiling to himself as her breath came ragged now. He knew he could probably dally about and work them both into a froth, but that could wait for a more leisurely moment. He wanted inside her and that was where he went.

Ever the gentleman—or maybe the barest sybarite who ever trolled the planet—he allowed her to climax twice before he took his own pleasure. He should have been more quiet; he could only hope Ianthe's children were sound sleepers. Heaven knows he had done the mating ritual before, but Ianthe took him by surprise as she wrapped her legs around him as though she would never let go. Well and good—nothing could have moved him from her bed then.

God help them both, she burned like a torch and so did he. If anyone were to ask him in years to come, what was the supreme moment of his interesting and challenging life, he would have to lie and say it was Trafalgar, or maybe the Battle of the Nile. Only Ianthe needed to know it was the first time he made love to the woman he adored, and whom he had proposed to years ago, in letters sent through another.

When they were warm and naked in each other's arms, he quietly told her how Jim died, how the splinter had pinned him to the deck, nearly dividing his body. "He suffered, but not over thirty seconds, dearest. My arms were tight around him and I was lying next to him, so he did not die alone. He thought only of you, and I suppose me, when he told me to watch over you. God bless the man."

She let out a long, shuddering sigh, and threw her leg over him to pull him closer. He knew he could sleep now, probably better than he had in years. He was bathed, clean and whole.

With only the slightest of misgivings. "I probably should go to my virginal pallet in Jem's room, dearest."

Her answer was a snort as she tightened her leg. "Well, perhaps," she admitted, but did not loosen her grip.

This was a good time to tell her his next scheme. "Ianthe, I'm still sailing to Australia this spring."

"I understand. I'll be here when you return."

"I have a better idea. Maybe there is some good to come of peace, after all. We'll send Diana back to Bath, but might you and Jem be interested in an ocean voyage?"

She moved her leg and sat up then, alert. "Are you *serious?*"

"It happens all the time, when things are peaceful. You probably won't be the only woman on board. If I get the sailing master I want, he'll likely bring along the missus." He tickled her. "Never interrogate a naked man, Ianthe."

She kissed him soundly. As little as he knew of marriage politics that sounded like aye to him.

The room was cold and she was letting air under the blanket, sitting up like that, so he tugged her down beside him again.

"How long is a voyage like that?"

"Six months, if conditions are favorable, dearest."

"Will there be a surgeon along?"

"Most certainly. I have a favorite one to requisition, if he's available."

"Six months back, too?"

He realized what she was hinting. "Aye, plus time in Australia before we wear ship and return home to Torquay.

Are you thinking we—or you, more specifically—could possibly require the services of a doctor?"

"I'm not an antique, Miah," she informed him.

Their recent breathless exertions left no doubts in his mind. "No, you are not. Neither am I, apparently, even though Diana probably thinks I am old enough to be in a grave, pulling soil over my head."

"Silly child," Ianthe said, her voice drowsy now.

He hugged her, then tried to rise. His love clamped her leg over him again. "They'll sleep late tomorrow."

Content as never before, he still could not believe his good fortune. "Ianthe, you should know better than to marry another tar."

He sighed as she ran her strong hands over his shoulders, then spoke into his ear. "Of course I should not marry another deepwater man. Sir, I am still a woman of the West Country and you are not the only one with salt water in your veins."

Nothing else she could have said would have touched him more, or aroused him so much. They made love more slowly this time, savoring their common joy in the sea and the knowledge of their mutual satisfaction with the world they were born to.

He held her close when they finished, content not to move beyond gathering her in his grasp and smiling when she hesitated, then laid her head on his chest, her arm around his body. In a euphoria of immense satisfaction, he told himself never to think of the time he'd wasted by not contacting her much sooner. Truth to tell, there had been precious few opportunities, not with war as the main course of his life's meal. *Now we have moved to dessert,* he thought, and kissed her sweaty hair.

"Since you named him Jeremiah, I wonder you did not

call him by my old nickname," he said, "I never could have misheard that."

She shook her head and kissed his chest. "Would you have had me in daily tears, thinking of you even more than I did?"

"I'm not much, Ianthe," he assured her, flattered, but ever the realist.

"You are everything," she contradicted. "Hush a moment, and let me savor the bliss of complete contentment. Parts of me haven't felt this refreshed in years!"

He laughed softly.

He waited until she was asleep to leave her bed. She said something drowsy to him when he kissed her bare shoulder, but did not wake when he bundled up his clothes and left the room. When he was more or less chastely clad in his nightshirt, he looked in on Ianthe again. She slept peacefully. He longed to climb in beside her again, but that could wait until Mr. Everly spliced them.

Diana was sound asleep, too, the hatbox on the floor right beside her bed. He watched her a moment, wondering how he would fare with a fifteen-year-old who probably knew all the answers to life's pressing questions. Time to worry about that later.

Jem had taken the telescope to bed with him. *You're a good lad,* Faulk thought. *I doubt your father would mind if I called you son. I already think of you that way.*

He stood at the window in Jem's room and spent a long moment looking out at the bay and the channel beyond. *Thank you, Jim,* he thought. *You laid a heavy charge on me, but apparently we have all been watching out for each other.*

He had never felt so content. A realistic man, he put it down to utter release in Ianthe's bed, where he had belonged for years, but never found until now. As he stared at the dark waters, he knew it was more than that, and even more than

Christmas working its magic. He had spent many Christmases looking at dark water, and he hadn't felt like this.

He decided it was peace. Maybe there was a use for it, after all. He would work his gun crews on the voyage to Australia, same as he always did, but there would be no need to fire the guns in anger now. Ianthe would be with him; Jem, too. Maybe in years to come, if there was time between the sea, and children and duty, he might have time to write his memoirs.

He smiled at the bay below. Peace had brought its own Christmas gift: choice. He looked up at the sky and gave a small salute to the God of war he had invoked many a Sunday from his quarterdeck as shepherd of his flock, and then another to the God of peace.

He stayed at the window until his feet were cold, then tiptoed into the hall. Another choice. Hopefully, Ianthe was right, and the children would sleep late. He went to her room and back to their bed. She didn't even squeal when he put his cold feet on her warm legs. Good woman, this.

* * * * *

A LITTLE CHRISTMAS

Gail Ranstrom

Dear Reader,

When I was first invited to contribute to this anthology, I was thrilled. Then I realized I would have to come up with a story. To set the mood, I began to hum Christmas carols, and soon the one that caught my imagination was "We Need A Little Christmas" by Jerry Herman. Though the song was more modern than my story, the lyrics inspired Sophie's yearning for just "A Little Christmas."

Many, many happy returns!

Gail

With Love, for Sarah and Lendie,
May you always make merry!

Chapter One

Near Greystoke, Cumberland
December 17, 1818

"The vultures are gathering, my lord." The butler, a stiff elderly man with a fine mane of silver-gray hair, said and handed him a toddy.

"Have they all arrived, then, Potter?" Viscount Sebastian Selwick stood in the library of Windsong Hall, warming his hands by the fire. He could not seem to chafe the chill from his bones, which was only partly caused by the coolness in the air. The rest, dash it all, was caused by the task ahead.

"Mr. and Mrs. Evans have come with their servants. I have put them in the east wing. Mr. Jonathan Arbuthnot arrived early this morning, and is in the south wing. And, most recently, Mrs. Emma Grant along with her son, Master George, also in the east wing."

Sebastian wondered if Potter had a reason for the room assignments. Quarreling parties that had to be separated? He wished, not for the first time, that he knew more about the family. "How many have yet to come?"

"I believe only Miss Sophia Pettibone. I have had the servants prepare a room for her in the south wing."

"Ah, yes. The spinster niece." He glanced over his shoulder to the window and the midday gloom. There must be a storm gathering. "Should we send someone along the road to see if she is stuck?"

Potter shrugged. "Surely she will not be long. We can send someone out if she has not arrived by supper, sir."

Supper. Sebastian sighed. He'd have to get through luncheon first. He did not relish sitting down with a table of strangers and breaking bread. He'd much rather be toasting by the fire in his library in London, dodging the merrymakers and well-wishers.

At least he would not have to worry about merrymaking here. All he had to do was inventory the personal effects, supervise the interment of Mr. Oliver Pettibone, read the will to the gathered heirs and return to his blissfully quiet life in London. Only one thing troubled him.

"Why must this particular part of Mr. Pettibone's will be carried out at Windsong Hall? Would not London have done as well?"

"It was his last request, sir. It had always been his intention to return to England once he retired, and that is why he acquired Windsong Hall." Potter paused to clear his throat before continuing, and Sebastian wondered if he was still grieving for his employer. "Thus, when he learned that he was, er, dying, and would never occupy Windsong Hall, he expressed his desire that his funeral and the reading of his will take place here, as soon as may be after his demise."

As much sense as that made, Sebastian still resented the inconvenience of a trip to Cumberland for the sole reason that he was the eldest son of Oliver Pettibone's also deceased partner and had read law at Cambridge. And, perhaps, that he would feel guilty if he disrespected his own father's memory. He sighed. "Families…"

"They are a great deal of trouble, sir. Not for everyone, I think," Potter agreed somberly.

Certainly not for Sebastian, at any rate. After his father remarried a woman with three daughters, there had never again been a moment's peace in the house. And it only worsened after his father died. He'd rather face Napoleon's army than his stepmother and stepsisters in high dudgeon.

He sipped his toddy, relaxing as the hot brew worked to loosen the knot that had formed in his stomach. "And the remains?" he asked Potter in a sigh.

"They should arrive tomorrow, sir. Or the next day. The London dispatcher assured me he would act with all due haste."

Drat! He was stuck at Windsong until Mr. Pettibone's remains arrived. There was nothing yet to bury in the frozen cemetery overlooking the valley, and the will could not be read until afterward. At least he could use the interim to perform the sorting of Pettibone's personal belongings.

The luncheon bell rang and he finished his toddy in one large gulp, fortifying himself. The time had come to deal with the task at hand—the gathering of the family. He squared his shoulders and headed for the dining room.

God save him from families.

After introductions, they were seated and the soup, an excellent chicken bisque, was served. Stilted at first, the conversation soon turned to the only absent guest.

"It does not surprise me, my lord, that she has not arrived in a timely fashion. Why, I shall be surprised if she arrives at all," Mrs. Marjory Evans proclaimed over her bowl.

Unpredictable, Sebastian gathered.

"An unconventional gel," her husband, Thomas, agreed. "Never biddable—she jilted a duke, you know—and disaster follows her everywhere."

Scandalous, too?

Mr. Arbuthnot, a handsome blade from London who seemed to be annoyed by nearly everything, sniffed as if he smelled something vaguely unpleasant. "Really, Thomas? I hardly think you'd be impartial. The duke was not the only suitor she refused if I recall."

"Are you implying I was Thomas's second choice, Jonathan?" Mrs. Evans asked with an arched eyebrow.

"I am implying, Marjory, that Thomas is perhaps not Sophia's most impartial critic. As for her jilts, I seem to recall some twaddle about her not wishing to be 'controlled.' Sophia would not be a spinster if she did not want it so."

Sebastian clenched his jaw, steeling himself for another week or two of bickering. Since the family could not be relied upon for an impartial description, he tried to recall what he'd been told about Miss Sophia Pettibone.

The sole surviving child of Oliver Pettibone's older brother, Miss Sophia had been taken to live with her mother's side of the family when she was quite young. Later, there had been some scandal in London—likely the jilt Mr. Evans had just mentioned. He'd heard the words *headstrong, odd* and *exotic.* Put them together with unbiddable, unpunctual, scandalous and disastrous and he couldn't imagine such a creature. She was bound to be trouble, that much was certain, and he couldn't abide troublesome women. He wondered if the groomsmen he'd sent out had found her yet.

"I was just making the point that we cannot expect anything ordinary from her," Mrs. Evans said under her breath. "I warrant that she will be without a chaperone when she arrives."

"You shall see, my lord, and I do not envy you having to deal with her," the usually shy Mrs. Emma Grant added.

"Hmm," was his only reply as he stood and dropped his napkin on his chair. With a slight bow in the ladies' direction, he left the room. If the woman was going to be that much trouble, perhaps he ought to help the groomsmen look for her. Nothing would happen to the chit while he was responsible for events at Windsong Hall.

Sophia Pettibone scrubbed her gloved hand across the frosted coach window as she tried to peer out at the countryside. Her excitement was growing. How lovely it would be to see her father's side of the family again. Yes, this would undoubtedly be an opportunity to build a relationship with them. They so rarely saw each other that they were not exactly what she would call "close," but she had longed to feel that way. To belong to something larger than herself. She sighed and put her melancholy thoughts away.

"I have heard the lake district is the loveliest landscape in all the empire," she told her maid. "I brought my paints along. At the very least, I shall do some sketches to complete later."

"Aye, miss. I warrant there'll be plenty o' spare time, but what could you find to paint with the leaves gone and everything so cold and bleak?"

"Bleak? Do you not see beauty in the winter sky? The patterns of frost and the pristine blanket of falling snow? I am fascinated by the way the bare branches of trees etch a silhouette against the gray." Sophia caught the hand strap attached to the inside wall to steady herself when the coach rocked as it hit a rut. "Goodness! Hold tight, Janie! I hope the rest of our trip will not be so rough."

"We must be nearly there, miss. The groom at the last

inn said 'twould only be a few hours. We have already missed lunch, I fear."

Before Sophia could answer, the coach lurched and began to slip sideways. "Heavens!" She raised her voice and shouted to the driver. "What has happened, sir? Have we broken a wheel?" And just then, as slowly and easily as you please, the coach tipped over on its side.

Sophia reached for Janie and pulled her against her chest to cushion the girl's fall. They landed with bruising force against the door. Sophia prayed that the window would not break and cut them. Her knee had jammed into the door latch and a sharp pain shot through her leg. She and Janie scrambled to right themselves and held on to each other in the dim light afforded by the single frosted window above them. Janie was moaning and shaking, and Sophia prayed she would not give in to hysteria.

Suddenly there was more shouting than could be accounted for by her driver and footman, but the sound was muffled by snow and the position of the coach. "Miss? Miss! Is everyone all right?" her driver called.

"We're whole, sir!" she called. "Can you pull us out?"

The coach rocked as someone stepped up on the axle and a moment later the door above them was thrown open. The silhouette of a man's head and shoulders appeared above them—black against the gray sky and not their driver from the size of him.

He reached down with a gloved hand for her, but she slapped at the insistent reach and nudged her nearly hysterical maid. "Take Janie first, please."

The man hoisted the plump maid without the slightest difficulty and they disappeared, no doubt to examine Janie for injuries. She held her breath as the coach slid sideways again and she pressed her lips together to keep from crying out. Oh, pray the coach was not perched on the edge of a cliff!

"Hold the axle!" an unfamiliar voice called.

The coach creaked as he climbed again and appeared through the window. "Now you, miss."

She stripped her gloves so she could clasp better and reached up to him. When his hand closed around her wrist, she gripped his wrist in return and he hoisted her upward, too, without hesitation. There was strength and confidence in that hold, and she knew he would not falter.

Before she could see him clearly, he swung her down to the waiting arms of her driver, who caught her with a slight stagger. "Are you well, Miss Pettibone? You look… overset."

"*Overturned* would be more apt, Mr. York. But I am well enough. How is Janie?"

"Here, miss," the maid called from the road. "I am whole."

Relieved, Sophia exhaled a breath she hadn't realized she was holding. "Thank heavens! You may put me down now, Mr. York."

The driver placed her on her feet, but a sharp pain shot through her right knee. She grimaced and seized Mr. York's arm to steady herself. "Just a bruise," she assured him. "Give me a moment to adjust and I shall be quite fine."

"Are ye sure, miss?"

"I—"

"Will not put weight on it until it has been seen to."

Sophia turned to the pleasantly masculine voice that had finished her sentence and recognized the silhouette of the man who had pulled her from the coach. Oh, my! He really was quite handsome. The wind had mussed his dark hair and a sweep of it had fallen across his brow to frame the most interesting eyes she had ever encountered—somewhere between gray and green. He had a strong chin with the shadow of a cleft. He smelled of fresh linen and wool with a hint of shaving soap—a very pleasant scent that caused something to tingle deep inside her. His mouth, though, was pursed in concern as he bent over her.

Before she could respond, he swept her up and began carrying her to a coach a few yards away. Little alarm bells went off in her mind. The man was handsome, yes, but how could she possibly know his intentions?

She wiggled, trying to get down. "Sir, put me down."

"I do not think so, Miss Pettibone. We must get you to Windsong Hall with all due haste."

Windsong Hall? "Are you one of the guests, sir?"

"I am the executor of your late uncle's estate."

Sophia had received a letter from a Viscount Selwick with instructions to come at once to Windsong Hall for the reading of the will. This, then, must be the unknown viscount, but that did not help her with her dilemma in the least.

"Lord Selwick? Really, you needn't carry me, and I must wait with Janie and the coach."

"I have already assured myself that Janie is sound. If I have learned anything from my stepsisters, it is to ignore demurs. Save your breath, Miss Pettibone."

She raised her eyebrows at his tone. "My reticule—"

"Your maid will see to it."

She was not used to being commanded. In a household of women, she was often the one who took charge. Still, this could be interesting in a curious sort of manner.

Chapter Two

The viscount placed Sophia in his coach, pulled a fur throw over her lap and climbed in to take the seat opposite. He rapped on the roof and the coach took off at a stately pace.

"Now, if you will allow me, Miss Pettibone, I would like to have a look at your injury."

"Really, that isn't necessary. I just landed against the door latch when the coach overturned."

But it was too late. He had leaned over and lifted her right foot to rest on his knee. She felt a heated blush rise to her cheeks when he pushed the hem of her gown up to midcalf. Her pale blue stockings were exposed along with her sturdy traveling boots.

"Good Lord," he muttered without looking up at her. "I doubt you could sustain much damage through such sensible traveling gear, but we cannot leave it to chance." He began loosening the laces of her boot.

This was a bit more than Sophia could endure. A retort rose to her lips. "My lord! You must not!"

He looked directly at her for the first time, the hint of a smile twitching at the corners of his mouth as he cupped her heel and tugged the boot off. "I shall close my eyes, Miss Pettibone, if that will preserve your modesty."

Speechless, she watched as he closed his eyes and slid his hands, strong and steady, from her ankle up over her calf to her knee. She could have sworn there was something...seductive in the way his hand skimmed her leg. And did his hand go a bit higher than necessary? He flexed her knee slowly, almost as if he were waiting for a moan or gasp. She complied against her will when a sharp pain burst into life. His hand slid over a tear in her stocking, shocking her with the intimate heat of his hand against her bare flesh.

"I fear I shall have to take a look, Miss Pettibone. Your cry and the torn stocking tell me a vastly different story than your words." And, very slowly, he opened his eyes—those chameleon eyes. His gaze dropped immediately to her exposed limb.

She looked down, too, and was surprised to see blood soiling the pristine blue of her stockings and a ragged gap exposing an oozing cut across her knee—neither too deep nor too long, but sufficiently painful. He removed a handkerchief from his jacket pocket and ripped it in two, folding one part into a pad, and the other into a twist to tie around her knee to hold the makeshift bandage in place.

"Wash that well with hot water when we have you home, eh?"

She missed the warmth of his hand when he withdrew it and a tiny shiver shot through her. She thought, from the set of his features, that he was a bit unsettled, too. Heavens, this would never do!

He reached for her hem and pulled it down over her legs in a quick motion, almost as if he'd just realized he'd seen too much. "I believe that will hold you until we have you back at Windsong, Miss Pettibone."

And thank heavens for that! Much more of his handling and she'd have been incoherent. Living in a household of females, she was unused to a man's touch, or the feelings it could evoke. Her cheeks burned when she realized this stranger had seen more of her than any man ever had. Even the duke.

He allowed a slight smile now that the danger was past. Sophia smiled back, the irony of the situation not entirely lost on her. Since he did not seem inclined to break the awkward silence, she cleared her throat and tried a neutral topic. "Am I the last to arrive, my lord?"

"You are. We expected you for luncheon." He folded his arms across his chest and settled back against the cushions.

"I apologize. We were delayed in our departure this morning. A deficit of fresh horses, it seems."

"Such inconveniences are not uncommon in the country, Miss Pettibone. One should prepare ahead for them."

Was that a reprimand? The prig! She arched one eyebrow. "Or one could make allowances for them."

He merely stared at her, his expression unchanging.

Well, if he could be taciturn, so could she. But while he had probably forgotten his veiled reprimand already, she had not. In fact, she was now contemplating ways to make him pay for that. Ways, in fact, to dig beneath that harsh, controlling veneer and see what really lay beneath. Ways to make him forget himself and smile. The man really needed a bit of Christmas.

As he was not inclined to conversation, she watched out the window until she saw their destination ahead.

Windsong Hall was a massive Elizabethan manor house that towered above the trees and looked mysteriously imposing against the icy-blue horizon. Lamps glowed in several windows, and a glass globe protected flames in the lantern stands on either side of wide stone steps.

As they drew up at the entry, the door opened and her relatives burst forth—her cousin Marjory with her husband Thomas, cousin Emma Grant with her son, little Georgie, and cousin Jonathan Arbuthnot bringing up the rear. How nice it would be to visit with them again. It had been far too long.

A footman opened the coach door and Viscount Selwick hopped down. He lifted her out and set her experimentally on her feet. Alas, she faltered again. Not as badly as before, but enough to evidence a limp.

Jonathan hurried forward with a welcoming smile. "What now, Cousin Sophia? Have you had another misadventure?"

She laughed. "Just a little coaching accident."

"Lord! Never a dull moment with you, is there?" He reached to lift her in his arms, but the viscount preempted him by sweeping her up once again and casting a dark look in Jonathan's direction.

"Potter, run ahead and be certain Miss Pettibone's fire is lit. And tell cook to bring her tea and a bowl of soup."

An elderly gentleman with gray hair and a slightly stooped posture hurried off, a concerned look on his face.

Sophia could barely keep from sighing. Lord Selwick was so hopelessly handsome and so determined. Indeed, she had rarely felt so unaccountably feminine but, next to his blatant masculinity, it was inevitable. Oh, this whole event was far too confusing. And when she settled into his arms as he carried her up the front steps and into the great hall, she was certain that God would smite her for her wayward thoughts.

Sebastian took the grand staircase two steps at a time, less to rush Miss Pettibone to her destination than to escape the family. Her arrival had elicited everything from relief and joy to snorts of disapproval and he was uncomfortable with such a high level of emotion.

Especially his own. When Mr. Arbuthnot came forward to assist his cousin, Sebastian found he did not want anyone else touching Miss Pettibone. Odd, since he barely knew her. Likely it was his banked physical needs caused by the fact that he'd dismissed his mistress fully six months ago and had not found a replacement. Not that Miss Pettibone would be a suitable replacement. Far from it! He never dallied with young women of the ton. That spelled trouble. And *that* spelled marriage.

Still, from the moment he'd seen Miss Pettibone looking up at him through the coach window, her red velvet bonnet askew, he'd been entranced. Her luminous soulful eyes coupled with her dark glossy hair were a startling contrast to her fair complexion. She had the sort of beauty that was termed "exotic"—the sort that painters strove in vain to capture on canvas. Sebastian thought of it as sultry, deeply sensual and lush.

She was quite unlike any woman he'd known before. Most who'd been through a coaching accident would be swooning and demanding attention. She seemed rather annoyed with the fuss and impatient to get on. But she hadn't lost her humor. Sebastian had rarely been so expertly teased and he suspected Miss Pettibone might be a flirt, a skill which he could appreciate but lacked entirely.

Add to that the fact that Miss Pettibone's reputation was a bit daunting, and he was certain he'd be best served by avoiding her as much as possible.

He gave himself a mental shake and looked down into her face. She smiled at him and, in the bright light of the chandelier at the top of the staircase, he noted a bruise along one cheekbone and a scratch on her neck. His viscera twisted in response. "You said you were uninjured, Miss Pettibone," he said in his most intimidating voice.

Her smile widened. "Indeed, I am."

"I see evidence to the contrary."

"Bumps and bruises are not cause for concern, my lord."

He turned right along the south wing corridor, pleased that she would be lodged in the same wing as he. Now, if he could just think of some excuse to relocate Mr. Arbuthnot so he could have unimpeded access to her.

"What are you thinking, my lord? I can see the wheels grinding in your head. You are silent, but I collect your mind is never at rest for very long."

He'd blush if he were capable of it. He could hardly tell her he'd been thinking how best to seduce her—to the contrary of his decision only moments earlier. Instead, he tried a self-serving evasion. "I am attempting to sort the family out, Miss Pettibone. How long has it been since you last saw your uncle?"

"I was a babe in arms, I believe, and have no memory of the occasion. He was a young man, just ready to leave for the gold fields in America, and he never returned. Well, but for now. Aunt Nora said—"

"His sister?"

"No, my mother's sister. I was sent to Auntie Nora to be raised after Papa and Mama died. On Uncle Oliver's side there were only my father and my uncles Edward and Oliver and my aunt Beth. Marjory is descended from Edward. Jonathan and Emma are descended from Beth and I was my father's only child. Did Uncle Oliver ever marry, Lord Selwick? Shall I meet new cousins here?"

"Your uncle never married, Miss Pettibone."

She glanced around the room they'd just entered, filled

with costly antiques, paintings and the very best of everything. She quirked one eyebrow. "Though he did succeed in finding gold, it seems."

He smiled again. He rather liked the way she probed right to the heart of the matter.

"And you, my lord?" she continued as he put her down on the edge of her bed. "Your father was Uncle Oliver's partner?"

"More of an investor than a partner, since he never went to America himself. He profited nicely, though he had no more at risk than a few thousand pounds."

She laughed and he liked the way those sultry eyes crinkled at the corners when she did. "Do not underestimate the power of a few thousand pounds, my lord."

He never would again. Without thinking, he reached out and cupped her cheek, tracing the bruise with the pad of his thumb. No matter what she said, it must ache. She turned her face toward his palm and he felt the heat of her breath against his flesh. The sensation was warming. And disquieting. He dropped his hand and stepped back, changing his mind yet again. He could not dally with such a woman, and a dalliance was all he had to offer. He did not want a family, nor was he the marrying kind.

Potter had laid another log on the fire before he and Miss Pettibone arrived above stairs and Sebastian stirred the embers to release a bit more heat into the cavernous room. "I shall see that your maid comes to you as soon as she arrives. Meanwhile, is there anything else I can provide for your comfort?"

She untied her bedraggled red bonnet and dropped it on the bed beside her. "I think I can manage until then."

He could not resist giving her back some of her own teasing. "If you would prefer not to wait for her, perhaps I could assist—"

"No! That is…quite all right, thank you."

"Really, I would not mind in the least. Did I mention I have stepsisters?"

"I am fine, Lord Selwick."

"Your injury should be seen to."

"Janie will tend it when she arrives."

"Do you propose to just sit on the edge of your bed until then?"

Her expression changed and he gathered she was onto him. Her eyes twinkled as she raised an eyebrow. "I shall put forth herculean effort and manage as best I can."

He shrugged. "Very well, Miss Pettibone. I am just down the hall from you. I shall call for you when I hear the dinner bell."

When he turned at her door to close it, she was wearing an expression of bemusement. He wondered if it would be too much to hope that he was having the same physical effect on her as she was on him. That would only be fair.

Chapter Three

When Sophia woke from her nap, it was fully dark. Janie stood across the room, opening the draperies to reveal a heavy snowfall. "Awake at last, miss?"

"At last? How late did I sleep?"

"Nearly suppertime, miss. Lord Selwick wouldn't allow me to wake you. He said that, if you was sleepin', you must need it. Said he'd like to see your knee again when you are up. He's a familiar one, eh?"

She pushed herself up against the pillows, remembering Lord Selwick's steady touch. "He seems quite experienced, Janie. I do not know what his training might be, but I collect he knows what he is doing."

Janie lifted one sandy eyebrow. "You do? Well, I will trust you on that, miss. He seemed a right enough gent when I spoke with him earlier. He asked if there was anything he could do to make us more comfortable. He said to call him when you're ready and he'll come carry you down."

As much as she'd enjoyed his attention, she could hardly spend the next fortnight expecting it. She swung her legs over the side of the tall bed and lowered herself experimentally.

There was still a fair amount of pain and she winced as she hobbled to the nearest chair. "I'd rather you dress my wound, Janie. I do not wish to…impose upon Lord Selwick."

Experienced in treating the ills of Aunt Nora's household, Janie clucked, fussed and finished with her quickly. "Nothin' so bad, miss. You'll be right as rain in a day or two. Best get you ready for supper before his lordship knocks."

"I shall wear my lavender gown." That was her favorite, with a low scoop at the neck and trimmed with white lace. The sleeves were puffed at the shoulders and then fell in a slim line to a point at the middle of her hand—quite suitable for evening.

That thought brought a smile to her face. How nice it would be to visit with her cousins again and catch up on all the family news. They had not been close, as families go, but they were all that was left of the Pettibone family tree. And she was inordinately fond of them as only an orphan who yearns for connections can be. She was forced to acknowledge, though, that they did not harbor the same fondness for her. She hoped to remedy that before they all left Windsong.

Once she had donned her underpinnings and Janie had fastened her into her gown, she brushed her teeth, dabbed lilac water behind her ears and in the hollow of her throat and sat again to rest. As much as she wanted to walk, she had no desire to be subjected to another lecture from the straitlaced viscount. Really! How could such an appealing man be so stern? She must have imagined that last puckish exchange with him.

The sound of a distant bell ringing was followed by a knock on her door. Heavens! The man was punctual, as well as stern. Or had he been standing outside her door the whole time?

Janie curtsied and admitted him with a silly grin—one

she understood when he turned to her. As handsome as Lord Selwick had been earlier, he was even more so in dark evening clothes. Janie was smitten. And, were she to be honest, she was a touch smitten herself.

He stared at her for one long moment, his eyes warming as he did so, then his gaze slid down her body to her knee. "I trust your knee is properly cleaned and bandaged?"

She stood and clasped her hands in front of her. The last thing she wanted was to give him an excuse to lift her skirts again. "Quite so," she said.

He smiled and nodded. "Excellent. Are you ready to go down for dinner?"

"Yes, though I really think I can— Oh!" Before she could complete her sentence, he had crossed the room and swept her up in his arms. She could still hear Janie chortling as he headed down the corridor with her.

"Really, my lord, I think I can walk. Truly, I feel better already."

"Tomorrow, Miss Pettibone, will be soon enough to test your leg. Until a new owner is named, I seem to be in charge here, and I would not like it if you were to sustain irreversible injuries during that time."

"You would have no one to answer to but me," she said breathlessly.

"And I warrant you would be quite stern with me."

"Bearish," she agreed.

"I would not want to face anything quite so fearsome as that, Miss Pettibone."

When they entered the dining room, Thomas and Jonathan stood to greet them and Georgie scrambled to follow their example. Lord Selwick put her on her feet beside a chair between little Georgie and Emma. He held the chair for her, then took a seat across from her.

"Selwick has explained about your unfortunate accident, Sophia," Jonathan said. "I gather we are fortunate that you were no worse injured."

"I am grateful we only slipped off a rut instead of a mountain."

"Your driver says the coach will be easily repaired. He has taken it to town and will stay with it until it is done."

She nodded, hoping "easily" translated to "cheaply." "Thank heavens Lord Selwick happened along when he did."

"Selwick didn't 'happen along,'" Thomas growled. "He went looking for you when you failed to appear."

Sophia tried to banish her unkind thought of her cousin's husband and turned to the lad beside her. "My goodness, Georgie, you have grown so big since I last saw you!"

The apple-cheeked boy grinned. "Mama says I am going to Eton next year, cousin Sophia."

Thomas snorted and she was certain he was about to comment on the fact that Georgie should have been sent to Eton two years ago. A diversion was in order. "Do not forget to send me your address at school so that I may post you packages. Would you like me to send some of my special ginger biscuits?"

He nodded and picked up his fork as dinner was brought. Maids began to serve them under the watchful supervision of Potter, whom Janie had informed her had been her uncle's butler. When the maids were done, they departed, leaving Potter standing at his post again, ready to ring for anything that might be needed.

Emma resumed the conversation. "That would be very kind of you, Sophia. I shall miss him dreadfully, but I am told it is beyond time for him to go. If only his father were still here to—"

"Now, Emma, we should not dwell on the past," Jonathan soothed. "You know it only makes you sad."

"Well," Marjory proclaimed with her usual authority. "I cannot see what difference it would make. Sad for this or sad for that. This is a somber occasion, after all. Dear Uncle Oliver—"

"Whom you never met," Jonathan interrupted with an arched voice. "Bloody hell! As soon as we bury Uncle Oliver, I am leaving. Pray I can be back in London by Christmas."

"Nor did you meet him," Marjory snapped.

Embarrassment nearly caused Sophia to choke on her first bite of roast beef. She glanced at Selwick over the rim of her wineglass to see if he had noticed. He had. The hint of distaste hovered in the frown lines between his eyes and the thin line of his lips.

Thomas cleared his throat. "Nevertheless, we are Oliver Pettibone's heirs and it would behoove us to observe a modicum of propriety."

"We?" Jonathan asked. "Hmm. Seems to me you are likely the only one here not mentioned in Uncle Oliver's will, Thomas."

Thomas turned deep red and Sophia said a silent prayer that he would not remind everyone at the table that, as her husband, he would have full use and control of any funds or property that Marjory came into.

Georgie began to fidget as he glanced between his mother and her cousins. "Am I mentioned in Uncle Oliver's will?" he asked, obviously trying to sort things out in his mind.

"*You,*" Thomas snapped, "ought to have been given supper in the kitchen and sent to bed. Dining with the adults! Really, Emma, what were you thinking?"

Emma's lips moved, but no sound issued forth. Sophia might have mistaken that for hurt or embarrassment, but she knew Emma well enough to know that she was merely trying to control her temper. She was not assertive for herself, but when someone attacked her cub she was fierce, and if something was not done quickly, there would be worse to come.

"I rather like having Georgie with us," she said. "It balances the table nicely, don't you think? Three ladies and three gentlemen?"

Georgie grinned, but Thomas glared at her, then turned his attention to his plate.

Potter, standing quietly in the corner, cleared his throat as the servants brought the next course, and Sophia thought it sad that a butler would have to remind them of their manners in front of the servants. She slid another look in Lord Selwick's direction. Heavens! He must be thinking them the most ill-bred lot on earth.

The table fell silent while everyone applied themselves to their dinner. She picked at her roasted potato and wished she could excuse herself and flee to the quiet sanity of her room. After a reasonable length of time, she offered her apology and pled fatigue.

Selwick hurried to her side. He wordlessly lifted her in his arms and nearly ran for the door. "Really, Lord Selwick, you needn't interrupt your dinner on my account."

"Not at all," he murmured, his brow lowering over his eyes, gone deep green in the gloom of the great hall.

At the bottom of the stairs, Sophia noted that there was no sign of Christmas. No decoration. No frivolity. No acknowledgment that the season was well underway—a concession to the sobriety of the occasion.

Selwick had her at her room before she could blink. The door was ajar and he pushed it open with his shoulder. Janie had evidently gone to join the staff for dinner in the kitchen.

"Thank you," she breathed as he sat her on her bed. "You've been quite the gentleman. I vow I shall be much better tomorrow."

He turned back at the door and bowed. "A pleasure to be of service, Miss Pettibone."

Bloody hell! Sebastian had thought he'd be safely tucked away for the holidays in Cumberland, free from dramatics, histrionics and petty disasters. Instead he was saddled with a quarrelsome family, an eccentric spinster and a tardy coffin. Even the most innocent comments were an occasion for dissent. Were it not for his duty, he would hie back to London in a trice. Alas, he had been well schooled in duty and honor.

Well, he had enough to do to keep him reasonably distant from the family. He hadn't even begun the inventory of the trunks and crates that had arrived from America. The thought had occurred to him that he really ought to have the assistance of a family member in the inventory, but that dreadful dinner had not yielded a single candidate. Except…

A smile came to his lips. Miss Pettibone was certainly the most pleasant of the lot. She may be eccentric, but she knew her manners and seemed competent enough. And she smelled good. Lilacs, if he wasn't mistaken. He could still feel her contours in his arms and against his chest—nicely rounded, though not overly so. And she had a wit about her that amused him somewhat. If he had to spend time with someone, it might as well be Miss Pettibone. She would make the time less tedious.

Very well, then. He'd stay, but he bloody well wasn't going to like it!

Chapter Four

Between her nap and her early bedtime, Sophia woke before the others and was unable to go back to sleep. Her knee was considerably better when she tested her weight, so she would not have to summon Lord Selwick to assist her. She rang for Janie, dressed and limped downstairs. Turning toward the back of the house, she followed a narrow corridor that led to another door and down a half flight of stairs to the large open kitchen. A tall, slender middle-aged woman was directing two scullery maids while the silver-haired Potter applied himself to the task of tending the fire. Wonderful smells filled the air and she sighed happily. She hadn't realized how hungry she was until that very moment.

The slender woman noticed her first and straightened her apron. "Have you lost your way, miss?"

"I think I have found it," she said. "I am Sophia Petti-bone, and I woke early this morning. I wondered if I might trouble you for a bit of breakfast. Toast and jam, perhaps, or a bowl of porridge?"

The man gave her a slight bow and a smile. "I shall have the staff prepare you a tray. Where would you like it served?"

She gestured at the wide plank table in the center of the room. "Here, if you please. I am quite at home in a kitchen."

"Of course, miss," the slender woman said. "I am Mrs. Cavendish, the cook."

Potter brought a stool to the table while Mrs. Cavendish ladled a creamy porridge into a bowl and placed it on a dish with a slice of buttered toast. She placed a sugar bowl and a pot of jam within reach and went back to preparing trays for the family. Sophia applied herself to the meal with gusto. She'd left the table still hungry last night, but she made up for it now.

"Delicious!" she pronounced after her last bite.

"Ah, another early riser!"

Startled, Sophia glanced to the stairway. Lord Selwick! A rush of pleasure swept through her.

"Your maid told me she did not know where you'd gone."

"I was hungry."

He inclined his head in acknowledgment. Still, he did not look pleased. "I was waiting to assist you downstairs. I gather you are much improved?"

She nodded. "Much." She hesitated, studying him. The cleft in his chin deepened. She assumed that did not bode well and suspected she was about to discover the truth of that.

"I wonder if we might have a word, Miss Pettibone. In the library."

"Of course."

Noting her limp, Sebastian offered his arm, relieved that the young lady was not going to be a problem. In fact, he gathered that she was more self-sufficient than most young women and seemed quite at ease in a kitchen. And she was certainly more accommodating than the rest of her family.

"You are looking fit this morning, Miss Pettibone."

"Thank you."

"I trust you slept well?"

"I did, thank you. The accommodations are excellent. Are you responsible for that, Lord Selwick, or someone else?"

"I believe you can thank Potter."

"I shall. I did not realize Uncle Oliver had sent…that is, had our uncle arrived in England before his demise?"

"No, Miss Pettibone. Potter was charged with returning his remains to his homeland and making the necessary arrangements. Since this was your uncle's property, he had expressed a wish to be laid to rest here."

"I see. Well, he has come home at last, and we shall have to be content with that."

She did not look at him again as they made their way to the library, and that gave him an opportunity to study her. Her gown was subtly seductive—prim but for the cut of her neckline. There, a definite shadow suggested a division between the soft, lush swells of her breasts beneath the embroidered edge. Heat seeped through his vitals. Lord! This deuced attraction to her was going to be a nuisance. Thank heavens she seemed oblivious to it, especially in view of the offer he was about to make.

When he had her safely seated by the fire, he took a chair opposite her. She looked at him with a quizzical smile and folded her hands in her lap. "This is most mysterious, Lord Selwick. Are you about to deliver more bad news?"

"No. At least, I think not. You have said you did not see your uncle after his departure for America, but how well did you know him?"

"Very little, and that only through annual letters. In fact, I think none of us did. As I mentioned last evening, we were all babes in arms or still in the nursery when he sailed to the Americas. We had his annual letter at Christmastime, but that is all. I wrote him frequently, but I never knew if my letters were received or read."

That, at least, was refreshing. The other members of the family behaved as if Pettibone had been their dearest relative. "Then you will not dissolve into tears should you see something of his?"

She tilted her head to one side, that enigmatic smile playing at the corners of her mouth. "I believe I can withstand it."

He breathed a sigh of relief. "We cannot have the reading of the will until after Mr. Pettibone's burial services, and we cannot have *that* until his remains arrive. Alas, the weather has delayed the wagon from London. The chore I have in mind, at least, will be one task we can acquit in a timely manner. You see, in addition to the reading of the will, I have been charged with the sorting and disposition of Mr. Pettibone's material belongings. I thought the task might be easier if I were guided by a member of the family."

She blinked, and he wondered how lashes could possibly be so long and thick. "And you thought of me? Well, I thank you, my lord, but would you not be better served by Jonathan's assistance? Or Thomas?"

"Mr. Evans is not your uncle's flesh and blood and Mr. Arbuthnot seems to have little patience for this whole affair."

She nodded. "Jonathan has always disliked anything that hints of duty or work, but he is quite a charming companion."

If so, his charm was completely lost on Sebastian. "If you would prefer not—"

"Of course I will assist you, Lord Selwick. A diversion will be lovely. And I shall welcome the opportunity to learn more about Uncle Oliver."

He hadn't realized how very much he'd been hoping she would accept until relief washed through him. The task he had least looked forward to was now the most interesting.

She stood and smoothed her lavender skirts. "Shall we begin at once?"

"His trunk and other effects have been put in the largest bedroom in the south wing. I shall inform Potter where we will be, and then, if you will follow me?"

She actually dimpled! He furrowed his brow in consternation as he grew warm in response. Had he not decided to give Sophia Pettibone a wide berth? And had he not just put himself in her way rather neatly?

Sophia could only stare at the complete opulence of her late uncle's bedchamber. She'd never seen a bed the size of a barge before. Why, an entire family could sleep there! A stool with three steps stood beside it to aid access. The gilt headboard with carvings of angels and flowers was so ornate that she could scarcely think of a man choosing such a piece. The golden satin coverlet and bed hangings only heightened the impression of a king's quarters.

Tall mirrors set into the paneling of the walls reflected both the light and the sight of her on the threshold, almost too timid to step over and enter such a world. As she stood there, Lord Selwick crossed the room to a bank of windows and pulled the golden draperies open. The last brave flakes of snow falling through the heavy overcast dulled the natural light of day. If not for the roaring fire in a marble-framed fireplace, the room would have been dim.

With a deep breath and a feeling that she was embarking on a fateful adventure, she stepped over the threshold and closed the door behind her. Plush red-and-gold carpets cushioned her footsteps as she went forward, curious what other surprises the room might hold.

His lordship turned from the window and watched her, almost as if he expected her to bolt. Her heart dropped and she glanced toward the extravagant bed. Oh! What was she thinking? They were only going to perform a small service for her uncle. It was the least she could do for the last of her father's siblings. "Where shall we start, Lord Selwick?"

Was it her imagination, or had his gaze slipped to the bed, too? He came toward her, another of those secret smiles hovering behind the stoic facade. "At the beginning, I should imagine. I shall bring his personal trunk in here, so we may have the benefit of the fire."

He gave her a polite bow and disappeared through a side door. She used her moment alone to complete her study of the room. Two chairs and a round table stood before the fire, almost as if awaiting them. A tall bureau to one side of the bed would never hold Uncle Oliver's things and a small escritoire had been placed in the opposite corner. She imagined the door through which Lord Selwick had disappeared would lead to the dressing room with a washstand and shaving mirror.

There was a *thump* and a moment later he was dragging a large wooden trunk into the room. He glanced at her as he unbuckled the straps. "There are two other trunks, Miss Pettibone. I doubt we'll be done today."

He lifted the lid, removed the top tray, which was filled with odds and ends, to reveal stacks of clothing beneath, with miscellaneous items packed between to cushion them from breaking. And there were two more? Heavens! Even with the whole day ahead, she doubted they would be done.

Sophia went to look at the items in the tray and noted shaving soap and a straight razor, items so personal and so intimate that a twinge of nostalgia pricked her heart. She wished she had known Uncle Oliver. Wished she could have been a part of his life. Perhaps they could have been friends. The yearning to be a part of something more than herself, that same yearning for connection and belonging that had plagued her most of her life, rose to cause a prickling behind her eyelids. Oh, she would not cry!

A black leather-bound volume rested atop a mahogany lap desk. She lifted the volume and opened it to the middle, expecting to find poetry or a rousing adventure. What she found instead was handwriting. Dated entries were followed by passages of narration. What a treasure! Here was an opportunity to learn about Uncle Oliver from his own words. She put the journal aside to take with her to her room.

"How shall we begin?" she asked.

Selwick retrieved the lap desk from the trunk and handed it to her. "We should make a list of items first, then determine to whom they should go. I think it would be best if you sat, Miss Pettibone, while I call them off to you."

Very efficient. But she gathered Lord Selwick was always efficient. She took the lap desk and sank into the chair by the fire. She found paper, a small bottle of ink and several pens beneath the lid and arranged them on the writing surface.

"Straight razor and strop," he began.

When they finished the contents of the upper tray, Sophia put the lap desk aside and stood to stretch her legs. Her knee had stiffened and she stumbled slightly. Lord Selwick was beside her, steadying her until she regained her balance. A frisson of heat warmed her and she looked up at him to confirm that he felt it, too.

He smiled down at her, but said nothing. She mumbled an apology and turned her attention to pouring the tea Potter had brought as they worked. Lord Selwick took his cup and sat in the chair opposite hers.

"This is rather more tedious than I thought it would be," he admitted.

Sophia took a sip of her tea and watched him over the rim of her cup. How, she wondered—not for the first time—could such a handsome man be so stern? She had seen a playful, almost puckish, expression in his eyes, and the tiny smile that would occasionally lift the corners of his mouth from its usual straight line, but he controlled it so closely that she wondered at his reasons.

"You are looking at me with a query in your eyes. What is it, Miss Pettibone?"

"I am wondering why you are so determined to be unhappy."

He looked surprised. "I am not unhappy, Miss Pettibone. What you see is my usual demeanor. I apologize if it displeases you."

"It does not displease, my lord. I only wish you would smile more."

And, to her surprise, he did. His eyes creased at the corners and a spark of something lively glittered in the depths. She returned his smile. "You have a very nice one, my lord."

"As we are now fairly well acquainted, I think you might call me Selwick. After all, I have seen your dashing blue stockings."

She laughed. Here was the man she wanted to know— part naughty and part proper. A nice combination in a man. "Very well, Selwick. And you may call me…Miss Sophia. After all, I have been in your arms."

He laughed, and she liked the sound of it. "You are not like your cousins, Miss Sophia. They are quite somber and contentious. I had thought they were in mourning but, if they did not know your uncle, I am left to think they are affecting it because they think it is proper."

"Emma and Marjory have ever been sticklers on propriety. Jonathan…well, Jonathan is variable by the day. They all think I am a bit scandalous, and I suppose I am."

He sat back in his chair and stretched his legs out in front of him. "Do tell?"

She thought for a moment and then pointed out the obvious. "We are closed up in here alone—an unmarried man and an unmarried woman. I shut the door to keep the warmth from escaping, but they will be wondering what we are doing in here. So you see, I think I am sensible, but they will be thinking me scandalous."

As if to punctuate her statement, there was a sharp rap at door. "Sophia?"

She lifted an eyebrow at Selwick and he grinned in return. "Come in, Emma," she called.

The door opened cautiously and Emma peeked around it, her wide blue eyes sparkling with curiosity. "Oh, here you are. Georgie and I have been looking for you. You know how he likes to play chess with you."

Selwick stood in deference to Emma's presence.

"We have just taken a rest from inventorying Uncle Oliver's things. Would you like to join us? I could ring Potter for another cup."

"Oh, no, Sophia. Quite all right." She touched the edge of a handkerchief to her eyes and sniffed. "These things must be settled, I suppose. So nice of you to take the burden for the rest of us."

Selwick cleared his throat and Sophia noted the light of amusement in his eyes. "We shall be stopping to join you for lunch, Mrs. Grant. Miss Sophia will have time for chess then."

Emma's mouth formed an O at the familiar use of Sophia's name and Sophia stifled a chuckle. Jonathan, Thomas and Marjory would know this development within minutes. Emma glanced toward the open trunk and the neat piles of items stacked on the dresser. "I see," she squeaked.

Sophia stood and tucked the journal under her arm before she put her cup down with a mockingly reproachful look at Selwick. "I shall come now, Emma, if it is important to Georgie. You know I would not disappoint the boy."

Emma flushed. "That would be...lovely."

Sophia made a little curtsy to his lordship and could not resist one last scandal. "I shall see you at lunch, *Selwick*."

He smiled at her as if he knew just what she'd done. She rather liked the idea that they had become conspirators.

Chapter Five

After her match with Georgie and an uneventful lunch, Sophia and Selwick went back to work, keeping their attention on the business at hand and sharing occasional self-conscious glances. The attraction between them was undeniable. In fact, Selwick was the first man she'd been drawn to since...the duke.

When they were done for the day, she pled a headache and escaped dinner for the privacy of her room. Once undressed, she dismissed Janie and climbed into the four-poster bed, retrieving her uncle's journal from the nightstand drawer. She noted the date of the first entry, then flipped to the back. Heavens! Here was Uncle Oliver's life in a single volume.

There were few entries in the beginning, as if he had no pens or ink—just a few words here and there about missing his brothers and hoping they were well. Then she came to a jubilant passage where Uncle Oliver recorded that he'd discovered gold. She was spellbound by the next entries of how he'd purchased the land, secured his claim and employed workers. The following years unfolded with barely a mention of family or England. Uncle Oliver was far too busy protecting his claim and reaping the rewards.

Then his entries became melancholy. He missed his home and family. He regretted not having returned sooner when each of his brothers died. He missed the pastoral grace of England, and the customs of civilization so absent in the gold fields of South Carolina. Then another Christmas came and went, with memories of holly and mistletoe, Christmas pudding and Yule logs, evergreen boughs and candles in the window to welcome guests. Then his account of employing an estate agent to purchase Windsong Hall and his intention to return one day. And then, in August, the entries stopped. Uncle Oliver had died without coming home.

Sophia's heart ached for him, so far from home and everything he held dear. His brothers had died, and no one he knew was left at all. Oh, if only he had come home. If only she could have been his family. They could have found the connection they had both wanted so desperately.

She closed the journal, placed it in her drawer and turned the wick down on her lamp.

If only…

Sebastian prowled the lower rooms the next morning, looking for Miss Sophia. She hadn't joined him in Pettibone's room to continue the inventory and he was concerned that her headache had worsened. Her maid told him that she'd risen hours ago and dressed to go out. Cook said she'd eaten an early breakfast. Potter mentioned that she asked for heavy shears. And, when he came down for breakfast, Georgie said he'd seen someone trudging across the back lawns from his bedroom window.

The warnings of disaster following in Sophia's wake

echoed in his head. He was tired of waiting and fetched his greatcoat. He headed for the back lawns, thinking it odd that her cousins did not seem in the least concerned.

The grounds of Windsong Hall were vast, but it was easy to follow Sophia's footsteps in the snow. The newly fallen blanket was deep enough to evidence the drag of skirts and the heels of small boots, not the sturdy ones she had worn for her trip. He would have to scold her for not dressing more appropriately.

Her footsteps led to the stables, then out again, heading in a line toward the cliffs. His heartbeat thumped as he imagined what could become of her there, and his own footsteps sped in her wake.

Through a gently falling snow, he finally caught sight of her. She was bent over the bushes surrounding a summerhouse that had been perched on a bluff to overlook a lake. Her back was to him and she was so caught up in her task that she did not hear his approach.

The heavy snowfall piled on the octagonal copper roof of the summerhouse began to slide, dropping a pile to the ground with a heavy plop. Sophia did not heed the warning and kept her attention trained on her task. Horrified, Sebastian watched as the entire section begin a rapid slide to the edge.

He ran for her at the moment of disaster but too much distance separated them. The full weight of the snow engulfed her, driving her to the ground and leaving a mound of white covering her.

Stillness settled over the scene and Sebastian knelt by the mound, scooping handfuls of snow away. "Sophia! Miss Sophia! Can you hear me? Are you injured?"

Layers of snow crumbled away as she struggled to sit up. He offered his hand and she took it with one hand and began brushing the snow away with the other. He was so relieved that she was uninjured that he laughed.

She sputtered and brushed the snow from her face. Framed by her worn red bonnet, she was a study in confusion. Snow glistened in the dark hair peeking beneath the bonnet and her lips were wet with it, too—full reddened lips that parted slightly in a smile. Thank the gods she was whole.

"Good morning, Selwick," she said in a breathless voice.

He smiled. "Good morning, Miss Pettibone."

The moment drew out and suddenly there was only one thing to do—the very thing he had dreamed of all night. He lowered his lips to hers, tentatively at first, savoring the cool moisture and soft plushness. He nibbled his way to one corner, then returned to take her mouth fully. She stiffened with the first sweep of his tongue, then lifted her arm to slip it around his shoulder.

He could tell this was not her first kiss, but he also knew no one had kissed her like this before. She was shy, hesitant, but willing. Blissfully willing. He paused to whisper in her ear. "You are beautiful, Miss Pettibone. The most beautiful thing I've seen this morning."

She smiled and offered her lips again. He did not make her beg. This time she wrapped both arms around him and held nothing back. Her eager inexperience was more intoxicating than anything he'd known before and he hardened in response. He wanted her. All of her. He wanted to take her here in the snow. Here, with nothing held back. He wanted to teach her how to make love and give herself with abandon. He wanted Miss Sophia Pettibone as he'd never wanted anything in his life.

He broke the kiss with a muffled groan and stood up, showering snow down on her. He offered his hand, and she took it. "We had best get back before they come looking for us, Miss Pettibone."

"Y-yes. I have been gone longer than I intended."

"What did you intend?"

She stood patiently while he brushed the remaining snow from her coat, then gestured to a pile of green stems with bright red berries attached. "I need a little holly." She gave him a shy smile, gathered up an armful of the stems and berries, and started trudging back toward the hall with only the slightest limp.

Holly? She'd risked life and limb for holly? Why the deuce did she want holly?

Sophia perched on a stool at the kitchen table with scissors, ribbon and twine. She had worked through lunch to finish her sprays and garland quickly. Now she had simply to hang them and then join his lordship after tea to continue their inventory.

But only if she could purge her mind of that remarkable kiss in the snow.

The duke had importuned her for kisses, but never one such as Selwick's perfect kiss—heated but tender, consuming but patient. Selwick, she gathered, was practiced in the art of seduction and she was undecided what to do about that. Avoid him? Encourage him? Ask him to behave himself?

If she were to be completely honest, she rather thought she might be in love with the man. From the moment she had looked into his eyes and he had swept her off her feet to carry her to his coach, she'd been alternately amused and annoyed by him, but consistently intrigued. *Coup de foudre,* the French called it. The thunderbolt. And though it could not go anywhere, Sophia had never felt anything remotely like it before.

Potter hovered while Mrs. Cavendish chatted happily about her family and how they were all grown and gone now. And how very fortunate she was to have been hired in London and brought to Cumberland where everything was so lovely.

Potter, however, was interested in what Sophia was doing. "If you do not mind, miss, may I ask what you are doing with those boughs?" he asked as he polished a silver teapot.

"I am making decorations for the hall."

"Why?"

"Because it is Christmas, Potter. And I think this house could use a bit of cheer. Long overdue, is it not?"

He inclined his head with a small smile.

"How long were you with my uncle, Potter?"

"Since his arrival in America, Miss Pettibone."

"Was he happy?"

"Happy?" The question seemed to confuse him. "I imagine he was. He never mentioned it, miss."

"And yet he never married. He had no children. I think he must have been lonely, sir."

A long silence ensued and Sophia finished tying the ribbon bow on the last spray of holly before she looked up. Potter was watching her intently. "We never had Christmas, miss."

She smiled. "I know. But we are going to have one now."

A glance at the case clock on the wall told her it was not quite noon. "Would you have someone bring a ladder to the great hall, please?" She had tested the chandelier rope in the hall earlier and found that it was hopelessly knotted.

"Miss?"

"These things will not hang themselves, you know."

He gave her another of those little half smiles and went

to find a ladder. She and two footmen gathered armloads of the sprays and the long garland and hurried to the great hall, stopping along the way to place a spray here and there.

The ladder was set up beneath the elaborate chandelier in the center of the hall and Sophia took one end of the garland and began to climb.

"Miss Pettibone," Potter said as he stood back to observe the scene. "I believe you should allow me to place the garland."

"Not at all, Potter," she told him. Indeed, for all his sprightliness, Potter was still an elderly man. She lifted her skirt an inch or two to reach the next step.

"I do not think Lord Selwick would want you on a ladder." Potter's voice was stern.

"Lord Selwick is not here," she pointed out. Someone cleared their throat and she looked over her shoulder to see her cousin Jonathan standing below her, his arms crossed over his chest and a look of disapproval on his face.

"But I am."

"Excellent! Lend Potter a hand, will you?"

"What do you think you are doing, Sophia?"

"Why, I am adding a little Christmas to Windsong Hall."

Drawn by the activity, Marjory, Thomas and Emma came from the parlor, followed by little Georgie. They all looked up at her as if she had lost her mind.

"This is a house in mourning, cousin!" Marjory reminded.

"Completely inappropriate," Thomas agreed.

Emma sniffed and pressed a handkerchief to the corners of her eyes. "I hardly think this is proper at all, Sophia."

But Georgie's eyes sparkled with excitement. "May I help?"

She remembered how she had felt when she was younger, always wanting to be a part of things but never quite feeling as if she belonged. "Yes, Georgie. If you will climb the stairs and direct me, I would be ever indebted."

Thomas harrumphed. "See here, Sophia, could you not be a bit more circumspect?"

"I believe I am, Thomas," she said as Georgie climbed the staircase until he was level with the chandelier. She draped the first end of the garland over the iron frame and pulled another arm's length up as she turned the chandelier. "Are we still even, Georgie?"

"Aye, cousin Sophia! It looks beautiful."

Potter, she noticed, was smiling at the lad. Thank heavens she had two allies, though they were still outnumbered. She draped another length of the garland and turned the chandelier again.

Holding it in place, her back to Georgie, she asked, "And this? Is it even, Georgie?" When there was no answer, she turned to look at the stairway. Selwick was standing beside her little cousin, looking very stern indeed.

"May I ask what you are doing, Miss Sophia?"

"Why...decorating the hall for Christmas." She saw that sensual smile again, so quickly gone she wondered if it had been there at all.

"Risking life and limb again," he admonished.

As if his words had caused it, the ladder teetered and she released the garland to catch herself on a rung as it rocked to and fro. Jonathan made a dash for her, but by the time she looked around again, Selwick was waiting beneath her, steadying the ladder. "Come down, Miss Sophia, before we have to scrape you off the floor."

She descended, feeling a bit sheepish. First the coach, then the snow this morning, and now the ladder. Was she cursed to look inept in front of Selwick? As she neared the bottom rung, his hands spanned her waist and he lifted her the rest of the way down. The heat and strength in that grip steadied her.

When she was on her feet, he went to the chandelier pulley anchored in the wall. Three good yanks had the knots loosened and he lowered the entire chandelier to the tiles. He turned to her and grinned. "Next time, Miss Sophia, send for me."

The hall was silent as he began to climb the stairs again. Sophia couldn't help herself. She began to laugh at the picture she must have made perched on a ladder when lowering the chandelier had been so simple for Selwick. Georgie covered his mouth with his hand but could not contain his laughter.

Selwick did not pause, but he looked over his shoulder and she could have sworn he winked! Staid and somber Selwick?

She ruffled Georgie's brown hair as the servants took the ladder away. "Come, Georgie. We had better finish this soon or Selwick will have our hides."

Chapter Six

Sebastian had taken his lunch in Pettibone's apartments. He wanted a few hours to organize the deceased's more personal belongings. Miss Sophia, as a spinster, should not be subjected to handling such intimate items.

But even as he inventoried and packed the last article away, his mind remained on the sight of Miss Sophia swaying on the rickety ladder and the way his heart had jumped to his throat. The scene had given him a very bad turn, even though he'd thought her quite adorable trying to bring cheer to the solemn household. The blasted holly could have been the death of her! He would have to keep a close eye on her.

Fortunately, that would be fairly easy. Between working with her on Pettibone's inventory and her family's penchant for raised voices, he'd only lost track of her when she'd gone out this morning. He was beginning to feel like a nursemaid.

"Come," he called, in response to a soft knock on Pettibone's door.

The very object of his musings peeked around the

portal and smiled that infectious smile of hers. "Am I too late to help?"

"Not at all. Your timing is impeccable," he told her. "I have just now finished with your uncle's personal items. We can move on to the crates."

"Crates?" Her eyes widened. "How many crates?"

"According to the manifest, twenty-two. There are four in his dressing room, three in the cellar and fifteen in the attic." A frown knit little lines between her eyes and he had the sudden urge to smooth them away.

"So many?"

"Windsong was to have been his home, Miss Sophia. Perhaps he purchased the things he wanted here from America, or perhaps he was merely sending on the items from his previous home."

She nodded. "It just seems so…daunting."

"If you are not up to—"

"No! No, of course not. I was only thinking of how little I knew of my uncle and now I am helping to catalogue and dispose of his goods. That is quite humbling in view of the fact that I have not the tiniest notion of what he would have wanted."

He smiled, knowing precisely how she felt. "I believe there is a list provided with his will for some of the items. Perhaps it will give us the direction he would have taken, had he known what the future held."

She sniffed and absently picked up an ebony trinket box from the escritoire. She lifted the lid and her lips parted in surprise. Curious, he looked over her shoulder to see a small gold broach studded with amethyst stones in the shape of a heart.

"Oh, dear. Did Uncle Oliver have someone special in his life?"

Selwick searched his memory for the things he'd been told about the odd man as the floral scent of Sophia's perfume tweaked his awareness of her. "Not that I can recall. Did he mention anyone in his journal?"

"I confess I only skimmed the passages. I shall go back and take a closer look. If there was someone he wished to give such an object to, she should have it."

"He is dead now, Miss Sophia. You do not owe anything to anyone outside the family—"

"But we have an obligation."

"Perhaps you or one of your cousins would like such an object as a memento."

She traced the heart with one slender finger and sighed. "It is lovely, is it not? But how much more precious to the one for whom it was intended. I shall look for a name tonight."

He was touched that she was so determined to honor her uncle's intentions, as well as his instructions, and found it refreshing that he could detect no greed in her. Admirable, really.

Thomas Evans, her cousin Marjory's husband, had already come to him to ask how much the estate was worth. In fact, none of Pettibone's heirs, with the exception of Sophia, had missed an opportunity to question Sebastian as to the disposition of Pettibone's wealth. And he'd told them all the same thing. *No one is to know that until the reading of the will.* The document had been given to Sebastian sealed, with instructions to open it only at the reading.

"You are not much like the rest of your family," he ventured as he took in the delicate flush of her cheek.

She looked up at him, her eyes twinkling, then smiled as she replaced the broach in the box and put it back on the escritoire. "We were raised differently. After Papa died, Mama took me back to her village. We were—" she shrugged her shoulders "—the genteel poor. Good family, but a bit strapped for the ready. After Mama died, it was just my aunt and female cousins. We did not have many extras, but we always had what we needed to get by."

"Were you happy, Miss Sophia?"

"Happy?" She paused. "Those were lovely days. Except for…" She turned her back to him and busied herself with counting a stack of linen handkerchiefs.

"Except for?" he prompted.

"You strike me as a man who has always known his place in this world, Selwick. Perhaps that is an advantage of being male and a peer. But I, well, never quite felt that I belonged after Mama died. Twice a year, I was sent off to holiday with my father's family, and I was given a season in London for my 'come out,' so I was not deprived of family contact. My aunt and cousins have been very good to me, but I am not quite one of them. I've always wanted to find that…that feeling of belonging and connection."

Sebastian felt a tug at his heartstrings. Yes, he'd always known his place in the world, but there was so much more he'd have done if he hadn't had the accompanying responsibilities. But Miss Sophia should not have had to learn that lesson. "You shall find connection when you marry and have a family of your own, Miss Sophia."

She laughed as she followed him into her uncle's dressing room. "Alas, Selwick, I shall never marry."

"Why? Do you not have a dowry? Perhaps your uncle has left you sufficient to attract a suitor."

"My dowry is respectable. But there are a variety of reasons not to wed. Not the least of which is a lamentable lack of proposals since my…ah, refusal of the duke."

"Ah, yes. The duke. A jilt, I heard."

She shrugged. "Refusal. Jilt. The same thing, actually."

"Not at all. A refusal happens privately, before offers are accepted and contracts are made. A jilt is a rather public sneer at an accepted fiancé. Much harder to live down. And a caution to future suitors."

She looked down and a lock of hair fell across her cheek, shielding her from his scrutiny. "There were reasons for that."

A long moment passed before he reached out and swept the lock back, the tips of his fingers leaving a tingling trail in their wake. His lips parted as if he were about to say something, then changed his mind. Instead, he pried the lid off a crate and set it aside.

Sophia wondered if she should tell him why she'd turned her back on the duke. But the duke had said her reasons were ridiculous. Childish. That she should put girlish notions aside and accept the realities of life. She could not bear it if Selwick thought her ridiculous, too. She sighed and looked down into the crate to see what surprises it held.

Selwick lifted a large object wrapped in wool bunting, and unwound the cloth to reveal a stunning painting surrounded by an ornate gilt frame of a forest scene with a rocky precipice and waterfall. She drew a long breath in appreciation. The painter had been gifted. Sophia could almost feel the mist rising from the water.

"Such beauty…" she said, and sighed.

"Breathtaking."

She glanced up to see Selwick studying her, and she suspected he was not talking about the painting.

He cupped her face and ran his thumb over her lips. The intimate touch left a tingling in its wake. Oh, she should stop him. She should run. Her eyelids, suddenly heavy and languid, drifted shut and she parted her lips in an invitation. She had loved the feel of his tongue earlier, and she was surprised how much she wanted it again.

He obliged with a slow, hesitant brush of his lips. Was he testing her? Drawing her out? Sophia felt herself melting into him, so close she could feel his heart beating. And then, when she had nearly grown accustomed to it, he deepened the kiss. She was drowning in him, unable to breathe or even think coherently.

He held her to him with one hand splayed at her back, and the other moving, caressing along her spine, as slow and unhurried as his kiss. And when she had grown to crave that touch, his hand slipped around to her side. She moaned when he broke the kiss to nibble his way down her throat.

The curve of his body as he bent to his task opened a breach between them, and his hand brushed across her breast. She gasped in shock, but a fire kindled inside her, so delicious, so arousing that she thought she would die if he stopped. The heat of his hand as he cupped her breast was seductive and her firmed peaks were so sensitive that Sophia shivered with the sheer pleasure of it.

And then he was kissing her again, fitting himself against her until she could feel every line of his body. When the hard length of his arousal pressed into her softness, she knew she should stop him. Should break the embrace at the very least. Oh, but how could she? Her body had a mind of its own and she could only press closer.

He moaned and parted from her, cupping her shoulders to hold her away from him. "I should not have done that, Miss Sophia. You have my apology."

She blinked. What had she missed? Twice in one day he'd owned her entirely and had retreated. The heat of a deep blush crept all the way up from her toes. "If you do that one more time, Selwick, I shall doubt your sincerity."

* * *

When Miss Sophia went to her room to change for dinner, Sebastian did not follow her example. He worked well past dinner, his mind in a turmoil.

It seemed he could not please anyone. Even Potter, when he'd brought a dinner tray to Sebastian, had looked at him in disapproval. "I believe I saw Miss Sophia with Mr. Pettibone's journal, my lord. Is that quite the thing for a young woman to be reading?"

"I hardly think there is anything objectionable in there, and if there is, I believe Miss Sophia has the fortitude to withstand it," he'd growled. Now he was answerable to the servants, as well as the family?

His every instinct for self-preservation urged him to finish at Windsong quickly and hie back to London. This chaotic Christmas was not what he had bargained for. And Miss Sophia Pettibone was evidently more temptation than he could reasonably resist.

Perhaps his lust had been heightened by the crisp northern air, or some spice in Mrs. Cavendish's cooking. Whatever it was, it made him—yes, he who had always been firm in his resolutions—waver like a schoolboy when it came to that cheerful bit of muslin so different from anything he'd known. She had his mind wandering toward a relationship he'd never contemplated before.

He shuddered. What sort of fool was he that he kept playing with fire, stoking it hotter and hotter at each encounter? The kiss this morning had been bad enough, but the kiss in Pettibone's dressing room made him certain he'd lost his mind. And it was getting more difficult to put her out of his thoughts.

The worst of it, though, was that he knew she was likewise enthralled. He'd had enough women to know an ardent, if innocent, response. She wanted him almost as badly as he wanted her, but it was unlikely she knew what lay ahead for her if she gave in to that temptation. Unless…

Unless her relationship with the duke had been more intimate than it should be until after the wedding. Could she have jilted him because he was clumsy? Inept? Had he hurt her? The mere thought of that made Sebastian's blood boil. It would be bad enough to have the duke despoil her, but to ruin such promise and sensuality would be unforgivable.

He laughed in self-derision. He had no business thinking of Miss Sophia in that way. And no right. And he bloody well knew if she looked at him the same way one more time, kissed him like that, touched him, he wouldn't be able to stop himself. To make matters worse, he was responsible, as the older and more experienced, to see nothing happened between them. To accomplish that, physical proximity must be avoided at all costs. Yes, that was the ticket. Like it or not, he would keep a safe distance from the chit.

Chapter Seven

Sophia rose early the next morning, and Janie helped her dress in a drab mauve gown and added a muslin pinafore. There was much to be done today between going through the crates and helping Mrs. Cavendish with the sweetmeats she'd requested. Georgie must have sugarplums, and there should be mincemeat and a nice Christmas pudding for all.

Janie pinned her hair up in a loose knot to keep it from falling over her shoulders and then Sophia hurried downstairs to the kitchen. Mrs. Cavendish was sending the breakfast trays up with the servants and Potter was adding wood to the cookstove.

"Good morning," she said with a cheerful smile.

Mrs. Cavendish waved to the worktable where her breakfast had been set out. "I'll be with you in a moment, dearie."

She sat on the stool and poured herself a cup of tea while Potter came to stand beside her, ready to fetch her whatever she needed. But she had other uses for Potter this morning. "Please sit down, Potter. I'd like a word with you."

He looked a bit nervous and Sophia hurried to reassure

him. "I would like to ask you a few questions regarding my uncle, if you would not mind."

"I, uh…" was his only response.

"You needn't worry about keeping his confidence, Potter. He is gone now and I only want to do what he would have wanted. I promise I will not repeat anything you tell me."

The color in his cheeks heightened. "If you say so, Miss Pettibone."

She poured a cup of tea for the butler and applied herself to her porridge. "I found a broach yesterday. A lovely thing in the shape of a heart with jewels all around. Had Uncle Oliver meant it for anyone special?"

There was a short silence while Potter thought, then, "Mr. Pettibone was accustomed to purchasing items he found attractive with no particular person in mind, miss. Perhaps he meant it for one of his nieces. You, perhaps?"

"Then there was no one special in his life?"

"Mr. Pettibone was hardworking early on, Miss Sophia, and had no time for social engagements. Later, he became a bit reclusive. He feared people would like him only for his money, you see. The curse of great wealth, I believe he called it."

The thought saddened her and she blinked back a wayward tear. "I wish he'd have come home." She sighed.

"I believe he did, too, miss."

She pushed her sadness aside and braced herself for the business at hand. "Very well, Potter. We shall determine the best home for the broach, and meantime I think we should start the sugarplums and mincemeat. Then I must go help Lord Selwick in the attic."

He started to rise from his chair and then sat again, a smile on his face. "Is this why you are making a little Christmas despite your cousins' opposition, miss? For your uncle?"

She looked down into her porridge. "In his journal, he mentioned missing Christmas with his family. The food, the decorations, the rollicking times. This is our last chance to give him that. One Christmas at Windsong Hall. Do you think me silly, Potter?"

He reached out and covered her hand with his. "I think it is the nicest thing anyone could have done for him, miss. Far nicer than a funeral."

"Then will you bring me candles for the windows? We shall keep them burning until…until he arrives."

Tears glittered in Potter's eyes as he nodded.

Mrs. Cavendish was free to turn her attention to them and made shooing motions with both hands. "Get on with ye, now. No tears in my kitchen. And you, missy, hie to the attic. Lord Selwick went up an hour ago."

"But the sugarplums—"

"'Twill not be my first sugarplum, nor my first Christmas pudding. I can manage without ye. Lord Selwick, now, that's a different matter. Stacks and boxes of things to go through. He needs ye more than I. I'll see to it that someone brings your lunch. Ye won't want to take the time to freshen up to sit at the table. Sooner done, sooner gone," she reminded.

Sophia needed no reminder that everyone but her wanted to leave Windsong Hall. She finished her porridge quickly and headed for the servants' stairs that passed through the south wing and climbed with the same rising expectancy she always felt when she was about to see Selwick.

The top of the attic stairs opened to a massive room the width and breadth of the entire south wing. The floorboards gleamed from a recent polishing and the rafters had been swept clean of cobwebs. A dormer window at each end allowed meager light from outside to stream in.

Crates had been clustered at the far end near one of the windows, and a small table had been placed to hold writing materials. An oil lamp hung from a beam to dispel any gloom from the lowering clouds.

Selwick, his back to her, was prying the lid off a crate with a crowbar. His muscles strained against his shirt-sleeves and the way the pull of fabric defined his lean flanks left her feeling flushed. He really was the most striking man. And when she could tease him out of his stern countenance… But that was in the past. All she wanted now was to finish the inventory quickly so she and her cousins could return to their homes.

She marched forward, the heels of her slippers making soft thumps on the polished wood floor. He turned to look in her direction and she could have sworn she saw something akin to pleasure in his expression.

"I did not expect to see you so early, Miss Sophia."

"I have been remiss, Selwick. I agreed to help, and then promptly abandoned you to perform other chores. You have my apology." She rubbed her hands together and swept her gaze over the waiting crates. "How many have you done?"

"This is the first. I finished in your uncle's room last night once I got Potter to help me move a crate. Just these and the ones in the cellar to go."

Just these? There were fifteen crates in all! She could at least be glad he'd chosen the attic next rather than the cellar. She didn't much relish the thought of working in a dark, dank cellar all day.

Selwick lifted an item from the crate and said, "A painting. Landscape of a meadow."

She went to the table and wrote the description down beneath the previously inventoried objects. There were two pages already filled, and suddenly Sophia wondered if he was as anxious to have this done as she.

A glance over her shoulder revealed that he was watching her with a gleam of speculation in his compelling eyes. What on earth could the man be thinking?

Miss Sophia had a steady hand and worked without complaint throughout the morning. They barely spoke, but for him calling off the items and she repeating them as she entered them on the inventory sheets. He regretted the awkwardness, but he did not know how to remedy it. If he was to keep his resolve—and his distance—he would have to discourage any personal discourse.

Oh, but he was bursting with curiosity. The little she had told him, and her mention of the incident with the duke left him hungering for more information. What, precisely, had been the reason for Miss Sophia not receiving any more proposals? Was the jilt not all it seemed to be? Was there something more?

They worked in tandem, neither passing a personal word or thought. They might have been strangers, to all appearances. "Wooden carving of a bear," he said, and set the figure on a canvas sheet until the remains of the contents had been identified and repacked.

"Wooden carving of a bear," she confirmed.

A new crate held furs, the pelts stored flat to prevent creasing. He took them out one at a time, laying them on top of one another as he called off the descriptions. "Furs. Three small brown, likely mink. Two large black, bear, I think." The next three were large and white, reminding him of sheep before shearing. "Three…mountain goat?"

He heard her pen scratching across the paper and sighed. He did not need that reminder to feel her presence. The signs were thick around him. Her scent, her soft sighs, the rustle of her gown as she turned or moved. All were incredibly evocative. He was like a schoolboy again, growing hard and ready at the slightest provocation. He marveled that his intellect and his body could be at such odds— knowing she was trouble, yet responding to such bone-deep need that it shook his very soul. He turned to look at her, drawn by her silence.

She glanced up when he did not call out an item, confusion in her eyes.

"What is it, Miss Sophia?"

"Furs." She gestured at the pile he'd made. "Why do you suppose Uncle Oliver had so many furs?"

"They are much in demand amongst furriers and tailors. From beaver hats to fur-trimmed coats, cape lining and lap robes. I imagine he was able to purchase them in America more reasonably than here." He paused at a sound from the bottom of the stairs.

Potter carried a tray up the stairs and glanced around the attic. "Where shall I leave this, sir?"

Sebastian was surprised that it was lunchtime already. He gestured to the only place to leave the tray—the table where Miss Sophia worked. "Thank you, Potter. We shall eat when we have a chance. Do not worry about fetching the tray. I shall bring it down when we are done."

The butler looked around and raised his eyebrows. "You have accomplished quite a bit, my lord. If you would like, I shall do the same with the crates in the cellar. I believe those are mostly wines and spirits, and perhaps a few tools."

Sebastian nodded, relieved. He'd been on the verge of pressing Jonathan Arbuthnot into service, but with Miss Sophia's warning that he disliked anything smacking of duty, he'd resisted. "Leave the list in my room when you are finished, Potter," he said as the man took his leave.

Miss Sophia stretched her arms over her head and arched her back, and he realized he'd been working her rather hard. "If you do not mind, Selwick, I could use a bit of hot tea and a nibble of something solid."

Lord, the curve of her breasts as they strained against the prim white pinafore just about undid him! He cleared his throat. "Of course."

He looked around, realizing there were no chairs. Miss Sophia had been writing as she bent over the table. No wonder she ached. Potter was gone, attested to by the click of the latch as the stairway door closed. Too late to call for chairs.

Ah, but the furs would make a soft place to sit. He gestured to them and Miss Sophia smiled, kneeling on them with as much ladylike poise as anyone could muster.

"A picnic," she said with pleasure.

He took the tray and joined her, grateful for her cheerful nature. Were she one of his stepsisters, or his former mistresses, she would be complaining.

Mrs. Cavendish had prepared a wedge of cheese, bread, sliced ham from last night, tea, pared apples and assorted cakes. As if an afterthought, she had included a sherry decanter and two crystal glasses. Very fine fare for a rough working luncheon.

"Thank you," he said as he handed her a china dish with the apple slices.

"Whatever for?"

"For being so cooperative. And congenial."

She laughed. "That surprises you?"

"I was just thinking that not many women of my acquaintance would give up their day to help me and then make a game of eating on the floor."

"Then you must widen your circle of acquaintances, Selwick."

"I think I ought to introduce you to my stepsisters. They could use a bit of coaching in congeniality."

"I am sure you exaggerate. I am quite ordinary."

Lord! How could she look in the mirror and ever think herself ordinary? How could she make him smile every time he saw her if she were unpleasant? He shook his head. "Miss Sophia, my stepsisters never miss an opportunity to make mountains from molehills. Catastrophe is their constant companion. And, since my father died, they and my stepmother expect me to smooth every bump in the road for them. They have quite put me off families altogether."

He expected sympathy, but she smiled instead. "Do you give them your attention when they do not have a disaster?"

"I have found my own lodgings to avoid their crises."

"Has that had the desired effect?"

He chortled. "Not in the least. They merely send for me."

"Do you visit them regularly when there is *not* a crisis?"

He reached for the sherry bottle.

"Ah, I thought so," she said. "I suspect their crises are manufactured to claim your attention."

That notion intrigued him. "Why do you think so?"

"Because they have lost everything *but* you. Twice, apparently. Their father and husband, then their second father and husband. The world must seem a very precarious place to them. They must be feeling uncertain and a bit frightened."

Sebastian wanted to contradict her, but she had given him something to think about, a new way of looking at his contentious family. Perhaps they had needed him more than he had thought, but in a different way.

"Have they come out yet?" Miss Sophia asked as she nibbled a crust of bread.

"Next spring."

"You will have to find them husbands, Selwick. It would be best if you knew their dispositions well, and their preferences, before matching them with any suitors. And it would not bode well if it were known that you were anxious to be rid of them."

He laughed. "I shall try to hide my anxiety."

"I know you will not fail them."

He poured her a glass of sherry and lifted his own in a toast. "To an uncomplicated life."

Her confidence in him was flattering, especially in view of the fact that he was determined to spend his life dodging the marriage trap.

Chapter Eight

Sophia smiled and sipped. "I hope you will introduce me to your stepsisters, should we attend the same fetes come spring. They sound rather amusing."

"Amusing? That would be one word for it, I suppose. But I should be delighted to introduce you, so long as you promise you will not advise them to jilt a duke."

"I promise," she said, torn between chagrin and amusement. "Though you are naughty to remind me of it."

He laughed, confirming her suspicion that he'd been teasing, and she loved him for that. How endearing. She took a small sip of the sherry and shivered as a lock of hair came down from the knot on the top of her head and tickled her cheek.

Selwick reached across the distance to brush the lock back and tuck it behind her ear. Something quite delicious kindled a fire deep in her center, and a glance at Selwick told her that he felt it, too. She wondered if he would kiss her, but after a moment, he dropped his hand and asked an unexpected question.

"What happened between you and the duke, Miss Sophia?"

She paused while she put her thoughts in order. Would he think her as foolish as the duke had? She sighed. Though she had no wish to look ridiculous in his eyes, there was no point demurring. He could have it from her or from her family. "Evidently I was a silly schoolgirl, expecting more than he could give me."

"He was a fool if he did not give you whatever you asked."

She smiled. "I doubt he was a fool. If he had a fault, it was his honesty."

"How so?"

Sophia sighed, the humiliation of that night coming back to her afresh. Would Selwick ever look at her the same after he knew the truth? Or would he always see her as somehow flawed? Less desirable? Too naive?

"Tell me, Miss Sophia," he urged. "You can trust my discretion."

"We…we were at our engagement ball, quite the largest of the season, and I saw him waltzing with a woman I'd never seen before. She was beautiful, and she appeared to be flirting with him. I asked him about her, and he took me out to the terrace for a private word. He said he hadn't meant for me to find out in such a public manner, but that the woman was his…his mistress. A courtesan."

Selwick's expression was incredulous. "He flaunted his mistress in front of you? At your own engagement ball?"

She nodded. "I could have borne that, I suppose. I knew he was a man of the world, after all. But then he told me that, although he loved me, he loved her more deeply, and that he would never give her up. I would carry his name, his heir, but she would carry his heart." She gritted her teeth, remembering how much that had hurt at the time. She had fancied herself in love with him, after all. Even so, "I could not imagine going through the rest of my life always being second best, or something that had to be endured for the sake of his public personage and to produce an heir. I wanted love. I wanted…belonging. A family of my own. He could not give me that.

"So, if he was not brave enough to defy society to have the woman he loved, then I had courage enough for both of us. I gave him his freedom, and told him that what he did with it was up to him. He, however, did not see it that way. He reproached me and said I was naive and should put my girlish notions aside and accept the realities of life. But I could not endure being…*used* in such a manner. To lie with him, knowing he did not want me, but…"

"That was incredibly poor manners." He placed his large hand over hers. "But he must have been fond of you, Miss Sophia, or he would not have wanted to shackle himself to you for life."

She gained strength from that touch and forged ahead, determined to make him understand. "Though he professed his fondness, I believe he chose me for other reasons. My dowry is respectable, but a duke could have expected much more. No, he chose me because I was a country girl of good family and he thought I would be so flattered to be marrying a duke that I would overlook his infidelities, his love children and his disregard for my feelings. In any event, fondness would never have been enough for me, Selwick."

"What *would* have been enough?"

The absurdity of what she was about to say brought heat to her cheeks. "I wanted to be my husband's greatest passion. His best friend. I wanted to belong to him, with him, and wanted him to belong to me. All, Selwick. All or nothing at all."

"That does not seem so unreasonable to me."

She looked up at him again, surprised that he agreed with her. But his next words sobered her.

"Perhaps, had you wed, you could have won him over."

"If not? By then, for better or worse, I would have been bound to him forever."

"And forever is a very long time." He stood and held his hand out to help her to her feet. She rose and swayed against him on the uneven surface of the furs. He tugged her against his chest and for an endless moment, she stopped breathing. Then, very slowly, he pulled her tighter until she was forced to tilt her head back to hold his gaze. She knew she should turn away, do something to stop him, but she merely parted her lips and lowered her lashes in a shameless invitation.

And he accepted. Not softly or gently this time, not in a tentative request, but hard and demanding, drawing forth a matching fierceness in her. She accepted that it would not end here. She could feel his desire in both the response of his body and the nearly frantic claim he made on her senses. By the time he relinquished her mouth, she was breathless and burning.

"I am glad the duke was a fool," he growled, his voice hoarse with his vow. "But I—"

"If you apologize again, Selwick, I shall scream."

"You'd have every right," he mumbled against her lips. "I'm not in the least bit sorry."

He lifted her off her feet, laid her on the furs and came down beside her. As he kissed her again, she longed to feel his hand on her breasts, as he'd done the last time they'd kissed, but he lingered, giving exquisite attention to her mouth and making her head swim with the arousing sensation.

She slipped her arms around him, pulling him closer, though there was not a single space separating them. He was solid and warm against her, but that was not enough. She slipped her hands beneath his jacket and the muscles of his chest jumped at her touch, and then that, too, was not enough. She fumbled with his cravat, hungering for the feel of his bare skin.

He seized her wrists and stopped her, pressing her hands back against the soft fur. "Please, Sophia, let me…" His long fingers worked the knots free and slipped the button from its loop, then tugged his shirttails from his breeches.

She marveled at his grace, and at the raw masculine beauty of his form as his chest was bared to her view. She'd never seen a man so…so undone, and the sight was playing havoc with her senses. He turned his attention to her and had her pinafore in a heap beside her before she realized it, then the buttons of her old-fashioned dress and the top laces of her stays were freed.

A flash of fear rose in her and she opened her mouth to protest, but he kissed her again and all her good intentions dissolved in an instant. His mouth was something magical, making her forget caution and good sense, especially as he kissed his way downward to the slopes of her breasts. Her heart beat wildly as he nudged fabric aside, drew one exquisitely sensitive peak into his mouth and rolled it with his tongue.

She whimpered and tangled her fingers through his hair, begging for more. How could she be both drawn as tight as a bowstring and fluid beneath his touch? He swept her skirts up her legs and paused to smooth over her healing injury before he lifted her knee to slide along his hip. She sighed at the texture of his trousers against the inside of her bare thigh. Was she wicked to be so wanton with a man she'd only known a matter of days?

"Sebastian," she whispered, and then could think of

nothing to say. But what need had she of words? He seemed to know her better than she knew herself.

"Sophia, by all the saints, you have bewitched me." He lifted himself on one elbow and unfastened the knot of her hair to bury his face in it. "You smell of evergreens and sweetmeats, and you look like an angel. I will never have another Christmas that I won't remember you thus."

She touched his cheek. "A wanton?"

"Not yet, Sophia, but soon."

He applied himself to her mouth again, then to the hollow of her throat, while he pushed her chemise higher, skimming his hand along the length of her bare thigh above her stockings and leaving trails of fire in his wake. But when his hand found her inner heat, that secret part of her no one had ever touched, she gasped. She wanted, *craved,* more of that touch.

A deep shudder passed through Sebastian and she felt him grow still and distant. He was going to stop! "No," she cried. "You cannot leave me thus."

"Sweet Sophia. You cannot know what you are asking. The consequences to you—"

"I do not care." She only knew she could not stop now. This closeness, this intimacy and belonging was all she'd dreamed of for so long. She wiggled against him, trying to recapture the warmth and closeness.

With a groan, Sebastian gave in to her pleadings, resuming his ministration with a renewed fervor. And when he invaded with one finger, and then two, testing, stretching, she could not catch her breath. Her hips rose of their own accord and her fingers bit into his strong arms as he balanced above her, cooing encouragement.

He murmured short breathless sentences, telling her what he needed from her, when she should move, and when she should not. He was gone for one heart-stopping moment and then was back, parting her thighs and positioning himself between them.

Inappropriate. Dangerous. Naughty.

The words whispered across her consciousness and were quickly disregarded. *Too late,* she sighed. *Too late.* She was already addicted to his touch.

He lowered himself, probing, finding her core with that wholly masculine part of him. She thought she would faint from a tension that caused an unbearable desperation for something as yet unknown. He gained a shallow entry and she grew light-headed. Then he pushed harder into her and she cried out in surprise at the stinging discomfort.

Sebastian stilled, embedded within her, and kissed her eyes, her nose, her mouth, with a mingling of tenderness and anxiety. "Hush, sweet Sophia," he murmured. "'Twill be easier now. The worst is over."

He began moving again, a gentle rocking that sent little thrills from her center in every direction, heating her, lifting her, consuming her, until an unexpected shock and heat shot through her, raising gooseflesh throughout her body. She stiffened and Sebastian followed her, panting, his forehead gleaming with perspiration.

"Sophia…" he groaned, a world of regret in his voice.

Chapter Nine

For the first time in his life, Viscount Sebastian Selwick had been completely out of control. An animal! A blasted rutting bull! He was no better than the most base of God's creatures. He'd ruined Sophia Pettibone, and he hadn't a single excuse for his conscienceless behavior. From her first sigh to her forlorn plea not to stop, then her last cry of passion, she had utterly possessed him. He'd been as powerless to stop as he'd been to pluck the moon from the sky, and he'd never once stopped to think of the consequences to Sophia, or his responsibility to her. But he did so now.

He shook his head in disgust. After he had taken Sophia to her room, he returned to the attic to pace out his frustration. The weather was too cold to go for a ride, and the snow was too deep to walk, but he needed some way to deal with the turmoil in his mind.

She was an enchantress, casting her spell about him so that he could not think straight. In the few short days they'd been together, he'd grown fonder of her than of any woman of his acquaintance, past or present. That, in itself, was not so alarming, but the fact that he had even been entertaining the notion of marriage…

But Sophia had been an innocent—the very sort he'd always avoided. He was experienced, a man of the world, but he'd never trifled with an innocent woman's future. Before today. And now, because of his actions, Sophia Pettibone would be considered damaged goods by any prospective suitor of good family. Yes, he'd utterly ruined the girl.

He lifted a heavy object from the crate and unwound the flannel around it. It was a bronze of nude lovers locked in an embrace, done in the Greek style. His mouth went dry and his heart skipped a beat as his mind went straight to Sophia and their tryst.

He spun on his heel and glanced toward the pile of furs—the place of Sophia's ruin. There was no trace of that act but for the impression of their bodies on the soft pelts. He threw his sherry across the room, taking savage satisfaction in the shatter of glass. He paused to see if he could hear the gods laughing and fancied they were.

Sophia. Sweet, dear Sophia. So misunderstood by her family, and so taken for granted. She deserved better than she'd received—from her family, from the duke, from him. And through it all, she'd behaved with such grace and courage that it left him humbled. Indeed, she had not seemed in the least bit angry or disturbed. No hysterics. No demands.

He took a few deep breaths and cleared his mind of self-loathing to deal with the problem at hand. There appeared to be no solution but that he would marry her. Of course he would marry her. The matter was out of his hands now and he must deal with the consequences. He, who had regarded marriage as an anathema, was about to step into the parson's mousetrap willingly, and all because he could not control his lust for a sultry dark-eyed enchantress. An *innocent* enchantress.

Sophia sat quietly, alternately torn between horror and happiness, so that Janie could put the finishing touches on her coiffure. When she faced Selwick again, she wanted to be as self-possessed and nonchalant as possible. She prayed he would not betray their earlier indiscretion in some way. And that she would not blush too vividly.

Selwick. Not at all the sort of man who ordinarily attracted her, though she seemed to have fallen rather seriously in love with him. He was more commanding, more confident than her usual sort. And very much less in need of her.

And, alas, he was a gentleman so he would possibly offer her marriage. Of course, she would refuse. As much as she admired Selwick for his integrity, she could not commit herself to a marriage built on obligation. She could never go through life loving him and knowing he had married her for the sake of a moment's indiscretion any more than she could have married the duke.

"Ye look so lovely, miss," Janie said when Sophia stood and faced the tall looking glass.

"I think my gown is somber enough to satisfy Marjory's requirements," she allowed. "And I really do not want to give Thomas cause for complaint."

"Prig," Janie muttered under her breath. "Ye look as beautiful as any queen, Miss Sophia. That was the duke's favorite gown."

The duke aside, Sophia was well aware the cut was flattering by the number of heads she'd turned that season. She looked toward the door and smoothed the drape of the heavy green silk as Janie arranged the sweep of her small train.

She took a deep breath and headed downstairs even as

her chest tightened with anxiety. She would simply do as she'd always done. She'd be as bright and cheerful as possible and behave as if nothing untoward had happened. If Selwick feared she would be like his stepsisters, he would be pleasantly surprised. It was the least she could do for him, considering what he'd done for her.

She heard the sound of conversation as she approached the dining room and hoped the family had not been seated yet. Jonathan would sigh and Thomas would make some comment about punctuality, no doubt.

Selwick noticed her first, a look of appreciation crossing his features, and stood to give her a polite bow before rounding the table to get her chair. Jonathan followed suit, and even Thomas grudgingly got to his feet.

"I apologize for my tardiness," she said as Selwick held her chair. His hand brushed her shoulder as he moved to return to his own place across the table from her. She was certain her expression did not change at that veiled intimacy, though her heartbeat accelerated.

She tried to dismiss him from her mind as she turned her attention to her family. "I trust everyone is well? And you, Master Georgie, have been making snowmen in the garden, have you not? I saw them from my window."

"Potter helped me. We are going to make a whole family, Cousin Sophia."

Sophia smiled at Potter, who was standing by the servants' door awaiting the next course. Selwick glanced at him, too, as if he could not believe Potter might have a bit of fun in him. She turned back to Georgie. "Then you shall be quite busy."

The boy grinned. "Mama says I must have as much fun as possible since we will be going home soon."

Thomas snorted and she was certain he was about to

comment on the inappropriateness of "fun" under the circumstances. A diversion was in order. "Then you are right to make the most of the time you have, Georgie. I am certain Uncle Oliver would have approved."

He nodded and went back to eating his pudding.

"That is very kind of you to say, Sophia," Emma said. "He has so little joy at home in Wiltshire. If only his father were still here to—"

"Now, Emma, we should not dwell on the past," Jonathan soothed. "You know it just makes you sad."

"See here," Thomas interrupted. "We should respect the sobriety of the occasion instead of treating it as as opportunity for frivolity. One could excuse a snowman from a child, but this business with holly and evergreens is absurd."

Anger and embarrassment nearly provoked Sophia to a sharp retort. She glanced at Selwick over the rim of her wineglass to see if he had noticed. He had. The hint of a scowl hovered in the frown lines between his eyes and in the thin line of his lips.

"I rather like the evergreens," Jonathan said. "Puts a freshness in the air, don't y'know. Old manors tend to go musty in winter, eh?"

"Nevertheless," Thomas persisted. "You ought to cease with the merriment, Cousin Sophia. Surely you can give up one Christmas for the sake of your deceased uncle."

She sighed. How could she make them understand that the little Christmas she'd been making was for their uncle? Even if she explained, they'd find fault with it. Perhaps she was never going to win their approval. Would never gain their acceptance. She remained silent, trying to salvage what remained of her dignity. A gulp of the deep red wine eased the knot in her stomach.

Selwick saved the moment. "Miss Sophia is not being

frivolous," he said. "She alone has stepped forward to assist me in inventorying your uncle's belongings. There are still crates upon crates in the attic. 'Tis like a maze up there."

Thomas lowered his brow, his expression ominous. "I say! Is that not what you are paid for?"

"I am acting without compensation," Selwick said, his lip curling slightly as he met Thomas's gaze. "As a favor to your family and in recognition of my father's relationship with your uncle."

Georgie's eyes grew wide and he looked from one family member to another as if he feared his uncle and Selwick would come to blows.

Again, Sophia took a gulp of wine. Oh, Selwick was sure to turn and run as far from her family as possible and as soon as he could.

"Easy, old girl," Jonathan warned. "We wouldn't want the servants to have to carry you to bed."

Another glance at Selwick warned her to action before he could interfere. She laughed and winked at Jonathan. "Ah, cousin. That would be a first for me, but how many times have *you* made that particular assent?"

Jonathan chortled. "I own it. Boredom does not sit well with me. When all else fails, drink brings some relief from tedium." He turned toward the butler. "Potter, more wine."

She cringed and looked about. Only Selwick looked as if he had recognized the insult. He must be thinking that his own family was a pattern of decorum measured against her own. Oh, she could not wait to excuse herself.

As the library clock struck the hour of midnight, Sebastian sat before the fireplace, warming his brandy glass between his hands. The soothing action helped him think.

He'd waited until the family was abed, then rang for Potter several minutes ago, and anticipated his imminent arrival.

If what he believed was true, everything would change for the Pettibone and Arbuthnot families. The implications were astounding, and his rational mind could not accept the possibility. Still, all the signs were there, subtle but undeniable.

Potter arrived in his nightshirt and robe, his silvered hair mussed and sleep clouding his eyes. "My lord?"

Sebastian waved at a chair facing his own. "Sit, Potter," he said as he stood to pour a brandy for the man.

A look akin to panic passed over Potter's face, but he did as he was asked, accepted the brandy Sebastian offered and took a quick drink. Fortification? "Is something amiss?" he asked when the liquid settled.

"You tell me, Potter," he said, sinking into his own chair again. "Or should I say, Pettibone?" The man blanched and coughed. A myriad of emotions passed over his face, and Sebastian knew he was considering denial. He shook his head. "Unless your plan is to impoverish yourself when everything is turned over to your heirs, I wouldn't bother to refute my conclusion, sir."

Pettibone heaved a long sigh. "How did you know?"

"There was not a single thing that gave you away, sir, but a collection of small things. Your distress when Miss Sophia took your journal to read, your readiness to be her accomplice in making a bit of Christmas, taking over the inventory in the cellar, building snowmen with Master Georgie. And your melancholy way of watching the family—half proud, half distressed. What were you thinking when you concocted this charade, sir?"

Pettibone's eyes welled with tears, quickly blinked back. "That they did not know me and likely wouldn't rouse themselves to attend me here. Not that they'd have reason to. I've been an indifferent uncle at best. But I wanted to see what sort of people they were before my money clouded their vision and bought me a superficial acceptance. Aye, I wanted just one Christmas at Windsong Hall before I was alone again."

Something of Pettibone's longing reached Sebastian—something he'd not felt for a very long time, and that surprised him. Pettibone, sad and pathetic man that he was, and Sebastian himself, were very alike in a fundamental way. They'd both made their own way from a very young age. Both had shied away from family and familial obligations. Both were essentially alone. But that had been Sebastian's choice, and that knowledge made him uncomfortable.

"You could have gone to them, Pettibone. Asked their forgiveness for your long absence."

"I was afraid they would not be natural with me. Money buys kindness, but lacks sincerity. I wanted to meet them as a common stranger. To see them as they are, not as they would be with a wealthy uncle. I have never been at ease with people, nor have I the gift of conversation. I do not know how to be an uncle, how to talk to family. It seemed easier to pose as my butler."

"And what do you think?"

"For all their peculiarities, I like them. Jonathan could benefit from a bit of hard work, but he is a good lad. Marjory and Emma try to do what is right, but are a bit too rigid regarding propriety. Georgie and Sophia, though, have won my heart. Both are so honest and natural, so bright and kind. And vulnerable." Pettibone turned a stern eye on Sebastian. "I would take it amiss if any of them were hurt."

If he'd meant to intimidate Sebastian, he failed. To his everlasting chagrin, Sebastian would ten times rather face

Pettibone's disapproval than Sophia's. He took a long drink from his glass and sighed. "What do you propose now?"

"I would prefer you keep your silence. I shall tell them when the casket arrives."

"There's actually a casket?"

Pettibone betrayed a slight smile. "Carrying my favorite books. It should arrive in another day. Two at most."

Sebastian did not like deceiving the family, especially Sophia, who had grown attached to the man in the journals, but Pettibone's dilemma touched him. "Only till then," he agreed.

Pettibone stood, nodded his gratitude and left the library, closing the door softly behind him.

Sebastian sat back in his chair and sighed. How in the name of God had he gotten into this mess? And he still had to deal with Miss Sophia—that daunting bit of muslin who'd given him her virginity and then behaved as if nothing untoward had happened. Her conduct over dinner had been so blithely casual that he'd wondered for a moment if he'd imagined the events of the afternoon. Oh, no, little Miss Pettibone was not going to get away with that.

Chapter Ten

On his way upstairs, Sebastian glimpsed the faint flicker of candles burning in the windows facing the road. Sophia? His smile died quickly when he recalled that, in her own way, she was mourning a man who was not dead. Blast and be damned!

He disliked keeping such a secret from her and the family, but he had to respect Pettibone's wishes. At least until the coffin arrived. He could only hope Sophia would forgive him when she learned the truth. The thought that she might be angry troubled him more than it should.

A muffled sound stopped him as he passed the room that should have been Pettibone's. The door was ajar and he nudged it wider, expecting to see Pettibone fetching some belonging. Instead he saw Sophia—barefoot, wrapped in a soft woolen robe, her hair falling down her back like a dark river—lighting a candle in the window. Keeping faith. Loving a man she never knew. Honoring him as if he'd belonged to her.

She sniffled and he knew he could not let her grieve a single moment longer—promise to Pettibone be damned. He crossed the room to her, his footsteps silent on the plush Oriental carpet. "Sophia," he said as he touched her shoulder.

She spun and he thought she would either swoon or scream. She did neither. She threw her arms around him and buried her face in his cravat. "Here now, Sophia. There is no need to cry. Your uncle—"

"Make love to me, Selwick. Make me feel as if I belong, if just for a moment."

The rawness of her voice twisted his gut and he forgot everything but the need to give her whatever she wanted. What *he* wanted. When she lifted her face to him, he met her lips like the unknown gift he'd longed for all his life. He placed her on the massive bed and came down beside her.

By the soft glow of the candle, he removed her robe and nightgown slowly, marveling at her lush curves and kissing each part of her as he laid her bare. No hasty, half-clothed coupling this time, but a long and lazy tribute to her perfection.

He undressed himself, divesting his clothes as he worshipped her with his mouth, paying homage to her lips, the curve of her ear, her throat, her breasts. Her sighs and little gasps guided him, and her dark hair tangled on the pristine pillow like strands of fluid silk as she twisted with passion unfulfilled.

By the time she reached for him and stroked his shaft, his need was as deep as hers. He'd never been so lost in a woman, so gone to passion. Sophia was consuming him, changing him into a man he barely knew with her sweet demanding body. He wanted to linger and savor the journey, but Sophia demanded the destination. She nearly pulled him atop her, her thighs tense against his hips.

"Please," she begged with a breathless sob. "Please... please."

Her pleading was an aphrodisiac to him and he needed nothing more to do the very thing he wanted most to do.

Mindful of her inexperience, he eased himself downward even as she rose to meet him. Her inner muscles were a tight, heated grip around him, creating the most exquisite friction he'd ever experienced. She was made for him—a perfect fit.

She found his rhythm and matched him thrust for thrust, robbing him of his cherished self-control. Thinking ceased and only the need to find the end of this remained. Her completion was as swift, blinding and intense as a lightning strike and he followed quickly, unable to delay when her muscles rippled and contracted, pulling him inward, commanding him, draining him.

He watched her in the throes of *la petite mort*. Her lids were closed, and translucent tears slipped slowly from the corners of her eyes. Her cheeks were flushed with the residue of passion. Her lips were swollen from his kisses and parted in a deep sigh. Here was another split second in time that he would remember always and, if luck was with him, that vision would be the last thing he'd remember as he slipped from this life. Dear God…he never wanted to leave the snug haven of her body. Never wanted to be a moment without Sophia.

How had this disaster occurred within the space of mere days?

"Gor! I've half a mind to give his lordship a piece of my mind. Just look at you," Janie muttered the next morning when she put the finishing touches on Sophia's hair.

Sophia looked at herself in the vanity mirror. Was there something that betrayed her activities of last night? Perhaps the blush that was creeping into her cheeks? "Whatever do you mean?"

"Why, look at the shadows under your eyes. Is he workin' you that late, miss?"

So late she'd barely gotten three hours' sleep, though it had not been work but pleasure. But she could not tell her maid such a thing. She managed a shrug. "We both want to finish quickly, Janie. There are so many crates. We've managed to empty most of them, but—"

"I've heard Mr. and Mrs. Evans talkin' and they want to be home by Christmas. So do Mr. Jonathan an' Mrs. Grant. Seems the only one enjoyin' his self is Master Georgie."

Sophia looked down to hide her disappointment. She had hoped they would all stay and spend the holiday together. And the thought of never seeing Selwick again was weighing on her. "I suppose it all depends upon when the coffin arrives," she said.

"An' it's overdue, at that," Janie said over her shoulder as she went to answer a soft knock at the door.

Sophia watched the reflection of the door in her vanity mirror, hoping it was Potter or Mrs. Cavendish bringing a pot of tea. Alas, it was not.

"I would like to have a few words alone with Miss Sophia, please," Selwick said to the maid.

Janie turned and waited for Sophia's nod before exiting and closing the door behind her.

He was so terribly handsome this morning, she thought. As if he'd slept an entire night, had risen early to bathe and shave and dress in impeccable black. She remained motionless as he came to stand behind her, watching her reflection in the mirror. He placed his hands on her shoulders with an intimate little smile that made her heart skip a beat.

"Sophia, my dear," he began. "I have come to settle matters between us before we face your family."

Surely he was not going to tell them what they'd done?

"When this business with your uncle is settled, we shall

go back to London together. I shall acquire a license to wed, and we shall marry before the new year."

She stood and turned to him so quickly that her little chair tumbled to the ground and forced Selwick to take a step backward. "Marry? I do not recall discussing this."

He gave her a crooked grin. "We did not do much discussing, Sophia. We were…otherwise engaged."

She pressed her fingers to her temples, trying to think. Oh, under any other circumstances, she would not hesitate. But she'd lain with him, and that made all the difference. His proposal now was driven by obligation because they'd been intimate. He would be thinking she'd caught him rather neatly. He would be thinking he was honor-bound to make an honest woman of her. Oh, he was being gracious enough, but it would not be long before he felt trapped. Before he grew to resent her. Could she bear that?

She shook her head. "No. I thank you, but no."

"No?" He repeated the word as if he thought there must be some mistake.

"I am mindful of the honor you have done me, Selwick, but I…I simply cannot accept. What I…what *we* did…was a simple lapse of judgment on my part. Please believe me when I say that I had no ulterior motive in bestowing my favors. Indeed, had I known you would feel obligated, I never would have proceeded."

"Never…" He furrowed his brow in a puzzled expression—half incredulous, half angry. "Lapse of judgment? I begin to sympathize with the duke."

Oh! How could he throw that up to her? It was not the same thing at all! "The duke has nothing to do with this, Selwick, and you know it."

"Very well, madam. I shall not importune you with this

again. Believe me when I say that I thought I was doing the right and honorable thing."

"I *do* believe you, Selwick. There is absolutely no question in my mind on the matter."

He bowed sharply, spun on his heel and left her room.

Sophia could not move for her shock. She could scarcely even breathe. She stared at the closed door and gulped. Marry? But of course. She had suspected he would propose after their first coupling. But last night had been, well…different. All need and no thinking. He'd only been responding to her plea for belonging—a plea that she'd forgotten her pride to make. Why should he have to make the ultimate sacrifice for that? Had he really thought her so shameless and conniving?

She lifted her chin and squared her shoulders. Well, that was done, then. She would go forward as if nothing untoward had happened and never mention it again. If Selwick thought she had schemed to trap him, he would be happily relieved.

Preparations in the kitchen were reaching a fever pitch, and Sophia sent word to Selwick by way of Potter that she would join him to resume the inventory after luncheon. Mrs. Cavendish needed her to decorate the biscuits with icing. He hadn't replied to her note, so she assumed he would proceed without her.

Strands of hair had come undone from her ribbon and curled around her face from the humidity in the kitchen. The wispy curls tickled her nose and she blew them away just as the luncheon bell rang.

Breakfast and lunch had been casual affairs since the family's arrival at Windsong Hall and Sophia hoped that would continue. She would much rather Selwick take his lunch in the attic than come to the table. Facing him in the presence of her family would be more awkward now than later. Alone.

She put the bowl of icing aside and covered it with a damp towel. "I will finish this after lunch, Mrs. Cavendish. I need to talk to the family regarding our return to London. I have not heard from Mr. York and I fear he is still waiting on a new axle. I may have to leave my coach behind, so I would beg a ride from one of them."

"Aye, miss. But I warrant Lord Selwick would convey you."

She was glad her face was already flushed from the heat in the kitchen so that the cook would not note her blush. "Perhaps, but I dislike asking him. Surely Jonathan or Emma—"

"Come now, miss. Ye don't have to play coy with me. The entire staff has remarked upon what a fine couple ye make."

She put the bowl aside and tried to smooth her hair back. "You are all mistaken. We are merely...friends."

By Mrs. Cavendish's raised eyebrows, she knew the woman did not believe her. And then she thought of Uncle Oliver's bed. Oh! She had not put it to rights. Had a maid found it in disarray? She removed her apron and headed for the dining room without another word. Pray she could live this down.

Only Marjory and Thomas were at the table when she arrived. A maid served her as she sat. "Where are the others?"

"Can't say about Selwick, but Emma has a headache and Jonathan has gone riding. To town, likely, looking for a pint in the local tavern."

Or to find more congenial company? Sophia took a sip of her wine and wondered where Georgie might be. Sent to the kitchen by Thomas? Or reading in his room? She squelched a pang of conscience. She really should have been paying more attention to the lad. It cannot have been fun for him, shut up in a cavernous house, no one to play with and subject to the bickering of his family. Yes, she would finish the remaining inventory as quickly as possible and then devote hours to coddling the lad.

She set her spoon aside and took a deep breath. Lord, how she dreaded asking. "I was wondering if, perhaps, you wouldn't mind my company on the return to London. I've not heard from Mr. York, so it may be necessary to leave him with the coach until the axle is repaired."

Marjory barely looked up from her plate. "If it comes to that."

"So long as you do not have more than our coach can comfortably carry," Thomas amended. "Or I suppose we could hire a cart if we are to leave with Pettibone's legacy."

Sophia nearly snorted. She, the church mouse among them? She'd arrived with one small trunk and would leave with one small trunk. She was about to tell them she would beg a ride from Jonathan when a footman cleared his throat from the doorway.

"A wagon has arrived, sir."

Thomas looked a bit confused, but Sophia realized what this meant. She stood and dropped her napkin on her chair, a tightness forming in her chest. She hurried to the foyer, Marjory and Thomas fast behind, and met Selwick, who was just coming down the stairs, followed by Emma.

The wide door stood open, admitting a blast of cold wind and the imminent threat of more snow. Outside, Potter and three footmen were removing a covered coffin from the bed of the wagon.

Chapter Eleven

Sebastian watched Sophia carefully for signs of distress, then cast a reproachful glance in Pettibone's direction. His hour of reckoning was at hand and, for better or worse, the family would know the truth by dinnertime. One of the footmen faltered and he rushed forward to lend a hand.

Mrs. Evans took control. "Take the coffin to the back sitting room, if you please. I have prepared a table there. It will be out of the way, and we can leave a window open to…to…"

How unnecessary of the woman to remind them that a body would be in an unpleasant state by now. He saw the first crack in Sophia's stoic demeanor, quickly controlled as she assumed the endearing little quirk of squaring her shoulders to brace for a difficult task. And he knew better than she that there would be difficulties ahead.

She glanced at him and he gave her an encouraging nod. She returned a little half smile and he imagined she was thankful that he was not still angry. Indeed, he had controlled his astonishment at her refusal hours ago, and now he was trying to be relieved that he would not be saddled with her eccentric family. Without much success.

The meager gathering made a small funeral procession as they followed Mrs. Evans up the entry stairs and into the great hall, the remainder of the family trailing behind the casket. Emma Grant began to sniffle and Sebastian prepared himself for a swoon. To his great relief, there was none.

A long library table had been placed in the middle of the back sitting room and draped in black crepe. Mrs. Evans had been busier than he'd thought. She and Sophia held the crepe in place as he and the footmen slid the coffin onto the table.

Perhaps Pettibone had been right. The entire family was anxious to be gone from Windsong Hall, including Miss Sophia. And once she was gone, would he ever see her again? The very idea that he might not gave rise to a twist of nostalgia in his gut. Quick memories flashed through his mind—Sophia covered in snow, her cheeks rosy from the chill, Sophia's dark hair tangled on the pristine white of a pillow, Sophia swooning from the effects of his lovemaking. How would he ever forget her?

Mrs. Evans straightened and cleared her throat. "I sent word to the vicar in the village that we would have need of his services and that I would send word to him of when. Potter, will you see to that, please? Shall we agree upon tomorrow morning?"

Mrs. Grant could not tear her eyes from the coffin. "S-should we open the coffin? I would like to say my goodbyes."

Pettibone looked disconcerted. "Oh, Mrs. Grant, I think not. After all…it has been months since…since…"

Thomas stepped in. "I believe we can eliminate that step, Emma. Potter has overseen that. Under the circumstances, I believe we should have the burial as soon as possible."

Mrs. Grant dabbed at her eyes. "Where is Georgie? He should be here."

Miss Sophia frowned. "I have not seen him all morning, Emma. I thought he was with you, though I found it odd that he did not come to the kitchen with the smell of sweets in the air. Potter?"

"No, miss. I saw him walking toward the stables this morning, but have not seen him since."

"I'm certain he is around here somewhere, Mrs. Grant," Sebastian said, keeping a rein on his misgivings. It was not like the lad to miss a meal, let alone forgo a sweetmeat.

Arbuthnot appeared in the doorway, his face reddened by the chill air and snow still clinging to his trouser legs. He glanced at the coffin and sighed. "So Uncle Oliver has come home at last?"

Mrs. Grant wrung her hands. "Jonathan, did you see Georgie in the stables?"

"Just one groomsman," he said as he removed his gloves. "Why? Is he late for luncheon?"

"Oh! He is missing!" Mrs. Grant wailed.

Sebastian stepped forward. He'd better stop this cater-wauling before it got out of hand and turned into outright hysteria. "I am certain he is around here somewhere, Mrs. Grant. Arbuthnot, did you see any tracks along the road?"

"None. How long has the boy been missing?"

"Potter saw him last at…"

"Before breakfast." Potter's brow furrowed as he tried to be more precise. "'Twas just past daybreak."

"Good heavens! And you let him leave the house alone?" Mrs. Evans accused. "He could be anywhere by now."

Sebastian interrupted before another quarrel ensued. "Accusations and recriminations will not find Master Georgie. Arbuthnot, see if you can find the boy's tracks in the snow. Potter, have the servants search the entire house, cellar to attic. Miss Sophia, please take Mrs. Grant and Mr. and Mrs. Evans to the library and calm their nerves with a glass of sherry. I shall go to the stables and search there. Everyone report to the library within the hour."

As they left the house, Jonathan muttered under his breath. "The villagers are predicting wind and snow, Selwick. Pray we find him before the storm sets in."

The search took much longer than an hour. Darkness was falling by the time the house had been thoroughly searched and Arbuthnot had reported back. Sebastian did not even apologize for the small bits of manure sticking to his boots as he entered the library to face the family. He'd searched the tack room, every stall, every nook, the stable boy's quarters, and had even raked through the hay in the loft to see if the boy was hiding there. To no avail. Georgie had simply disappeared.

The family turned to him, hope dimming in their eyes as they noted his expression. He did not speak on his way to the brandy bottle. His fingers and toes were numb with the cold and he needed to compose himself before he spoke. He glanced at Pettibone and gave him a nod.

The man cleared his throat before he began. "We have searched the house top to bottom. Master Georgie is not here."

Arbuthnot, still warming himself by the fire heaved a heavy sigh. "I followed his tracks halfway to the cliffs. They appeared to stop and turn back, but the snow had begun to blow and cover his footsteps. I've been to town and back, in the event that I missed him on my ride back here this morning." He shook his head. "The villagers say they have not seen any trace of a lone boy."

Sebastian nodded his understanding, glancing quickly at the family. Mrs. Evans and Sophia sat on either side of Mrs. Grant and were clinging together, united in their concern for the boy. Sophia's hands were clenched into fists in her lap, a sure sign she was tense, but her demeanor was grimly composed. Arbuthnot looked haggard and tired. Even Thomas Evans was harried-looking as he paced aimlessly in circles, his hands clasped behind his back and his head down.

The task was his, then, to state the obvious. The brandy was warming him from the inside out and he, too, heaved a sigh. "The stables were empty but for the horses and stable boy. I cannot accept that Georgie simply disappeared into thin air. It appeared as though he turned back from the cliffs. He is not in the stables. The villagers have not seen a lone boy. That leaves only two possibilities. Either Georgie met with a stranger or he is somewhere nearby. Potter, are there any close neighbors? Anywhere he might have found refuge?"

The man's eyes were pale and red rimmed when he answered. "I do not know the surroundings well. I have not seen any neighbors, nor have any come calling."

Sebastian sank into the chair behind the desk and stared at the gleaming surface, thinking back to the last time he'd seen the boy. Dinner the previous night. The family had been quarreling and even he had been testy. It had started with Thomas's exception to Sophia making a little Christmas and gone from there to the inventory in the attic and on to Jonathan's drinking. Nothing so unusual for the family as a whole, but had the boy been frightened? Good Lord! Had he run away from them?

As Sebastian had run away from his own family? Oh, not so obviously, but more subtly, more deviously, and just as absent. A rare tweak of guilt made him uneasy.

"Darling Emma," Mrs. Evans murmured as she comforted a weeping Mrs. Grant. "Georgie is safe somewhere, I just know it. We cannot lose him. You know we love him, too."

Mrs. Grant sniffled. "If only we'd paid more attention."

Sophia, sitting on Mrs. Evans's other side, held her cousin's hand, tears welling in her eyes. For all their quarreling and differences, their love for one another was obvious. How had he missed that? A glance at Pettibone revealed that the old man felt the same. They were family.

Sebastian stood again, deciding action was better than stasis for both him and Sophia. There would be no rest until Georgie was found. "I shall ride out and search the surroundings for neighbors—anyone who might have taken him in."

Arbuthnot put his glass down and straightened his jacket. "I'll do that, Selwick. I already have the lay of the land."

Sebastian knew better than to argue. He turned to the others. "Potter, send the servants to the cellar to start the search again. Miss Sophia and I will begin in the attic. Mrs. Grant, please search the boy's room, and your own, to see if anything is missing—clothing, cash, trinkets, or if there is a note. Evans, you and your wife keep vigil here and if anyone has anything to report, bring the news here."

Mrs. Evans's eyes widened. "You think he's run away!"

"I don't know what I think, Mrs. Evans. I only know that we cannot give up looking for him."

Sophia glanced around the attic. She hadn't been up here since she and Selwick had made love on Uncle Oliver's furs. That memory stirred a fluttering deep inside her. But she could not think of that now. There was too much at stake.

Selwick had made progress since then. Another crate or two had been opened, one had been tipped on its side and a sheaf of papers lay on the lap desk, an open bottle of ink and a pen placed to the side. He hung the lantern he'd carried up from one of the rafters and glanced around.

He gestured at the disarray and smiled. "I see the servants made a thorough search."

She nodded, following the sweep of his hand. A candle burned in the attic window, now lighting the way home for Georgie, too. How thoughtful of Selwick.

Selwick glanced around and then settled his gaze on her. "I am sorry for this, Sophia. Georgie should be home, tucked in his bed. I cannot imagine what Mrs. Grant must be thinking. Your entire family, as well."

"I do not know what we would have done without you, Selwick. You have been a pillar of strength throughout this. I know how much you dislike crises and fixing other people's problems, but I am grateful that you are here." She clasped her hands together and bowed her head. She did not want to see his disdain. "You must be thinking us a great deal of trouble. As much as your own family."

He winced. "I wish I could deny that charge, Sophia, but that is exactly what I thought after your family gathered here at Windsong Hall. In fact, I've thought all families are a great deal of trouble. More than they are worth. But I've been a fool. I thought you could barely abide one another, but I've watched your love and concern draw you together. And ever since we discussed my family, I've been thinking about my stepsisters and stepmother. I believe you are right—that they only want my attention and the assurance that they are secure, and I have been too blind and selfish to see it. Indeed, I've thought I would be happiest avoiding all the traps and trappings of marriage and family."

Sophia glanced up and met his gaze. "You needn't go on,

Selwick. I am well aware how you feel about encumbrances. And I've already told you, I do not expect you to marry me."

"Hush, and let me finish, Sophia." He took her hands and drew her close. "Yes, families *are* a great deal of trouble but, in the end, they are the only lasting thing we have. The only thing that will never fail us. And worth any amount of trouble. You taught me that, Sophia. For that much, at least, I am grateful. And, should you need it, my offer stands."

Should she need it? She supposed he meant that, if she found herself enceinte, he would marry her. Noble, but unnecessary. She disengaged her hands, afraid he might feel her yearning through her fingertips. "I appreciate the offer, Selwick, but I—"

"Ahem."

They spun toward the head of the stairs. A red-faced Potter stood there, his hands clasped behind his back in an attitude of waiting.

Her heart raced. "Did you find Georgie?"

"I am afraid not, miss. But I thought you should know… that is, cook mentioned that someone has been pilfering in the kitchen."

"Pilfering?" Selwick repeated. "Have you questioned the kitchen staff?"

"Aye, my lord. No one will admit to it."

"Thank you, Potter. Please continue the search."

Potter nodded and returned the way he'd come.

"How odd," Sophia mused. "Why would he bother us with such a thing now?"

Selwick smiled and touched her cheek briefly before turning to scan the long attic from dormer to dormer. "Well, Miss Pettibone, I suppose it is time for us to resume the search for Master Georgie, eh?" he said in a louder than normal voice.

"Plainly the room is empty, Selwick."

He laid his finger over his lips as he moved toward the tipped-over crate. And then she understood.

"Before we leave, shall we right this crate?" He gripped the edges of the wooden crate and began to shake it.

A frightened squeal preceded Georgie's tumble from the open end. The boy had come here for sanctuary. He had somehow evaded the search, had lit the candle in the window and had pilfered in the kitchen for food—likely sweetmeats.

"Georgie!" She threw her arms around him and squeezed until he wheezed. "Whatever were you thinking of to frighten us so?"

"I...I didn't mean to, Cousin Sophia. But, last night at supper, when Lord Selwick said there were empty crates, I thought I could make a fort."

She bent over to look into the crate. He'd spread a fur to sit on and a plate heaped with gingerbread and iced biscuits sat in one corner. He'd spread his toy soldiers into battle lines and must have been playing war. "But why did you not come when you were called? Why did you hide from us, Georgie?"

He looked shamefaced. "I was watching from the window when the wagon came and I remembered that Mama said we'd go home as soon as we put Uncle Oliver in the ground. But I...I did not want to go. I like it here, and it's ever so much more jolly when we are all together."

Selwick took his hand. "I know just how you feel, lad. Come, let's go tell the others you are safe."

Sophia wanted to be stern but she laughed instead and hugged him again. "Do you know that Uncle Jonathan is out in the snow looking for you? You will have to polish his boots to make up to him."

Chapter Twelve

Another late night with the family safely abed. Another talk with Pettibone over another glass of brandy. Selwick waved him to a chair by the library fire. "Tomorrow morning, Pettibone. No more delays."

Pettibone gave him a wan smile. "I will honor our agreement. But I confess grave misgivings. They will be angry. Feel cheated of their inheritance. Ah, but I have memories, do I not?"

Memories. Is that all he'd have of Sophia? Last night in the attic, when he'd renewed his proposal, he'd hoped… "I gather you did not send word to the vicar?"

"You gather correctly, Selwick. Tomorrow, when they are all congregated in the back sitting room, I shall speak with them. No doubt we shall be supping alone tomorrow evening."

"No doubt." Selwick gave him a crooked smile. "But there's always the possibility that they might accept you." He thought Sophia, of all of them, would understand her uncle's need to belong and his fear that he wouldn't. Perhaps she would stay. And that thought gave rise to another question.

The old man's expression was wan and a bit harried. For the first time, Sebastian realized the depth of Pettibone's loneliness and fear of rejection. "Was it worth it, Pettibone? Risking their anger and rejection just to see them as they really are?"

Pettibone sank into a chair by the fire and stared into the flames, all traces of the butler fading away as the real man asserted himself. "Every moment of it. I've seen them for who and what they are, and I am exceedingly fond of them all. I've lived most of my life alone, Selwick. They are all I have, and if they leave me now, if they want nothing to do with me, at least I will have had these days with them."

Sebastian sighed. There was an unreachable melancholy in Pettibone's answer. A deep sadness and isolation. The man had lived in self-imposed solitude for his entire adult life. And Sebastian recognized himself in Pettibone—years from now, alone, a shadowy figure in other people's lives. He grew numb, unable to comprehend such emptiness now that he'd known Sophia.

"I intend to offer Emma and Georgie a home with me, if they will have me," Pettibone continued. "They need someone to look after them. Marjory and Jonathan do not need me, but I will offer them whatever they will take."

"And Sophia?" Would she have her "belonging" now? Would it be everything she wanted?

"Ah, well, I thought you'd be taking care of that, Selwick."

Sebastian drank deeply, wondering how much Pettibone knew and how much he merely guessed. "I offered. She refused."

He quirked an eyebrow in surprise. "She's all pride, that one."

"She rejected a duke. I am a lowly viscount."

"She is not holding out for a king, Selwick. But marriage will have to be on her terms. Did you meet her terms?"

"I..." He thought back to their conversation about the duke. He'd asked her what she'd wanted from the duke and she'd said something that he hadn't understood then. What was it?

"What, precisely, did you offer?" Pettibone persisted.

"My name and protection."

Pettibone snorted. "I can imagine her reply. Do you intend to settle for that answer?"

"You're a fine one—"

"You are right." Pettibone took a deep drink from his brandy glass. "All my life, I've settled for the easy way. The safe way. I've protected myself from hurt and trouble. I have shirked my responsibilities to those who depended upon me. And you can see what I have to show for it. But you, Selwick, have a talent for trouble. I've watched you manage my troublesome family, rally them and solve their problems without so much as turning a hair. I've seen the way you look at my Sophia, too, and the way she looks at you. You'd be a greater fool than I if you walk away from that."

Was he a fool? He did not want to spend empty years yearning for something he never had. He wanted Sophia Pettibone. He wanted her to take his name, bear his children and wake up beside him every morning. He wanted to shelter her from harm, protect her and smooth her path through life. He wanted her to belong to him...*belong*...

Bloody hell! He *had* been a fool She'd given herself to him, body and soul—a gift she'd given no other man. He'd satisfied her and taught her the pleasure of giving and receiving such a gift. He'd felt her fondness, if not her love, in what she'd given him, and he'd returned her gift with equal ardor. And he, blind fool that he was, had not understood what she needed most from him.

He raised his glass to Pettibone as he stood. "She has rejected me twice, Pettibone, but I believe I may just have one last chance to persuade her."

Sophia had dressed in black bombazine and a black woolen shawl to shield herself from the cold in the back drawing room. She sat on a straight-back chair, hugging herself, giving herself the comfort she could not find elsewhere.

Emma took a seat beside her, her lips moving as she read from her little prayer book. Georgie was somber and kept his hands clasped and his head down. Marjory and Thomas sat together on a small settee, and Jonathan stood beside Selwick in front of the meager flames of the only fireplace in the room.

They were ready to begin, but for the vicar.

Potter entered the room and closed the door behind him before coming to stand by the coffin and rest his hand upon the smooth polished surface.

"Potter, are you certain you informed the vicar when we would be expecting him?" Marjory asked, breaking the tense silence.

"No, Marjory, I did not."

Marjory's eyes widened at the familiar address, but she regained her aplomb quickly as she stood again. "Then we are gathered here for nothing. I shall send for him at once, and we shall have this finished by sunset. With a bit of luck, we can leave for home tomorrow."

"Sit down, Marjory," Potter said. "I have some things to say that concern the family."

By now Sophia was thoroughly intrigued. She rather

liked Potter, but this new man before them was quite mysterious. A little tingle of anticipation traveled up her spine and she sat a bit straighter. A quick glance at Selwick made her think that he knew what was coming.

"Here now!" Thomas rose to stand beside his wife. "You cannot speak to my wife like that."

A quelling glare was all it took to put Thomas back in his seat. "I know you are expecting a funeral, but you shall be disappointed. I would like to give you the news more gently, but I have been unable to think how. So I shall say simply that Oliver Pettibone is not dead."

"Wha—" Emma quickly covered her mouth with both hands.

"I say! Is this some sort of joke?" Jonathan came forward and stood across the coffin from Potter.

Sophia took another glance at Selwick. He did not seem in the least bit surprised. When she looked back at Potter, understanding began to dawn. She stood, too, tears of joy rushing to her eyes. Potter nodded at her, as if he had heard her silent revelation. "Uncle Oliver?"

Georgie sprang from his chair with a whoop. "Uncle? You are my uncle, Mr. Potter?" When the man nodded, Georgie ran to him and wrapped his arms around the butler's waist.

Marjory and Thomas looked stunned and incapable of speech for the first time in Sophia's memory. She dashed her tears away with the back of her hand and stepped forward. "Why did you not tell us?"

"I was afraid you would not stir yourselves to attend an old man you did not know. Or that you'd only come for what you might gain. You were strangers to me, after all. I did not want to risk your scorn."

Selwick moved to the bank of windows and began closing them, one by one. How like him to think of practical matters when everyone else was witless. Heavens! How he must be congratulating himself on a narrow escape from becoming a part of her eccentric family.

Thomas shook his head as if unwilling to believe this turn of events, then came to the coffin and lifted the lid. "Books..."

Marjory covered her mouth to stifle a sob as she went to stand beside their uncle, tears of joy in her eyes. Gone were her efficient manner and severe expression. She looked like a child again, eager for answers.

"I want to thank you, Sophia, for making a bit of Christmas for me. I cannot tell you how much it means to me that you wanted to give me that, even though you thought I was dead."

She took his hand, her heart too full to speak.

He looked about the room again and sighed. "I suppose now you'll all be wanting to go back to town," Uncle Oliver said, looking a bit shamefaced.

"No!" Georgie cried.

Emma clung to Marjory's sleeve and shook her head. "No, Uncle. Georgie and I shall stay for the entire season."

"I'd like to hear about the gold fields in America," Thomas added.

Sophia kissed his leathery cheek. "I want to stay, too, Uncle. We have so much to catch up on. And we shall make a proper Christmas now."

Jonathan laughed outright. "By God, I did not think there were any surprises left for me! Glad I was wrong, Uncle."

"Selwick is gone?" Sophia's heart sank. She hadn't really expected him to stay after his duty was done, but she had not thought he would escape within mere hours, and without even saying goodbye. Oh, but she should have known. He'd made it quite clear how he felt about obligations.

"Aye, miss." Janie made a fancy bow in the red ribbon holding Sophia's curls in place. "Just took up and left without so much as a by-your-leave. Closed up in the library with business matters while you and Mrs. Cavendish were preparin' a grand celebration all day, and Lord Selwick just slipped out while everyone was busy."

Sophia looked at her reflection in the dressing table mirror. Her white gown, trimmed in red and white velvet, had been for naught. She had meant to dazzle Selwick, and now he was gone. The low décolletage would not command his attention, and the bright flashes of red would not cheer him. While she'd been in the kitchen, finishing the tarts and mince pies, Selwick had been stealing out the door.

She chided herself for the tightness in her chest. If she meant so little to him that he could not spare her a farewell, she could not wish him back.

"Oh, miss! You look just like a Christmas fairy," Janie exclaimed as Sophia stood. "The maids say Mrs. Evans and Mrs. Grant are taking special pains tonight, too. This will be the first time Mr. Potter—I mean, Mr. Pettibone—sits at the table with you, eh? How odd that will be."

"Odd, but very welcome." Sophia forced a smile as she turned toward the door. "We shall let nothing spoil this celebration, Janie. It is far too important for Uncle Oliver to have a Christmas with family."

"Aye, miss. You go on then, and join them in the parlor for a bit of wassail."

Sophia hurried downstairs to the parlor and found she was the last to arrive. The last but for— "Where is Georgie?"

Emma's face lit up. "Changing. He will be down in a moment."

Uncle Oliver grinned. "The rascal has been out trudging through the snow with Selwick half the afternoon."

Sophia's heart raced as she accepted a cup of wassail from Jonathan. Selwick? He was here? He hadn't gone back to London yet? Thank heavens she would have a chance to talk to him before they encountered each other at a ball or soirée back in London. She did not want there to be any awkwardness between them, nor did she want him to think there was any need to avoid her.

Jonathan grinned. "Uncle Oliver has been regaling us with tales of the gold fields and red Indians. Makes me want to visit America someday."

"Red Indians? Georgie will want to hear about them. He has a book with illustrations and told me how fierce they look."

Her uncle came forward and took her hand. "You look especially lovely tonight, Sophia. I daresay you would turn heads in London with that gown."

She laughed, feeling a bit giddy now that she knew Selwick had not run off. "Thank you, Uncle."

Georgie came thundering into the room. "Red Indians? Have you seen them in real life, Uncle Oliver?"

"Georgie, where are your manners?" Emma reminded.

He halted and gave sober bows in the ladies' direction. "Good evening, cousins."

Thomas ruffled the hair on Georgie's head, one of the rare signs he ever gave of his fondness for the lad. "Are you old enough for wassail, boy?"

Georgie's eyes grew round with delight when his mother consented. "Half a cup, and that is all, mind you."

"What were you up to this afternoon, Georgie? You and Selwick were quite mysterious."

"Oh!" He turned to Sophia and gave another bow. "Lord Selwick begs me to convey his desire that you attend him in the library, Miss Sophia."

She chuckled at his formality, obviously coached by Selwick. "Now?"

"As soon as may be."

"Very well." She bobbed a quick curtsy to the gathering and left the parlor.

Selwick adjusted his cravat and took a deep breath. For better or worse, his future would be decided in the next few minutes. Everything hinged on Miss Sophia Pettibone— eccentric, walking disaster, jilt. Was he mad?

Since the day he'd met her, Sophia had him reversing his decisions hourly. Changing his mind twice as often. Rethinking his entire life at every turn. On reflection, he decided that she had him at a loss in almost every respect but one. In making love, at least, *he* had the advantage. And he would use that advantage if necessary.

The library door opened and Sophia entered, a vision in white and red. She was stunning, her dark sultry beauty set off by the pristine white of her gown. Her full lips parted in a dazzling smile.

"You wished to speak with me?"

He held out his hand, hoping that she would come to him, and she did. "Do you see what I see, Sophia?" he whispered as he looked up at the ball of mistletoe hanging just above them.

"You…you and Georgie were out looking for mistletoe? That is not like you, Selwick."

His heart twisted at the simple wonder in her voice. "What Christmas would be complete without it?" But why should she be surprised? She had him doing things he'd never dreamed he'd do. Indeed, he was not the same Selwick who'd arrived at Windsong Hall less than a week ago.

He lowered his lips to hers and kissed her rather more

thoroughly than he should, given the audience gathering at the library door. Blessed, responsive Sophia forgot to protest when his lips parted and begged an answering heat from her. She gave it, tightening her arms around his neck and molding against him until he could not tell her heartbeat from his own. And he kept kissing her until he felt her complete surrender. Yes, he was ruthless in wielding his only weapon—Sophia's deep passion.

Her eyes were still heavy lidded when he lifted his head moments later. He knew what she needed to hear, and he was not in the least surprised that he meant every word of it. "You, Sophia Pettibone, are my greatest and only passion, my best friend, my whole world. You belong to me, with me, and I belong to you. I love you, Sophia. Marry me, and save me from a dull and empty life."

Her eyes filled with tears. "You remembered," she said on a sigh. "Everything I said that day in the attic." Her voice restricted with emotion and failed her, so she nodded her consent.

"And you will not jilt me once you meet my troublesome family?"

"Never," she managed.

He threw his head back and laughed, feeling lighter than he had in years. He'd gained everything he never knew he wanted, and had shed the burden of solitude. "Oh, Sophia, you are a pearl beyond price. I thought this would only be another tedious fortnight in the country, but from the moment you began to make your little Christmas, I lost my heart."

* * * * *

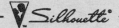
Silhouette®

SPECIAL EDITION

**FROM *NEW YORK TIMES* AND *USA TODAY*
BESTSELLING AUTHOR**

KATHLEEN EAGLE

ONE COWBOY,
One Christmas

When bull rider Zach Beaudry appeared
out of thin air on Ann Drexler's ranch,
she thought she was seeing a ghost of
Christmas past. And though Zach had
no memory of their night of passion years
ago, they were about to share a future
he would never forget.

*Available December 2009
wherever books are sold.*

SSE65493

Visit Silhouette Books at www.eHarlequin.com

Silhouette Desire

**FROM *NEW YORK TIMES*
BESTSELLING AUTHOR**

DIANA
PALMER

THE MAVERICK

**A BRAND-NEW
LONG, TALL
TEXAN STORY**

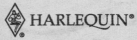

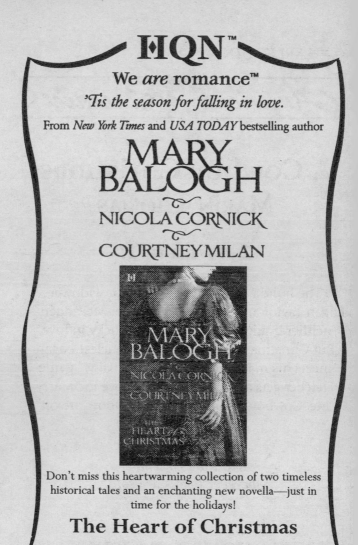

REQUEST YOUR FREE BOOKS!

 Harlequin® Historical
Historical Romantic Adventure!

2 FREE NOVELS PLUS 2 FREE GIFTS!

YES! Please send me 2 FREE Harlequin® Historical novels and my 2 FREE gifts (gifts are worth about $10). After receiving them, if I don't wish to receive any more books, I can return the shipping statement marked "cancel". If I don't cancel, I will receive 6 brand-new novels every month and be billed just $4.94 per book in the U.S. or $5.49 per book in Canada. That's a savings of 20% off the cover price! It's quite a bargain! Shipping and handling is just 50¢ per book.* I understand that accepting the 2 free books and gifts places me under no obligation to buy anything. I can always return a shipment and cancel at any time. Even if I never buy another book, the two free books and gifts are mine to keep forever.

246 HDN EYS3   349 HDN EYTF

Name	(PLEASE PRINT)
Address	Apt. #
City	State/Prov.	Zip/Postal Code
Signature (if under 18, a parent or guardian must sign)	

Mail to the **Harlequin Reader Service:**
IN U.S.A.: P.O. Box 1867, Buffalo, NY 14240-1867
IN CANADA: P.O. Box 609, Fort Erie, Ontario L2A 5X3

Not valid to current subscribers of Harlequin Historical books.

Want to try two free books from another line?
Call 1-800-873-8635 or visit www.morefreebooks.com.

* Terms and prices subject to change without notice. Prices do not include applicable taxes. Sales tax applicable in N.Y. Canadian residents will be charged applicable provincial taxes and GST. Offer not valid in Quebec. This offer is limited to one order per household. All orders subject to approval. Credit or debit balances in a customer's account(s) may be offset by any other outstanding balance owed by or to the customer. Please allow 4 to 6 weeks for delivery. Offer available while quantities last.

Your Privacy: Harlequin Books is committed to protecting your privacy. Our Privacy Policy is available online at www.eHarlequin.com or upon request from the Reader Service. From time to time we make our lists of customers available to reputable third parties who may have a product or service of interest to you. If you would prefer we not share your name and address, please check here. ☐

HH09R

COMING NEXT MONTH FROM

HARLEQUIN®
HISTORICAL

Available November 24, 2009

- **HER COLORADO MAN**
  by **Cheryl St.John**
  (Western)
  When eighteen-year-old Mariah found herself pregnant and unmarried
  she disappeared for a year, returning with the baby and minus the
  "husband." But now, with handsome adventurer Wes Burrows turning
  up and claiming to be the husband she invented seven years ago,
  Mariah's lies become flesh and blood—and her wildest dreams
  become a reality!

- **GALLANT OFFICER, FORBIDDEN LADY**
  by **Diane Gaston**
  (Regency)
  Ensign Jack Vernon is haunted by the atrocities of the war in Spain.
  Back in London he finds the comfort he seeks in beautiful and
  spirited actress Ariana Blane. With Ariana pursued by a man she
  fears and detests, her forbidden relationship with Jack is fraught with
  danger—but he is a man determined to fight for his newfound love....

- **MISTLETOE MAGIC**
  by **Sophia James**
  (Victorian)
  Miss Lillian Davenport is a paragon of good taste with an unrivaled
  reputation and dangerous American Lucas Clairmont challenges every
  rule she upholds! A confessed gambler who walks on the wrong side
  of right, Lucas is a man Lillian knows she should have the sense to
  stay well away from....

- **THE VIKING'S CAPTIVE PRINCESS**
  by **Michelle Styles**
  (Viking)
  Renowned warrior Ivar Gunnarson is a man of deeds, not words.
  He certainly has no time for the ideals of love; he gets what he
  wants—and mysterious and enchanting Princess Thyre is no
  exception to that rule!

HHCNMBPA1109